About Apollo Africa

The original Heinemann African Writers Series was launched in 1962 with the publication of Chinua Achebe's *Things Fall Apart*, Cyprian Ekwensi's *Burning Grass* and Kenneth Kaunda's *Zambia Shall Be Free*, with Achebe himself acting as an editorial advisor. Over the next 40 years, the series continued to publish the best writing from across the African continent.

One of the founding aims of the Heinemann series was to make books by African writers available to as wide a readership as possible. Apollo Africa – a collaboration between Black Star Books and Head of Zeus – is proud to continue this work, ensuring novels, essays, poetry and plays from the original series are once again made available to readers all over the world.

Sterile Sky

Sterile Sky

E. E. Sule

Black Star Books and Head of Zeus would like to thank the following organisations: The Miles Morland Foundation, The Ford Foundation, and Africa No Filter. This publication was made possible through their support.

First published in the Heinemann African Writers Series in 2012 by Pearson Education Limited.

This edition first published in 2023 by Black Star Books and Head of Zeus, part of Bloomsbury Publishing Plc.

Copyright © E. E. Sule, 2012

The moral right of E.E Sule to be identified as the author of this work has been asserted in accordance with the Copyright, Designs and Patents Act of 1988.

All rights reserved. No part of this publication may be reproduced, stored in a retrieval system, or transmitted in any form or by any means, electronic, mechanical, photocopying, recording, or otherwise, without the prior permission of both the copyright owner and the above publisher of this book.

This reprint is published by arrangement with Pearson Education Limited.

This is a work of fiction. All characters, organizations, and events portrayed in this novel are either products of the author's imagination or are used fictitiously.

9 7 5 3 1 2 4 6 8

A catalogue record for this book is available from the British Library.

ISBN (PB): 9781035900725
ISBN (E): 9781803288765

Typeset by Siliconchips Services Ltd UK

Printed and bound in Great Britain by
CPI Group (UK) Ltd, Croydon CR0 4YY

Head of Zeus Ltd
First Floor East
5–8 Hardwick Street
London EC1R 4RG

WWW.HEADOFZEUS.COM

For my DAD and MUM,
whose lives intersect with this story

1 | *The Tarred Street is Hot*

The tarred street was hot and I could feel it through my rubber sandals. I had passed Sabon Gari Divisional Police Station where Baba worked and had just crossed Airport Road when I saw people suddenly running helter-skelter.

I saw an old Fulani woman, a cock in each hand, trying to run while looking back. Her right leg hit the jerrycan of a motorist whose car had broken down. She stumbled and fell. The motorist rushed to her aid. The two cocks hopped around, squawking. A frightened runner hit one of the birds. The helpless bird collapsed on its side, one wing down, the other up. Its neck stretched out as it fell limply to the ground, its beak agape in terror. The legs kicked weakly.

The old woman, now up, sputtered, 'May Allah strike you for stepping on my cock! May Allah strike you hard!'

I sighted the chanting mob. Some had their fists in the air. Others wielded swords, spears and cutlasses. They were drawing closer. I turned and headed towards the station, looking back now and then. A clashing sound made me trot. At the station, I turned and saw thick smoke surging upwards behind the mob. A kiosk with Reinhard Bonnke's posters pasted on it caught aflame.

'God Almighty! God Almighty! Jesus Christ! Help! Help! My body o!' A female voice was shrieking in the burning kiosk. Loud and piercing. It pitched above the mob's chants and died down gradually. Nobody went near the kiosk as the fire razed it. Only a few policemen were around, standing in front of the station.

'They are burning houses!'

'They are killing people!'

Two terrified women stood by me near the station entrance. They carried on their heads trays of the fruits they hawked. One of them said, 'Dent say dey no wan Bonnke to come Kano. I no know why de man come by all means sef.'

'But e don leave na,' the other replied.

'Which time im leave?'

'Na now now. No be him dem dey follow go airport so?'

It dawned on me. For a week now, Baba's radio had been blaring adverts about the coming of a great man of God from Germany. He would perform unprecedented miracles like Jesus had. Blind people would see. Lame people would walk. The deaf would hear and the mute would speak.

I peeped into the offices through the windows to see if Baba was inside the station. He was not. After a while the chanting of the mob petered out. The chanters moved towards the airport. Thick smoke rose behind them as they went.

A Hausa man, across the street from the station, was trying to convince a group of people who crowded around him that the white man had gone to the emir's palace and had astounded him. What did the strange white man do? He simply said a kind word to one of the blind beggars in front of the palace, whereupon the beggar jumped up with a shout of joy, his sight restored. The white man would have been stoned to death right there by furious unbelievers who claimed he had brought an evil ring from India to hoodwink all of Kano City. But the emir begged passionately that, for political and diplomatic reasons, the miracle maker should not be killed. While the emir placated the raging mob, his men whisked the frightened white man to the airport.

I didn't know if the Hausa man was telling the truth. As I hurried home, I saw people in groups, defying the late afternoon heat, talking with mixed feelings about events. Why was this happening on the day I had started secondary school?

Baba confirmed the Hausa man's story when he returned home. 'Before boarding his plane, the white man pulled off his shoes and left them behind,' Baba told Mama.

'Isn't that what Christ said?' Mama replied. 'Shake off the dust of your footwear when they refuse to listen to you.'

'But he should have stayed in his land and preached to his people.'

The argument started all over again. Baba hated the endless noise about the coming of the white man. Mama thought it was heathen of Baba to dislike a man sent by God to perform miracles.

The previous night before falling asleep, I had consulted

Baba's dog-eared dictionary, searching for words with which to intimidate SMG, the biggest boy in my class, who bullied me. I found *scallywag* and *megalomaniac*.

In my sleep, a big monster with the face of SMG chases me with a long sword. I scream for help. He has almost caught me when Helen suddenly appears with an even longer sword. She stands between me and the monster, stoops and shouts, 'Climb on my back!' So I do. With me on her back, her body begins to enlarge, growing bigger than the monster. The monster, frightened, turns and takes to his heels. She gives chase with me still on her back, increasingly frightened, holding tight to her neck. Incredibly, she acquires huge wings and I feel myself lifted from the ground. She flies high on a strong wind at an amazing speed. When we are far above the ground, I feel my palms loosen. I lose hold of her! I land on my back in a pool of blood. Scrambling to my feet, I see swollen bodies floating in the blood. I scream, waking up.

Ukpo, my immediate younger brother, held me tight. 'Stop screaming. Stop screaming!'

'Okay, okay. Am I screaming?' I gasped, sweating. I wriggled out of Ukpo's hold and leant my back against the wall.

'What did you dream?' Ukpo asked, moving closer to me.

'I'll tell you when it's daybreak. I can't talk now.' I looked round the room. Yakubu and Oyigwu, our younger brothers, were sleeping soundly on a mat.

'Ukpo, there's this big boy in my class…'

'Speak on. What about him?'

'Well, never mind. Please, let's sleep. And… and… there's this girl whose bandy legs remind me of…'

'Helen?'

'Oh well, I think we should sleep.'

Ukpo grabbed my wrist, looking into my eyes. In the dim light of the lantern, I could see his bloodshot eyes.

'I saw Helen yesterday. She's sad that her father won't send her to secondary school. But does your nightmare have anything to do with her?'

'Let's not talk about it, please. Let's sleep.'

I stretched myself on the bed. Ukpo did the same beside me. Before we slept, Ukpo told me that he too had had a nightmare, in which he saw himself carried away by a monstrous whirlwind.

Next morning I was set for school a few minutes after six. I interrupted Baba as he shaved his beard and listened to the news, telling him that I was on my way.

'Good that you're an early bird. How was your first day in school?'

'Fine. I like the school, our teachers are good.'

'I'm glad I've finally got you back into school. Hope you understand the sacrifices. A hard time for us.'

'Thank you, Baba.'

Our schooling was irregular, because Baba could not afford to pay our school fees all at once. I looked too big for Form One. But not as big as the bully SMG.

The day before, after I had returned from school, my younger ones had crowded around me. Imatum, the eldest of my younger sisters, had just returned from hawking *chin chin*. She took one look at me and burst into laughter. 'Eze goes to school,' she said.

'Wrong,' I retorted. 'Murtala goes to college. Past the level of Eze.'

Anyaosu, next to Ajara by age, drew closer to me. Touching my uniform, she said, 'It's fine.'

'It's fine, *kwo* Anyaosu. But will we ever wear such a uniform?' asked Ajara.

Imatum turned to Ukpo. 'See, Ukpo, we must tell Baba to put us in this school too. And he must tell Mama to stop sending us to hawk.'

'Not when you have a coconut brain,' Ukpo snapped.

Ajara, Anyaosu and Yakubu burst into laughter.

'What about yours?' Imatum retorted.

'Better than yours.'

Yakubu, following Anyaosu in age, raised his voice and said, 'Mama said all of you girls will be taken to the village and married off soon. Only Ukpo and I will go to school.'

Imatum barked, 'Shut your mouth up! *Mumu!* Isn't it poverty that makes Mama say that? I'll look for money and take myself to school!'

When I stepped out of our house, the morning was bereft of its freshness. The smell of gutter was in the air. Two swollen mice lay near the gutter running in front of our house, stinking liquid seeping out of them. I saw Aminu, my primary schoolmate, on the main road and greeted him.

Instead of responding, he gave me a withering look and muttered something to a boy standing close to him.

I went a bit farther and saw an old woman wailing '*Laa a ila!* Why did they set the mosque ablaze? They have poked fingers in your eyes, my sons.'

I instinctively turned and began to hurry home. I came upon a fat, dark-skinned man sharpening a sword. Then I sprinted.

At home, although Mama and Ajara were ready for Yarkura Market where Mama sold *alubo*, they could not leave because of the tension. I told them what I had seen and heard. Baba had not dressed for work. We were all outside in our small, rectangular compound. Our house had three rooms on a single block. The first, running from the wall that separated Helen's house from ours, was for Mama and Baba, the second for my sisters and the third for my brothers and me. Near the main entrance was our bathroom combined with latrine. A long wall, across the front of the rooms, separated our house from another.

Voices drifted over the wall of the adjoining compound. 'Hhm, the *kafiris* have burnt the Sabon Gari main mosque.' It was Umar's mother.

Umar said, 'We'll burn all their churches! We'll kill them!' Mama froze, her arms across her breasts.

Umar was Ukpo's age-mate and he was talking of killing people. How did people kill people? I tried to imagine it.

'Who will lead you?' Umar's mother asked.

'Baba Sani,' Umar replied. 'They say he has a strong talisman. Inna, I'm hungry; anything for me?'

'Umar, real men set for war don't complain of hunger.'

'I'm still a boy. Will be a man someday. *Don Allah*, warm the leftover *tuwo* for me.'

'In that case, go make the fire. But they'll leave you behind because of food, my son.'

'They will blow a horn before we all move out.'

2 | *The Horn is Blown*

The horn was blown minutes later. It was so loud that its sound filled our house and when it died down, fear sprang in its place, gripping us. We came out of our rooms and looked at one another.

Mama broke the silence. 'Jehovah our Lord, we're in your hands. You've saved us from riots before. Save us from this.'

Oyigwu and Emayabo, the youngest ones, leant on her, their palms clutching at her wrapper. Baba stood near her, hands across his chest, his head bowed. Almost to himself he said, 'It's started again.'

Imatum, Ajara and Anyaosu stood in front of their room, staring at Mama. Ukpo was close to me, blinking his eyes, his left palm seeking my right. Yakubu leant on the door frame of our room, fingering the buttons of his shirt.

I heard Umar hurrying away. 'I can't wait for the food, Inna. *Insha'Allah*, I'll not be left behind because of *tuwo*. I'm a man.'

The atmosphere was still and calm, as if the world awaited something. Baba went to our main door and locked it. With heavy steps, he walked into his and Mama's room. I wondered what was going on in his mind. Baba was tall and had the brave appearance of a man who could withstand danger.

I looked up at the sky. Its blue brightness gave me strength. I thought I sensed the wind in the air and thought of Grandmama. I tried to stem the tide of my thoughts.

A woman's voice burst into a wailing pitch. I had never before heard such wailing. I felt a watery disorder in my stomach. I felt my body growing cold. I disengaged my hand from Ukpo's, walked to the wall, sat on the ground and drew up my knees. Mama pulled Oyigwu and Emayabo along as she also moved towards the wall and sat down. Her eyeballs rolled and her tears pooled. 'They're killing a woman,' she said, her voice shaky. I looked away from her.

I looked at the sky again and was shocked to find it clouded with smoke. The glare of the sun was dimming.

Suddenly, screaming garbled voices seized the air.

'Na dem! Na dem! Na dem!'

'My own don finish o! Papa! Mama! Paaaapaaa!'

'Wetin I do you? Wetin I do you? I beg…'

'*Iya mi o! Iya mi o!* I don die! I don die! I don…'

Tears streamed from Mama's eyes. My sisters, frightened, huddled beside her.

Other voices, really male, were chanting '*La ila a ila laa! La ila a ila laa! La ila a ila laa!*'

It was an odd mix: the terrifying screams and the chanting. I could no longer see the sun; the sky had gone totally dark. The wateriness in my stomach intensified. I felt an opening tug in my anus.

The chanting became louder, swallowing the screams, drawing closer to our house. Mama got to her knees, her palms stretched skyward as she muttered fearfully. Beads of sweat dribbled down her face. Apart from Baba, who had come out of their room and was staring towards our main entrance, we all joined Mama on the floor and did as she did.

The chanters moved away from our house. I sighed loudly. We all stood up slowly, but Mama did not. Baba cast a glance at her. He did not talk. None of us did. Our silence seemed to shield us. Baba returned to their room. In whispers, her tearful eyes tightly closed, Mama continued speaking. 'God of Abraham, Isaac and Jacob, do not let them eat our flesh. Send your angels to be on…' We froze in terror as a nearby scream stabbed the air. It diminished with each hacking blow. Still kneeling, Mama shivered and began to weep quietly. Oyigwu and Emayabo wept along with her. Imatum stared, her face contorted and her lips in a pout. Anyaosu held her hand, leant on her, her face sketched for crying. Ajara put her two arms across her head, looking bereaved.

'It's Helen's house,' Ukpo whispered.

Helen's parents occupied two rooms in a large compound beside our house.

Unsteady, I leant against the wall, my wet palms clutching at the block.

Baba came out and stood by the door, tilting his head to hear the voices from the adjoining compound.

'My own don finish o!'

'Jesus of Nazareth o! Where you dey? I say where you dey? I don die!'

'My father! My mother…'

'Dey don kill me o! Dey don kill me o! Dey don kill me o! Ahhh…'

I moved away from the wall. I picked out Helen's voice, raw, responding to each blow. Tears stung my eyes. I felt the pain of being clubbed to death. I felt as light as a leaf.

'Hold him! Hold him! Hold my son for me,' I heard Mama's voice distantly.

I felt Baba's hands around me, pulling me up. 'Murtala,' he called softly, his lips against my left ear.

He called again. I responded. He dragged me to near Mama. In that half-conscious state, I saw Mama's body quiver uncontrollably. I screamed. A heavy palm clamped over my mouth and the scream filled my mouth. I jerked violently, struggling for breath. With the strength I had left, I gripped Baba's palm with my two hands and yanked it off my mouth. I took a deep breath.

Baba said, 'You must remain quiet. Don't scream!'

Ukpo came close and took my hand. Baba left me and went back into his and Mama's room. The screams continued from Helen's compound.

'Jesus where are you? Come o! Come o!'

'My own don finish o! God na so you go let dem kill me and my children?'

'*Iya mi o!*'

'God na you I blame! Na you I blame! I no blame dem!'

'*Chei Chineke!* Na so life be? Me wey survive de Biafra war go die here?'

'Give me my son! Give me my son! Give me my J-e-r-e-m-i-a-h!'

'*Kai!* Bring that pregnant woman here! Rip the womb open! That child is a *kafiri*!'

'But if we…'

'Follow the instruction!'

Mama suddenly sprang up, startling us. It was Baba. He walked out of the room, hurriedly dressed in his uniform, holding his truncheon in his right hand as if he would strike someone.

'Going where?' Mama whispered.

'To rescue you from this place.'

'No, you can't go out. Can't you hear the voices of death?'

'I won't remain here and see us killed.'

'God forbid, they'll not kill us, in Jesus' name!' Mama looked into the sterile sky. 'O God, have mercy on us. We shall not die. He that lives in the secret place of the Most High…' She lapsed into sobs.

Baba walked away from Mama. Her recitation stopped short and, in a leap, she grabbed Baba by the waist. Baba could not move.

'Leave me. I'm no longer going.'

Mama let go of him, but moved in front of him to block his way. She struck a desperate pose, her body quivering. We all stared, wet-eyed.

Imatum rushed to the latrine and returned quickly.

The screaming voices subsided. I could no longer hear the grim voices. The smoke was still present, thickening. Intermittent gunshots drew sharp screams from afar.

Yakubu stood up suddenly and rushed to the latrine. His movement scared us.

Mama said, 'God of Abraham, Isaac and Jacob. It is this time we need you most. This period. Come to…'

As if Mama's prayer had invited it, we heard a loud bang on our door. Yakubu dashed out of the latrine, holding his shorts in his left hand, watery shit dripping from him. Baba sprang up and Mama froze awkwardly. Imatum and Ajara and Anyaosu held one another tightly. They wept silently. Oyigwu and Emayabo burst into fresh tears. I tried to stand up, but my legs could carry me no longer. *The hour has come.*

Another shattering bang on the door. The same grim voices.

'Yes, the policeman here is a *kafiri*.'

'I do see his family go to church every Sunday.'

'But I swear by Allah they have all fled.' It was the voice of the barber whose shop faced our house.

'*Mallam*, we don't have to waste time here. There are more people to kill.'

Ukpo attempted to climb the wall that separated Umar's house from ours. Baba pulled him down in a single move.

An utterly frightened Yakubu turned round, shit dropping in greater quantity down his legs and on to the ground.

Baba let go of Ukpo and walked unsteadily to the latrine. He did not enter it. He returned to his seat. He did not sit down. Then he made for the latrine again.

'They're not in. I swear by Allah.' A loud voice pleaded. 'They've left.'

'Set the house ablaze!'

'It belongs to Hajiya Halima. I swear by Allah.'

'We want to go inside and see for ourselves.'

'No use. I swear by Allah. *Haba!* Kabiru, don't you trust me for once? Accept what I've told you and leave this house alone. It's under my care. I beg you, in the name of Allah.'

With a wave of her hand, Mama ordered us to enter her and Baba's room. We scurried in as though it would save us. Inside, we were as light as ghosts. We knelt down with Mama. Her voice began to tremble again: 'Almighty Father of Heaven…'. The girls were also murmuring. The smell of Yakubu's shit filled the unventilated room.

The minutes dragged on.

We heard no more banging on our door. The voices were also gone. Ukpo and I emerged from the room. Baba sat on a small stool, gripping his truncheon. He sweated as profusely as if he had just wrestled with a man his size.

The sun was cowed.

Baba stood up quickly when he heard police whistles.

'The police are here,' he said.

Mama walked sickly out of the room, my younger ones following her. 'How do you know the police are here?' Mama had a distant gaze on her face.

'The whistles.'

Baba entered their room and began to pack.

'Go and pack your clothes in your bags,' Mama ordered us and disappeared into their room. Emayabo followed her, whining that she did not have a bag.

Ukpo followed me closely as we walked into our room. It appeared we had lost our tongues; we did not speak to each other. Our eyes spoke a lot though.

Baba opened the door of our house carefully, peeping out at first, despite the whistles blaring all over. Mama was behind him.

The air outside was heavy with the odour of burning flesh. I listened to the barber who lived opposite our house talking to Baba.

'I told them a lie to save you.'

'I heard your voice. May Allah reward you for saving our lives. I don't think we've done anything to deserve this salvation.'

'The breath of life is the same for every person. I value it. If I can help, I can't stand by and see you killed.'

Mama moved closer to Baba.

The barber continued. 'It was easy for me to dispel the first group because they're from here, they know me. The second group isn't familiar with this area, but I know the leader. He lives in this neighbourhood.'

'We're really grateful, Barber.'

'They killed all the people they found in the compound beside your house.'

'*Chaakokoo!* Jesus of Nazareth!' Mama was beating her chest with her palms.

'Ehm!' Baba stared vacantly.

Suddenly Mama said, 'Let's go.' She was trying hard to hold herself together.

Baba hoisted two big bags on his shoulders and began to move after thanking the barber again. We walked next to Mama, carrying our luggage.

We had just reached the main road when Mama let out another cry. Two corpses lay mangled on the floor, their heads chopped off. I turned my eyes away quickly. But where I turned, the corpses of a man and a woman lay side by side. The beheaded corpse of a boy lay across their chests. Next to that was the body of a girl, her head shattered. Her headscarf, part of a school uniform, still in shape although it had fallen off her head, was damp with blood and a whitish substance.

I noticed that the road was littered with corpses. I could also see many damaged cars and motorcycles. Some houses by the roadside smouldered with acrid smoke. We walked in silence, inhaling the stale odour of death.

Ukpo drew closer to me, whispering, 'Look up, Murtala.'

I looked up and beheld vultures flying in a circle.

'They're celebrating,' Ukpo said.

'They want to eat human flesh.'

Mobile policemen, armed like the very ECOMOG soldiers I had seen on TV in Helen's house, were mobilised, their guns at the ready.

One of them stood by the roadside as we passed. 'Officer, how are you?' he asked Baba.

Baba stiffened in a salute. 'I thank God, *Oga*.'

We stopped.

'I hope they didn't touch your people.'

'Yes. I'm lucky.'

'Take care of your people.' He turned to Mama. 'Madam, sorry ehn. It's part of life.'

'Tank you, sa,' Mama said, bobbing a curtsy.

There were other people wearing white clothes, a Christian cross in red on the front, carrying corpses and putting them in a big van. Red paint splashed a slanting *Red Cross* on the van.

Most Hausa people, looking sad and sympathetic, stood in front of their houses staring at us. The street had swollen with victims who looked unusually solemn. Corpses still lay haphazardly on the ground as though they had rained from the sky.

We flowed into a multitude of refugees, carrying their

baggage on their heads, eyes sunken with anguish. I heard the sounds of the slow, snaking vehicles of the mobile policemen and soldiers. Except for those and the intermittent gunshots from near and far, there was an uncanny silence.

3 | *We Reach Sabon Gari Police Station*

We reached Sabon Gari Divisional Police Station and met a crowd of refugees. A woman was thrashing about on the ground, shouting: 'My own don finish o! Na my only son! Na only him I get. Him papa don die for ECOMOG!' She wore a cloth of rich lace. Her wrapper came loose on her hip, revealing two tangled strings of beads over her underwear. Sprawled beside the crying woman was a young man with a deep gash on his right shoulder. A fresh cut ran down his left thigh. The T-shirt he wore was soiled with blood. His mouth opened and closed now and then. His chest rose and fell in heavy breathing. Some of the onlookers beat their chests with their hands, weeping and cursing the police.

'If na deir broda, dey for don bring motor carry am go hospital since. Wicked people!' a woman in front of me said.

'No mind dem. No be dent cause dis *wahala* for us? Dem know say Muslims go kill people and dey no do anything.'

'God go punish dem!'

'True! God go punish dem!'

'Which God?' The short, dark woman widened her eyes in indignation. 'E concern God? Na so we go dey look until dat boy go die.'

'Hei! *Olodumare!*'

'Let's stay here,' Baba said. His uniform was drenched in sweat.

A short policeman helped carry one of Baba's bags from the gate. He lived in the barracks. He started complaining that his apartment was flooded with refugees, that he had no space for us. I heard Baba address him as Sergeant Abu. He spoke a different dialect of our language.

We all sat on the floor, spent.

'I'm hungry. Mama,' Emayabo complained, as Mama untied Oyigwu from her back.

'Wait, I'll get you some food,' Mama said, cuddling Oyigwu who had also begun to cry. She drew Emayabo into her embrace and patted her consolingly on the head.

I looked around for food. There was none. People's lips were either dry or wet with drool as they wept.

'I'm hungry, Mama.' Emayabo had a way of turning such desperation into a song. I knew she was complaining for all of us.

The wind was gentle. I thought of its absence during the hours of killing.

'Murtala, move around and see if you can get a loaf of bread for your sister,' Mama said, loosening one end of her wrapper.

She gave me a ten naira note. I walked towards the gate of the barracks, which was not really a gate, but a relic of it. There I came upon a small circle of people, their hands against their chests in utmost despair. A small boy held tight to his mother's right leg, staring up at her. A woman staring at a man spreadeagled on the floor held her baby to her breast. The nipple rested on the baby's cheek, breast milk dripping. The baby, opening its mouth and tilting its head, tried in vain to latch on. It gave a sharp cry. The mother turned and hurriedly put the nipple in its mouth. As I approached, I saw that the man's left foot had been chopped off. His right foot was shod in a fine shoe. Still staring at him, I moved away and hit the leg of an old woman seated on the floor, her head bowed.

She yelped. 'Can't you watch your steps? Watch your dangerous steps, my son.'

The words *I am sorry* came to mind, however I could not utter them.

People did not talk much. Some conversed quietly, their eyes darting about frequently.

I saw Adejo, my primary schoolmate, sitting on the floor, his head bent downward. I did not move towards him.

Outside the gate, across the street, at the back of a two-storey building, I saw a brood of chicks with bright feathers and amazingly neat legs. They were crying. Their mother was out of sight. Where had their mother gone? I looked around, but did not see her. I walked to the only kiosk I saw.

In front of the kiosk was a large umbrella bent eastward. The man under it sold provisions. People crowded around him, looking very sober. He was reacting fast to their demands. Because most of them were adults, some of them impatient, I had to wait. By the time I was able to tell the man what I wanted, the bread was finished. I bought biscuits and returned to where we were staying.

Oyigwu and Emayabo had fallen asleep on our threadbare mat. Imatum, Ajara and Anyaosu stood together, looking around and whispering to one another. Ukpo and

Yakubu seemed to have strayed off. Baba was not around either.

Mama scowled at me, demanding, 'Why did it take you so long?'

'There was only one person selling and there were many people.'

I kept what I had bought and decided to wander around too.

I saw a plump man of about thirty in a pair of blue jeans and an ash-coloured T-shirt, moving around. Given the way he walked, I wondered if there were springs under the sneakers he wore. He had headphones on his ears that seemed to trigger the gaiety in his eyes. He drew closer to us, stood near me and winked at Imatum, a lecherous smile hovering on his thin lips. I missed Imatum's reaction. The man strutted away jauntily like an excited cock. Curious, I followed him. He moved towards a young woman standing alone, her cheeks seemingly puckered in a smile. Drawing near, I realised that she was not smiling. She was weeping. The man had already spoken to her.

'Get out of my sight!' she barked. 'You must be a madman!'

He winced, bouncing backward, almost bumping into another man who threw him a wicked look.

I followed him as he pranced about until I was tired.

When I returned to our place, I met Baba. He had opened his mouth to say something when our attention was drawn to a police van that had driven into the premises. Three policemen were struggling with somebody inside the van. The way they held him against the tailgate of the van, twisting his arms behind him, was so conspicuous that it made people stare. I walked behind Baba to the scene.

What I saw shocked me. Tall and wiry, but looking suddenly old, Helen's father was being hauled from the truck. He kicked weakly. They kept him on the veranda of the office block. I pushed my way forward and stood nearby.

He lay on his side, his face towards the onlookers, breathing heavily. His Afro, usually combed, was dishevelled. His eyes were bloodshot and blinked rapidly, the eyeballs rolling sideways. There were bruises all over his face. Spittle dripped from a corner of his mouth, yet his lips, half-opened, were dry and cracked. Also dry and cracked were his palms and feet. The safari suit he wore was filthy, smeared with blood and sand.

A pot-bellied policeman, wearing a uniform jacket, walked out of the office. Somebody shouted and all the policemen saluted him. He stood over Helen's father, bent down and turned the enervated man so that he lay supine.

A policeman moved respectfully closer to the pot-bellied officer and said, '*Oga*, the man dey fight us since.'

'Did he use any weapon?'

'No, *Oga*. But he carry stones.'

I pictured Helen's remains. I became weak and left. How could Helen have gone that way, after so much laughter and hope? Her voice rang in my ears: 'When next you go hawking bread, I'll go with you. When you're tired of carrying the tray. I'll relieve you.' She giggled. 'No. You can't stop hawking bread for your mother. She's helping the family.

I know how my mama is helping us, but she won't let me hawk. Our mothers are different.'

I met Madam Well-Well, Mama's neighbour in Yarkura Market, talking to Mama in our language about Helen's father, all my younger ones attentive. '…That he saw his six children, piled one on top of another, all slaughtered. And by their side was his wife, also slaughtered, her womb torn open.'

Mama winced. 'Oh Jehovah, my Lord.'

'And there beside her was the foetus, a mangled baby boy.'

'*Chaakokoo!* Violence even to the unborn?'

'They said he went berserk. He pulled an iron bar from a pile of rubble and attacked everybody in sight.'

'Oh poor man, poor man!'

'He struck a small girl dead. He was chasing an old man when the police got him.'

'God Almighty!'

In the evening, people became busier. A tall, slim policeman spoke through a megaphone consoling people. 'Contry people, my brodas and sistas, I bring you message from our military president. De situation dey under control now. Na religious fanatics and vagabonds cause de *wahala*. Dey don bring more soldiers to Kano. So abeg make una relax. Na dis be de message from His Excellency, our military president.'

People stared at him morosely.

Out in the open space, people used their kerosene stoves

to cook, although the harmattan disturbed them. Some gathered firewood from the surroundings to light fire. At the left end of the grounds, there was a clump of *dogonyaro* trees. To the right, just before a large gutter widened by erosion, stood a thicket of ferns.

Baba disappeared and returned with two food flasks filled with beans, watery and over-peppered. There were also two loaves of bread. We ate up the food in no time. It amused me that my sisters, who hated beans, ate up everything and even licked their fingers. After eating, Baba left us again.

Darkness stole upon us. The whistling movement of the wind was steady. I looked up, searching for the moon. It was not there. It occurred to me that for some days now, the moon had gone on its usual journey. Why, then, had it missed such a day as today?

Baba appeared briskly, carrying two damp blankets, dusty and smelly.

'We'll spread these blankets on the floor and sleep,' he told Mama.

Mama collected die blankets, without a word, and placed them on the ground beside her.

'They said they would bring relief materials tomorrow,' Baba informed us.

'What are they bringing?' Mama asked.

'Blankets, rice, beans, sugar, bread and other things.'

The darkness thickened. Flames of candles were dancing in the wind all over. I did not hear laughter or music. Many people had lain down. I thought of what the time might be. Beside us, a man and a woman, lying very close to each other, were whispering. I strained my ears in vain to grasp their words.

I noticed a tall man slinking around us. He edged towards Ukpo and me.

'What does he want?' I asked Ukpo.

'How do I know?'

When he was very close to us he switched on a torch. We were startled. I sprang up. Ukpo stood up and grabbed my hand. We said nothing. He raised the torch in such a way that our faces were in its glare.

Baba shouted, 'Who be dat?'

'*Oga* sorry abeg. I dey look for my son.'

'Okay o. Dese ones na my sons,' Baba said curtly.

We watched him move away slowly, his head bowed. He wandered amidst the people lying down, shining his torch now and then. I was still watching him when Ukpo whispered into my ear: 'Imagine that were me looking for you.'

'I can't.'

My sisters lay on one blanket, my brothers and I on the other. We covered ourselves with a large cloth Mama gave us. Mama and Baba lay down on the mat, her back against his stomach.

Suddenly a harsh scream tore the delicate calm of the night. The voice kept rising. We scrambled to our feet. There was no electricity. Most of the small flames had gone out. The three big flames made by the police and placed at strategic intervals still glowed. We could barely see ourselves in the dim light. Screaming voices rent the air.

'*Iya mi o!*'

'God of Israel!'

'Wetin dey happen?'

'Denis! Denis!'

'Make una no run! Make una no run!'

'Murtala, Ukpo, don't go anywhere!' Baba shouted at the top of his voice.

I heard Mama's voice. 'Imatum, hold your sisters.'

They held one another in a tight embrace: Imatum, Ajara and Anyaosu. Baba held Yakubu by the hand. Mama carried Oyigwu. Emayabo began to cry. 'Hold me, Emayabo. Hold me, don't cry.'

My palm gripping Ukpo's, I saw people rushing here and there in confusion. They surged towards the police office block, crashing into one another.

'My *bele* o! My *bele* o! My *bele* o! Ahhh mama me o! Mama! Mama!' The voice rose and fell. It rose and fell. It rose and fell again. My stomach tightened. Tears stung my eyes.

'It's a girl,' Ukpo whispered into my ears.

'Yes.' I could barely hear myself. My saliva was salty.

The voice with its terror grew weaker until it died away.

I turned to the left where I had earlier heard the whispering voices. A mat and a large cloth lay rumpled on the floor. Dust rose around them.

The voice of the man with a megaphone seized the air. 'Contry people, brodas and sistas, make una calm down. Nothing dey happen. Nobody dey come after anybody. Na one woman shout for im sleep because of bad dream. No be anoda fight o. Abeg…'

Silence returned, as suddenly as it had been broken. Then wails broke out as people crowded around the body of the girl. A policeman knelt and put his ear on her chest. He sprang up and lifted her up. 'We must to take her to hospital now!' he shouted.

'Wetin happen wey we dey run?' a woman asked Baba.

'I no know, Madam.'

Armed policemen moved around us as we lay, unable to sleep. I noticed that the whispering voices had returned. The night deepened.

'I can't sleep, Murtala,' Ukpo said, his mouth almost touching my ear.

'Nobody can.' I thought I was whispering, but my voice sounded loud.

Ukpo continued. 'If I close my eyes, I see many dead people.'

'My English teacher said that kind of thing was an imagination.'

'Interesting. Then I have an imagination. So how do you define imagination?'

'It's defined as something we create in our minds which does not really happen.'

'But the deaths happened and I'm seeing them when I close my eyes.'

'You can't see when your eyes are closed. It's an imagination.'

'I wish the killing were an imagination, Murtala.'

'Me too.'

A man, lying close to us, was shifting restlessly, moaning, 'Oh my God, it's hurting me so bad; it's my waist…'

'Sorry, darling. Please, bear it. I pray we'll get out of here first thing tomorrow. Sorry…' A woman was consoling him.

When Ukpo's voice finally dissolved into sleep, he produced throaty, meaningless utterances, a sleeper's version of our conversation. I heard the harmattan soughing through the clump of *dogonyaro* trees. Then I heard the footfall of the policemen patrolling.

I noticed that the whispering voices from our left had stopped. I was curious and raised my head to look towards them. In the faint light, I saw the two figures entwined, but not still. My eyes strained. The steady rhythm under the large cloth was unmistakable; buttocks rose and fell.

I fell asleep.

It was cold and misty. Emayabo and Oyigwu had woken up. Mama covered them with cloths to protect them from the cold. She sat between them, her hands resting on their shoulders. My sisters sat on their blanket. They were talking and Imatum was pointing her index finger to her left. I did not bother to look what was there. Ukpo, his face unusually taut, was staring towards the cluster of *dogonyaro* trees. Yakubu sat close to Baba, his brow puckered in a frown.

'What are you looking at?' I asked Ukpo.

He did not answer me.

I stood up and walked around. People moved about quietly, with light steps. Their eyes were swollen with grief. I looked carefully at the shape of their eyes, the colour of their eyes, how their eyelids moved, how the eyelashes protected the eyes. Some people's eyes dilated at the slightest noise. Others' narrowed in steady, cold stares, unmoved by sound. Most people stared without blinking. The eyeballs did not seem present for seeing alone. I stood at the gate for a minute before I returned, conscious that it was too early for me to be far from my family.

'Murtala,' Mama called.

'Yes, Mama,' I answered, moving closer to her.

'Go and look for food. I'm sure you know Sabon Gari well?'

I nodded. I saw men and women bringing food in polythene bags. Ukpo offered to go with me when Mama gave me some money.

People were milling around at the gate. There were also glaring, armed policemen. We avoided the gate, passing instead through the three blocks of the barracks. Because the fence had broken down in places, there were four outlets apart from the gate. The outlet we went through was busy, with many people walking in and out.

Just before we crossed the gutter to the tarred street, I saw a mother hen clucking loudly, wings half open in rage as she moved first in a circle, then towards the east. She seemed to be searching frantically.

With sunken eyes people walked past us, their feet dirty, their steps raising dust.

'I dreamt Mama was axed to death,' Ukpo said suddenly.

I froze. 'You dreamt Mama died?'

'Yes. And we were crying.' He was looking into my eyes, a wan smile on his lips.

'A bad dream, Ukpo.'

'Thought it was only you who had nightmares.'

'Wish I would not have nightmares anymore.'

Ukpo smiled. 'Overheard Mama and Baba saying dreams were a precious gift from our ancestors.'

'But how could you dream of Mama being killed?'

'I did. I was scared.'

I imagined Mama in a pool of blood, being hacked to death. I was terrified. How could she die? Who would be our mother if Mama died? Would we remain normal if she died? I did not think children without mothers were normal.

'They killed many people yesterday, Murtala.'

'Yes, many people including Helen.'

'I'm so sorry they killed her.'

'Maybe I'll find her someday.'

'But why are people killing people?'

'Don't know, Ukpo. Will ask my English mistress.'

'Never seen a goat killing a goat.'

'Me neither.'

'Would you kill somebody, Murtala?'

'I wouldn't. I don't know how to kill. Why?'

I cast my mind on the utterly wicked verb: *kill*. What did it actually mean? Why did it exist? Ukpo was not even afraid of using it.

'I think killing is not so bad, Murtala.'

'Why?'

'People who kill are happy. They sing and rejoice.'

I tried not to understand what Ukpo was saying. 'Let's stop talking about killing, I'm scared.'

Ukpo giggled. He always felt braver than I did, even

though I was older. Mama said he had actually been braver when we were younger. He was born just a year and three months after me and enjoyed better health in childhood. I did not care about that. Now he respected my views and made me proud with his bravery.

As we walked and talked, I looked to the sides of the street. Almost everywhere around us there were burnt tyres, long iron bars, huge sticks and heavy stones on the ground. Sabon Gari remained the same except for the ashes of the burnt tyres everywhere. I did not see any burnt houses, vehicles or any corpses on the ground. I noticed that people stood in groups outside their houses, talking in low voices or simply watching things going on in the streets.

'A woman is selling food over there,' Ukpo said, pointing.

'Yes, I can see her.'

We bought the food: rice, beans and tomato stew.

On our way back, we had just crossed Enugu Road when an uproar erupted. The abrupt screeches of speeding motorcycles deafened us. Three motorcycles carrying two people each appeared beside us. The passengers, giddy with excitement, were shouting: 'They're coming! They're coming!'

'The killers are here!'

'Everybody bring your weapons out!'

They raced past us. People were dashing into their houses upon hearing the message.

'Ukpo, what do we do?'

'We run.'

I looked back and saw a bewildered crowd rushing towards us. 'Ukpo, let's run.'

He flung away the food we had bought and grabbed me by the hand. He was ahead. I was slowing him down. I wrenched my hand free from his grip. 'Just go, Ukpo. Just go!'

People were shouting and yelling at the top of their voices. Going as fast as he could, Ukpo kept turning back to look at me. I understood but could not run any faster. *The tortoise*, Grandbaba once told me, *cannot suddenly acquire the speed of the hare.* We were lost in the pandemonium. Car horns blared furiously. I tried to keep my eyes on Ukpo. *Go, brother, go! You're the hare, son of the Wind.* He was at the last turn before the police station. Then in a split second a car emerging from the turn at top speed braked with a terrible screech. Ukpo disappeared from sight. I tried to slow down, to see properly. The saloon, its tyres grating the tarred road, swerved towards me. I must have leapt. I was on the bonnet of the car as it jerked and jerked and jerked to a halt. As I rolled off the bonnet, my eyes caught spattered blood and a mutilated figure on the ground. I saw the oncoming runners freeze. People crowded around me, their voices a din in my ears. A hulking man held me down as I struggled to stand up. 'Sit on the ground. Don't stand up!'

'*Chaakokoo!*' Mama collapsed, rolling sideways in the throes of sorrow when Baba finally confirmed Ukpo's death. All my younger ones burst into tears, kneeling around Mama. Imatum tried to hold her, to make sure that the hidden parts of her body were not exposed.

'Why now, when I thought God had taken sorrow away

from me?' Baba wailed. 'Where are you, sons of the Wind, my ancestors?'

'Hold her well. She'll injure herself,' Madam Well-Well said, helping Imatum.

'*Oga*, sorry, take am easy. Na so God say make e happen,' a scrawny man told Baba, draping his hand on Baba's shoulder.

A woman walked to me slowly, staring at me. Her eyes were wet. 'Na God say make you live. *Do*, sorry.'

The plump man with the headphones brought drugs for me to swallow. I shook my head. He barked at me, 'Come on, take! Y'know, what do you think you are? A monster? Y'know, these are just painkillers.'

I did not want anybody shouting at me, so I took the tablets.

A moment later, the loud voice of the policeman with a megaphone interrupted our mourning. I did not care to grasp his meaning. Those who stood watching us with blurry eyes began to move towards the voice. As they moved away, I got what the policeman was repeatedly saying. 'Contry people, make una join de line witout fighting. De relief material go do for everybody…'

I did not know what emboldened my legs, but I stood up and walked slowly, unsteadily, following the people.

'Murtala!'

I looked back and answered feebly, 'Baba.'

'Get back. You have no strength.'

I turned as if to go back, but dodged out of Baba's sight.

A small girl was carrying a big basin clumsily. She started running, but collided with a man. She fell, rolling to one side while the basin rolled to the other. The man hurried away without even looking at her. Whimpering, she jumped up and made straight for her basin with grim determination. She hurried towards the lines. I saw a woman with a large cup, trotting towards them. A man pulled off his shirt and stretched it flat as his container.

Two intimidatingly long lines snaked away. I joined the shorter one. A tall, dark policeman, his gun held horizontally, was pushing, shouting, 'Go join the line! You must join the line. Foolish people!'

Other policemen were shouting orders, wielding their truncheons.

'Aah my wound, my wound! Dis stupid man don brush my wound,' a slim woman howled. She supported her hurting left arm with her right hand, her face wrinkled in pain.

'Sorry abeg.'

Her eyes were full of tears as she blurted, 'Why you no go front go struggle with men like you. Na me you see to push. God punish you!'

'Make you no insult me o. I don tell yon sorry.' He turned his back to her, pushing his way.

The woman coughed, cleared her throat and spat at him angrily. The mucous saliva settled on the man's left ear. His left palm rose slowly to the ear, the substance dripping onto his fingers. Boiling with contempt, the man started towards her.

'Stop dere!' a policeman bellowed. 'If you touch am I go put you for guardroom now now. '

The man glared at the woman, glared at the policeman

and walked towards the end of the line, cleaning his palm on his trousers.

It was an awful din: the cries, the shouts and the curses that filled the atmosphere.

After a long time, during which I had grown weaker but refused to give up, I had in my possession a packet of sugar, a small sachet of Peak milk, a tinful of *garri*, a blanket thicker than ours and a bowlful ration of beans. Abruptly, I realised I was alone. 'Ukpo!' I called. It seemed he answered the call from behind me. I turned sharply. He was not there. 'Ukpo,' I called and turned again, dropping the things I carried. Then I saw his face. It was gory, but calm. The face multiplied into many faces. I started screaming, 'Ukpo! Ukpo! Ukpo!' My head was spinning.

Mama woke up the next day retching and wheezing. She began to vomit, though she had not eaten any food since the news of Ukpo's death. Her temperature ran high. She grew weaker by the minute. Baba was restless. My sisters and brothers jostled around her, staring and guarding her with unuttered prayers.

Baba left us and returned with some medicine.

'Ijaguwa, take these drugs.'

Mama muttered, 'Let me die and leave the problems of this world. Leave me alone, I want to die…'

'Your children are staring at you.'

Mama looked at Emayabo and Oyigwu. 'I'm tired of this life.'

'Take the drugs, please.'

'Leave me alone. Let me die…' Mama narrowed her eyes, staring vacantly.

Baba became exasperated. 'That's nonsense. And you'll leave these children for whom? Before you die, just make sure that all of them are dead, then you follow them.'

Mama started weeping, accusing God of bringing such sorrow upon her. Baba was frustrated, threw a look at me and stomped away, muttering.

At that instant, we heard the blaring of a lorry's horn. I turned my eyes. Outside the gate, two lorries, each half loaded, slowed to a halt. I heard a man who had just jumped down from the lorry shouting, 'Ojoma! Ojoma!'

A woman was also shouting as she strode briskly towards the gate. 'Michael! Michael! Bring our things!'

People began to rush towards the lorries, carrying their luggage. They were climbing into the lorries, whose tailgates were already flung open. Two men in dirty clothes were shouting: 'East, South and Central Nigeria!'

'Na south we dey go o. Come enter and save your life from killers!'

'Na one way. Cheap transport, one way!'

There were frantic movements as people rushed to get spaces.

Mama stood up slowly, her gaze intently on the scene. She walked slowly towards the gate, murmuring to herself. Then stopping halfway, she turned back to us. 'Imatum, Ajara, Yakubu, pack our things. We'll leave now!'

Where were we going? I could not ask Mama because of her countenance. She looked like an enraged mother hen.

I turned, helpless, and saw Baba coming towards us with more relief materials.

Imatum folded the blanket they had slept on and unzipped one of the bags to put it in.

'Why are you folding…?'

Mama interrupted Baba. 'We're leaving here.'

'For where?' Baba was perplexed.

I collected the relief materials and put them on the ground.

'My children and I have a home.'

'You want to go to the village now?'

Mama looked him straight in the eyes, her voice became low and each word came in emphatic cadence. 'I should keep my children here and allow the hawks to snatch them from me? All of them? My children shall not die. Go and look for a lorry to pack our belongings now!'

Baba was trying to contain his rising anger. 'I don't understand you. What about my work?'

Her voice rose, 'What kind of work, ehn, what kind of work?' She mimicked him. 'What about my work? You're not ashamed working in a place where death stalks our lives? Where is Ukpo, tell me, where is that young, strong, courageous son of mine? Tell me!' She stamped her foot and burst into tears.

My younger ones stared at Mama. People were watching us.

After a moment, as Mama was wiping her face with the edge of her wrapper, Baba answered, 'I don't have the money to get a lorry.'

With a swift movement, Mama untied her wrapper,

pulled out a cloth pouch from her waist, unzipped it, withdrew some bank notes and threw them at Baba. 'Get us a lorry!' Mama screamed. Then she lowered her voice again. 'My children shall not die.'

Mama and Baba glared at each other. It appeared Mama might let out a harsher scream. Baba took a look at us and walked off.

He returned some minutes later and found us, belongings packed, set to travel. We were eating soaked *garri* while Mama sat on one of the loads, her hand cradling her chin, her look surly. She carried Oyigwu asleep on her back.

Baba spoke calmly. 'They've given me a police truck to pack my load here until we get a house in a safer area.'

Mama did not answer him.

'Did you hear me?' Baba stepped close to her.

She burst out, 'The whole world is not safe, Father-of-my-children. The whole world! But we'll be comfortable in our village. That's where we want to go. Now!'

'You can't go now. Don't…'

'We must go now, my commander.' Mama stood up, invigorated, a weather-beaten woman in her last fight. 'Not on your cost, but on mine. I will use my money to save my children. Look around: people are leaving. We cannot stay an hour longer. I shall not watch while the hawks descend on my children again.'

Mama looked frail, as if she would be lifted from the ground by the harmattan.

Baba drew quiet, his head low and his arms across his chest. We watched him expectantly.

4 | *Mama Gets Her Way*

Mama got her way. Baba begged her like we had never seen before. But she insisted on leaving. Baba protested. 'But Murtala has to go to school here.'

'He's my first son, I can't leave him behind. There are schools in the village.'

'Not like the one he attends here.'

'Don't you have eyes? Can't you see what's happening around you?'

'Why don't you give me your eyes?'

'My children are my hope. I can't leave him behind in this turbulence.'

'Peace will come,' Baba said. He sounded confident.

At first, I was confused. Then I sided with Baba and said, to Mama's bewilderment, 'I'll stay with Baba. I'll go to school here.'

Mama threw me a cold look. She did not speak again. Imatum glared at me and hissed loudly.

Really, I felt pity for Baba. I knew that if he had the wherewithal, he would have agreed that we should all leave for the village. He wanted to carry Ukpo's corpse to our village, but he had no money to rent a car. I reasoned that if all of us followed Mama and abandoned

Baba, it would be unkind, especially as I knew he was helpless.

That night, we buried Ukpo in a cemetery within walking distance of the police station.

Mama and my siblings departed the next day, hungry and frail. Mama stared at me for a long moment, her eyes filled with uncertainty. Yakubu drew closer to me and took my palm in his, the way Ukpo used to do. He had never done so before. Our palms trembled on contact. He turned his face away when I looked at him. Little Emayabo, when she was sure they would leave without me, grabbed my right leg in a tight embrace, weeping and refusing to let go. I lifted her up. From her tearful eyes shone a strong fear, as if she would never see me again. I could not resist my own tears as I told her, 'Emayabo, I'll see you again.'

Ajara's voice quaked when she said goodbye to me. Anyaosu, quiet and shy, simply hid herself behind Mama. And it was a relief that Oyigwu was asleep.

It was two weeks now since they had left.

With a single trip in the rickety police truck, Baba and I moved our belongings from our former house to our new one at Kwanar Jabba. It was the third day after they had left.

The new house was a tenement house. I counted fourteen room-and-parlours. In one of the rooms, when I looked through the window, I saw dried blood on the floor, drawn from the centre of the room to the door. Most of the wooden doors were broken, hanging loosely on their hinges. Baba chose carefully, so that he would not have to replace the door. The blue paint of the house had flaked off with age. There was a low fence at the entrance to die house.

It had no door. Holes and scratches had made nonsense of the plastered floor inside the relatively large compound. A stunted *dogonyaro* tree stood at the centre of it and there was a mosque directly opposite the house. There were only two sets of tenants, Hausa Muslim couples, in the house.

I liked sitting in the front of our room, reading *An African Night's Entertainment*, or *Triumph*, the newspaper Baba brought home. I enjoyed reading the newspaper because of the variety of its headlines: *25 People Killed in Religious Riot in Kano; Normalcy Returns to Kano; Reprisal Killings Erupt in Enugu; Operation Desert Storm Rages; Ten Palestinians Killed in Gaza*. And so on. I read every sentence in every story. Baba's dictionary was handy. One of the words I saw regularly was *tragic*. There was also *SAP*, always in upper case, frequently in headlines. The longer words that entered my subconscious were *corruption, infrastructure, government* and *underdevelopment*.

One morning, a picture on the twelfth page of the newspaper struck me. A boy, Yakubu's age, was sitting on brown grass, staring at a flood of sunrays coming from the side. He was emaciated and his body was glistening in the sun. His head was a thinly-fleshed skull with elongated ears and drooping lips. Thick snot ran down from his small nostrils to his upper lip. Flies perched on the upper lip. His eyeballs protruded against his eyelids and only the lower parts of his eyeballs were visible. His neck was very thin and the collarbones were so prominent that they looked like those of an adult fixed on his small frame. The arms were bony, so bony that they appeared like sticks. His outstretched legs too. I had not seen such a picture before. Under it was the caption: *Child victim of war in Liberia*.

I went to the window where Baba kept the razor blades he used for shaving. I picked up an old blade. Carefully, I cut out the picture with the words under it. Then I went into the inner room and found two drops of pap on the floor near the kerosene stove that had not dried up yet. I wiped the pap from the floor, rubbed it on the back of the picture and pasted it in the outer room near my bed.

In the afternoon, tired of looking at newspapers, I decided to do something else. I cooked rice and beans in the *dafa-duka* way Baba taught me: I poured the rice and beans, including the various other ingredients, into the pot together. The beans were half-done. Baba insisted I cook this way to save kerosene.

Baba returned in the evening, looking depressed. His reply to my greeting was a grunt. He undressed silently in the outer room, the smell of his socks fouling the air. My eyes darted to him from my book periodically. He took his uniform into the inner room. He did not ask for his food. Instead he asked, 'Have you eaten?'

I said yes.

'Murtala,' Baba said when he came out of the inner room and sat on the chair opposite me.

'Yes, Baba.'

I did not look at his face. I had never really looked into Baba's eyes. I dropped the book I was reading.

'Your mother is a stubborn and senseless woman. Do you know that?'

I raised my head, averting my eyes. Did he expect me to

answer his question? He would be hurt if I did. I opted to remain silent.

He continued. 'I have a feeling my children aren't doing well in the village. Hhm, those village witches!'

I refused to respond. Mama often quarrelled with Baba over his belief in village witchcraft. During one of the quarrels in our Kwana Hudu house, an exasperated Mama had almost spat on Baba as she howled, 'A reasonable person doesn't hate his home the way you do.'

'If my home deserves hate, it gets hate. Simple and short,' Baba had blurted out.

Mama told us that Baba was hiding his reluctance to visit the village behind a fear of witchcraft. She said we should disregard him.

'Power is back,' I said, as our rickety ceiling fan began its noisy movement.

'She's taken my children there to expose them to witches.'

No. Certainly that was not Mama's intention. I did not know how genuine Baba's fear was. But I knew that Mama was a mother hen. Grandmama called her 'Mother-hen'. Mama could not possibly watch while the hawks of noonday violence picked her children away. Mama had been, to say the least, devastated when Ukpo died. Baba too.

'Murtala,' Baba called my name again.

'Yes, Baba.'

'Do you think your mother took a good decision?'

I knew he wanted me to say something. 'I don't know.'

'You should try to know something. At fifteen, you're becoming a man.'

'I hear you, Baba.'

Baba left the outer room for the inner one.

That night Ukpo crept into my dreams.

I find myself on strange sandy ground. I feel an uncanny blast of cold air on the back of my neck. I turn sharply to see a pained smile on Ukpo's face. The contours of his face are indistinct.

'Ah Ukpo, where have you been?'

'In the market square.' His voice is weirdly husky.

'Which market square?'

'A place for us who find ourselves in the naked path of violence. Look around.' He turns round, showing me people with his gestures.

I see several very faint human-like figures, suspended, sleeping in mid-air.

I notice Ukpo's shirt and shorts, ragged on his shiny skin, changing colour from white to blue and from blue to grey.

'But you shouldn't be here,' I tell him.

'Two brothers were walking on the road. And violence snatched one away.'

'Return home. We've changed our house.'

'We're here, waiting. Just waiting.'

'Come, I'll lead you.' I move to hold his wrist but grab empty air.

He is moving away from me without taking a step. I move closer to him. I cannot reach him.

The figures around us have disappeared. Terrified, I watch as, incredibly, Ukpo acquires wings and flies away like a huge vulture. My gaze is intent on him as he grows smaller, smaller, into the purple sky.

* * *

The day I resumed school, we counted losses on the assembly ground. The short and pot-bellied proprietor of the school was almost in tears. His chubby cheeks protruded as his lips remained tight. His teaching staff stood beside him on both sides, their faces stony.

Penetrating the harmattan's haze, the sun's rays settled on the two-storey building that contained our classrooms.

We were exceptionally attentive. I was sure no student had dodged assembly. We were not many, however, because most students had not resumed school. We sang gospel songs, led by a girl, graceful in height, humble in appearance and soft in speech.

'Our female Jesus,' a girl beside me in the Form Two line whispered to another behind her. They giggled quietly, covering their mouths with their palms.

The first song was *Soon and Very Soon, We are Going to See the Lord*. I wondered why we were singing it. Were we really going to see the Lord soon? Since one had to die to see God, it meant we wanted to die. Were we celebrating the deaths we had witnessed? The next song was *In my Father's House, there are Many Mansions*. I stopped singing and cast my mind on the wording. I wished God would either bring the mansions down to earth, so that the world would become better, or send an aeroplane to move all of us to heaven to occupy them there. Why were we living with mice in a dilapidated house while the mansions in heaven stood unoccupied? We also sang *Abraham's Blessings*. It reminded me of what our Sunday school teacher had said about Abraham in the Bible. Acting on an instruction from God, Abraham was set to slaughter his only son as an offering to God when the very same God gave him a ram so as to spare his son. I had totally believed the story until the day Imatum, who had a talent for doubting such stories, told me, 'Well, the day God will tell Baba to sacrifice his son, the first son for that matter, you're gone!' Though Baba did not look like someone who would obey such a command, fear had gripped me at the thought of being slaughtered.

After we had finished singing, the proprietor took two steps forward. He stood erect. Then he placed his hands on his large stomach.

His brow furrowed as he began. 'Good morning, students.'

'Good morning, Sir,' we chorused.

'On behalf of my staff and the school authority, I welcome you back.'

'Thank you, Sir,' some students said loudly.

'A terrible time for all of us. We sympathise with everyone. We're all casualties, as JP Clark says.'

We were silent.

'We've lost twenty-four of our students to the crisis.'

We were all gripped by the urge to weep, gasping and exclaiming quietly as he read their names from the list: 'Mary Nnamdi, may her soul rest in peace. Oladimeji Joseph, may his soul rest in peace. Yakubu Babayaro, may his soul rest in peace. Maryam Mohammadu, may her soul rest in peace. Jennifer Samson, may her soul rest in peace…'

Because he read slowly, as if his lips were unwilling, it took him some time before he finished. I saw films of tears on the cheeks of students. We observed a few minutes of silence for them, offering prayers in both faiths. A day before the crisis, when I had started school, there had been no Muslim prayers on the assembly ground.

As the prayers began, I recalled an argument Mama had had the previous year with Uncle Tony, her cousin, who was studying at Kano University. He was much younger than her. He often came to our house for weekends and holidays. Mama had entered our room, where Uncle Tony was lying on a mat, reading a book, and rebuked him for not going to church.

Uncle Tony sat up on the mat and shot a meaningful glance at me. 'Don't worry about me, Big Sister. Christianity and Islam are foreign religions that don't merit my attention anymore.'

Mama's eyes clouded. Then she stared at Uncle Tony contemptuously. I thought she would bark at him to get out of our house.

'Maybe you don't understand what I mean, Big Sister,' Uncle Tony said, his tone unapologetic. On his smoke-darkened lips was a triumphal grin.

'Because you're studying at university, you've joined those hell-bound bookish people who say there is no God, ehn Tony?'

'I wasn't talking about God, Big Sister. He exists. The ancestral way our fathers worshipped God is the best way for me.'

'So you don't believe in Jesus Christ?' Mama asked, her tone surprisingly desperate, like that of an evangelist expecting a sinner to say, 'I do'.

'Oh yes, I know he existed in history,' Uncle Tony enthused. 'Jesus Christ was a great humanist of his time. Every history has its great humanists.'

Mama sensed that Uncle Tony, who was studying history, would intellectualise the issue as he was fond of doing. She gave up with a sullen silence.

The prayers ended. I did not say amen. I did not wish to pray anymore within the religions that had triggered the violence in which Ukpo and Helen perished.

Helen and Ukpo lay heavy on my mind as I walked to class.

Once inside, I remained silent. I only nodded at my classmates who greeted me.

I should have gone with Mama. If I were in the village now, I would be with my thoughtful Grandbaba, listening to him. Or I would be playing with my funny Grandmama, who called me her husband, trying to wheedle a piece of smoked fish out of her. More eloquent than Grandbaba, she called herself the daughter of the Wind. She taught me to be brave, to fight whomever wanted a fight with me. 'I married your grandfather because he was the greatest wrestler of his time. Do you know how to fight, city boy? Come let me teach you.' And she would stand up and strut around, opening her arms and clenching her fists for a fight. I would collapse with laughter.

I did not wish to remain in the class. I was about to leave when Millicent, with whom I shared a desk, walked in, her school bag strapped on her back. She was clean, smart and cheerful. She struck me as a curious being. She looked as vivacious as Helen although, unlike Helen, her face was oval.

'Good morning. Please, I want to go to my seat.' She pointed.

I created a space for her. 'Good morning and welcome,' I said.

She took her bag off her back and sat down. Her name was printed on her bag. She placed her forehead on the edge of the desk and remained silent for some time. Then she raised her head and made the sign of the cross. She pulled up her bag and began to open it.

'Millicent, do you know that Stella was killed?'

'Jesus Christ!' she exclaimed and leant towards me. Her expression became sober. 'Oh, dear Stella star.'

'Did they kill people in your place?' I asked.

'They killed many people.'

'Where is your place?'

'Dakata.'

A student walked into the class, her right elbow bandaged. As she took her seat, other students went to her quietly.

'They killed many people in my place too.'

'Where is your place?'

'Kwana Hudu.'

A dark, plump girl waved at Millicent. She responded by grinning and waving back.

'My mother said Muslims started the killing.' Her small lips moved gently when she talked.

'It's because Christians burnt a mosque in Sabon Gari.'

'They burnt many churches and mosques in Dakata.'

'Did Christians fight in Dakata?' I asked eagerly.

'Yes. Christians killed many Muslims.'

'In Kwana Hudu, it was Muslims that killed Christians.'

'My mother said it was not the first time Hausa people had fought strangers. Before the civil war, they killed many Igbos.'

'When was that?'

'Long time ago. She was a small girl then.'

'That must be a long time ago, indeed,' I said, staring into her beautiful eyes.

A tall boy winked at Millicent as he walked to his seat.

'She said that was when the North and the South started hating each other.'

'But the crisis was between Christians and Muslims.'

A frown creased Millicent's smooth forehead. 'Most people from the North are Muslims and most people from the South are Christians.'

I understood Millicent's point. The majority of the students in my school were, like Millicent, Christians from the South. Prestigious and elitist, my school was considered a Christian private school. My primary schoolmate, Aminu, had sneered when I told him I had been admitted to Tony Cheta College and said, 'That school is full of *inyamiris* and *kafiris*.' I had not taken him seriously.

After a moment of silence she asked, 'Where is SMG?' A benign smile played on her lips.

'I don't know.'

I wondered why she had asked me about the bully. I also wondered where he was.

A teacher entered the class.

* * *

Baba returned home tipsy. He refused to respond to those who greeted him in the compound. He did not respond to me either. I stood up from a wooden stool in front of our room where I had been sitting, reading my social studies notebook. He flopped down on the chair, unbuttoned his uniform shirt and removed it. His white undershirt had changed colour and smelled of sweat. Then he loosened the long laces of his police boots. I watched him furtively as he retrieved some squeezed bank notes from his smelly socks. Raising his head, he caught my eyes. On his lips was a funny smile.

Baba went into his room and returned, looking sad.

A Christmas carol was booming somewhere in the compound.

Baba burst out unexpectedly: 'People are still killing people.' Loudly, he continued, 'People are slaughtering people in silence, in hiding. We are living in an abattoir.'

'We lost many students in my school,' I replied.

Baba was not interested in my words. A long moment of silence ensued. I listened to the whooshing of the December wind outside. Our frail windows, open, banged against the wall intermittently. I heard a woman calling her children. Then I heard their footsteps as they ran to her.

Baba, who had reclined on the chair, suddenly sat upright and stiffened his arms, his two palms locked together, his head low. 'People are still killing other people. Not soldiers, but ordinary civilians, using their loud religions and silent weapons.'

I did not say anything, but my interest peaked.

'Life can become terminal, even before death,' Baba continued.

Baba stood up abruptly, his face twisted aggressively as though he were quarrelling with someone. 'And yet she took my children to the village against my wishes.' He walked into the inner room.

Baba's logic baffled me. If people were still killing people, was it not safer that Mama and her children had left for the village?

Christmas passed silently. Baba did not receive his salary in January and February. He said the military president had not approved the year's budget. We survived on the naira notes tucked into Baba's socks. That was when he was on a good shift. On a bad shift, when he guarded banks and houses instead of doing patrolling, he brought home nothing.

'The bank gives me only five naira for lunch,' he told me one day though I did not ask. 'That's corporate wickedness, isn't it?'

I nodded.

'I carry an ancient gun that couldn't even save my life to guard the banks. And what I get is a meagre sum that the bankers would be too ashamed to give as offering in a church.'

We also survived on the amounts he pushed me to borrow from our neighbours who sold foodstuffs. Yes, Baba pushed me because, left to me, I would rather have died than ask any of those fat, slovenly Yoruba women to give me foodstuffs on credit. One of them stung me one day when she riveted her small eyes on me like a tough headmistress and said, 'Murtala, tell ya papa say credit get limit o.' The limit was that I never again returned to her kiosk to buy anything.

Baba got a new transistor radio before Christmas. When I was home on weekends or public holidays, I listened to the network news with him. Baba would respond to the news by saying 'Umhum!' to a news item, 'Ehm hem!' to another, or even a whole sentence such as 'Didn't I say it?' to others.

There was an expression that sprang frequently from his lips: 'Na wa for dis SAP!' He expressed it in different tones. I had been watching Baba mouthing it for some time before he called me one day after the news.

'Yes, Baba,' I answered him, yawning. At weekends, I hardly slept. Instead, I read late into the night.

'There's something called SAP. Heard of it?'

'I've seen it on paper and heard of it from you,' I answered him.

'That word is lashing every poor person with *bulala* in our country now.'

I took this as Baba's way of putting things. Baba had the habit of complicating simple things, like a teacher bent on impressing his pupils. I doubted if Baba knew that what he said was called personification. How SAP whipped people was what I honestly did not know. Though I read newspaper stories with headlines containing SAP, I did not understand them fully. SAP must be an adult worry. I did not like having adult worries, even though Baba had taken to calling me a man recently. All I wanted now was to wash my face and to start washing my clothes and Baba's. It was Saturday.

'Structural Adjustment Programme,' Baba burst out, startling me. He looked at me and chuckled. 'That's SAP.'

I tried to repeat what he said. 'Stru-ctu-ral adjust-men…'

'Aren't we doomed,' Baba interrupted me, 'because our leaders who can't adjust their own lives are adjusting ours? We're being adjusted into poverty and violence.'

I remained silent. I had little interest in what Baba was saying.

Baba continued as I was about to stand up: 'Do you know life is hard, Murtala?'

'Yes, Baba. We're always eating beans and *garri*.'

Baba looked into my eyes and said, 'Murtala, do you know that several people out there can't enjoy that beans-*garri* luxury?'

I was puzzled. 'Baba, are beans and *garri* a luxury?'

'I see, Murtala. You've hidden yourself inside your small books and you don't know what's going on around you. We call people like you the elite.'

Baba pronounced 'elite' as 'ei-lait', different from the way I heard my English teacher pronounce it.

'Baba, I'm just reading my books to do well in school.'

'Nice of you. Sometimes I see you as the lone ray in this darkness. That's why I insisted on sending you to a private school, even if I can't afford the fees! You'll meet your destiny. Ah, I have suffered in life. We're progressing backwards, Murtala.'

'I want to go and wash.'

'I bore you, don't I? You have no worries, because I worry for you. You're fed, your school fees are paid. Go and wash, but be watchful of SAP.'

I decided to stay watchful. Our compound was alive with people. Our big house had been occupied, except for two rooms. Most of the people that came initially, some former occupants of the house, were men. Later their families joined them.

Baba Tindele – for that was what I heard his wife call him – was a thin, dry man who occupied the double room opposite ours. He was quiet and reserved like Baba, only answering greetings with a couple of words, not caring to look at people. A week after he joined us in the compound, his family arrived. His wife was a huge, light-complexioned woman with pockmarks on her face. Her ten children were all like their father, thin and dry. You would swear that the children could not have come out of her enormous body. Three of them were severely ill and the woman spent her time attending to them.

A Fulani man who did not look like a herdsman had just occupied the room after ours. He was handsome, of light complexion and average height.

A man who limped because of a bad leg had already occupied the room beyond the Fulani man's. He was a Muslim from Bendel State. He moved into the double room along with his two wives and thirteen children. Since he had arrived, I had never seen him or any member of his family without wondering how they arranged themselves to sleep.

A fat, muscular man Baba once addressed as Mr Godwin occupied the room before ours. We later called him Baba

Eddy when his wife, two daughters and two sons arrived, all very eager to please people. They responded to ordinary greetings with extra enthusiasm, as if they had been done a huge favour.

Quite surprising to me was the appearance of a particular plump man in our compound. I recognised him from the police barracks: his bouncing steps, his headphones and his conspicuous exploits with girls. He talked, walked and did everything with style. I had not met such an unusual person before. The day I introduced myself by name, he flashed me a knowing smile and intoned: 'M-Boy.'

I smiled.

'I forced you to take medicine at the barracks. Call me Omodiale.'

I remembered and nodded.

People began returning to Kano City. The city that had shrunk to a ghost in the days of killing recovered quickly, fattened by people-filled streets busy with normal activities.

I saw heaps of debris along the road, near the burnt houses. Beside the cemetery that extended to the Airport Road lay a heap of burnt flesh, rotten. The odour was heavy in the air. A man and his wife, carrying Bibles, covered their noses with their palms as they hurried past me. I held my breath and quickened my step.

There were still burnt vehicles beside the roads. I felt uneasy each time I looked at them. They brought Helen and Ukpo to mind. Each day I yearned to discard these images and think beyond them. I wanted to become a recluse, hidden from the world.

Many roadside shops were locked up. Some of them remained vandalised. I saw the debris of burnt TV sets, radios, torches and electric lamps, swept into a heap. Beside the debris stood a man, well dressed but with only one ear. I drew closer to him to look at the stump of his roughly sliced-off ear. A short man in his work clothes was inside a shop, painting it.

As I walked along the police barracks, down towards Nomansland, I came upon a group of schoolchildren, staring at a skinny dog in the throes of death. It yelped, sprawling in a dry gutter littered with brown grass. Its legs and waist were smashed, with raw flesh and bones jutting out.

'James, it resembles our dog,' a little girl holding an older boy's hand said. She looked from the boy to the dying dog.

'It's not ours.'

I pondered over what fate had befallen the dog that morning as I walked to school.

I had just settled in my class when Ola walked up to me, a wide-lipped grin on his face.

'Happy survival, Murtala,' he said, stretching out his hand for a handshake.

I stood up as we shook hands. 'Same to you, Ola.'

I shifted to make a space for him to sit. Ola was the only boy who had confronted SMG when he was bullying me on the day I started school. I had sought an opportunity to befriend him. But the crisis had flung us apart. Although school had long resumed, Ola had just returned. 'Did they kill people in your place?' I asked.

'No.'

I didn't believe him. Could there be anywhere in Kano City they had not killed people? 'But they killed people all over the city.'

'No, Murtala. I live with my parents at GRA, close to the governor's house. Nobody would kill around there.'

'Oh I see. I thought they killed people everywhere.'

'We didn't even hear any sound of gunshots or fighting. We watched the destruction on our telly.'

'Then why has it taken you this long to resume school?'

'We travelled out of the country. My mum was not happy with the news of death around us, so we left for London.'

'That's nice. I welcome you back.'

'Thanks, Murtala. I hope nothing happened to anybody in your family? I was thinking of you.'

'I lost my younger brother.'

Ola suddenly became sober. 'Oh I'm so sorry. Accept my condolences.'

'Thank you.'

During the break, while Ola and I got chatting again, SMG walked up to us and stretched his hand for a shake. Ola hesitated before he took it. I took SMG's hand too. He had a shamefaced grin as he told me, 'Murtala, I'm sorry for that day.' I nodded.

5 | *I Reach Our Village*

I reach our village just after the rain, which has swathed it in a fresh, earthy smell. It ushers in an uncanny darkness. I do not see weaver birds on mango trees chirping their last tunes for the day. I do not see children hurrying to their homesteads with errands their mothers need to finish the cooking. I do not see latecomers hurrying from the stream, water splashing from the big basins they carry. I do not hear mothers calling their children loudly. I do not hear competing rhythms of pounding from various homes. Nor do I hear the loud laughter of young men returning to their homesteads. How could all these have given way to this eerie silence?

I walk faster. Reaching the village square, fear grips me. An unearthly wind whirls round me. I quicken my step, almost trotting, hoping to see somebody, anybody, whose appearance will reassure me of human beings still living. I had gone in the morning to Oweto Market while the village was alive with neatly-clothed women and children. Where are they now?

It is abrupt and terrifying: the loud, harsh, piercing cry of Owuna. He is in an angry masquerade with two short horns as eyes. He wears a red blanket and a red cap with an eagle's feather stuck on it. He wields a horsewhip to lash any teenagers who get in his way. I dread him. My heart pounds in panic as his voice fills the air. Horrified, I turn round. Where is he? Teereeeeeeyaaaaaaa! The cry pierces my soul. Then he appears unexpectedly before me. I run. As fast as I can, I speed away towards Ogam Road. I take a sharp corner, heading for Obagaji Road, hoping to elude him. But he comes after me angrily. Taking another sharp turn, I head for the village square. Try as I might, he gains ground and, alas, catches me by the arm and flings me into the air. I eddy up like a whirlwind, fall back into his arms and then he hurls me flat on the ground, pressing me down with his right leg. I squirm helplessly, my scream receding into my throat. Then he raises his horsewhip and I spring up to run.

I must have woken up screaming.

'Murtala! Murtala!' Baba stood beside my bed in the outer room. 'Tell me what you saw. Whom were you struggling with?'

I scrambled out of bed, sweating all over.

'What did you see in your dream?'

I remained mute. I looked into the brightness of the electric lamp. Power must have returned after I had gone to bed. My body was hot.

'What did you see in your dream? If you don't tell me I'll spank you. You must stop that habit of keeping nightmares to yourself!'

Baba was having one of his rare tantrums.

'It was Owuna chasing me.'

Baba's anger deflated. He sighed loudly and adjusted the towel around his waist. He stood with his hands on his waist looking at me, and then turned back to the inner room. As he walked away, he said, 'What else will you see, as she's taken my children to the witches?'

I heard him yawn loudly and the wooden bed creak. I stifled a yawn and rubbed my eyes. I heard the distant howls of dogs. Sitting down on a chair, I folded my arms across my chest and began to weep silently, taking care that Baba would not hear me.

Ukpo, where are you? I've lost my sleep to nightmares, as I have lost my laughter. When I close my eyes in sleep, thinking you'll come, all I see is Owuna bent on killing me.

'Murtala,' Baba called, his voice echoing.

I did not answer. I wiped the tears from my eyes.

'Murtala, am I not calling you?'

'Yes, Baba.'

'Stop crying. Sleep now. The world has heard too much of innocent crying. It has no respect for tears.'

I climbed onto my bed, but remained fearfully awake.

I took refuge in school. Not that home was uncomfortable, however. Baba gave me the comfort he could afford. When he had money, it showed in the food we ate. He would bring home goat meat and cook the food himself. But when times got tough again, as they always did, we reverted to beans and *garri*.

I became quite lonely, even in our big compound with its playful children. The thought of Ukpo and Helen, of Mama and my siblings took my mind away from the compound. Whenever I heard children playing, I thought of

Emayabo, of Oyigwu, of Yakubu and of the trio. Frequently, I imagined them suffering from terrible illness, on the verge of death. I pictured a helpless and frustrated Mama, crying and praying. Much as this image haunted me, I did not mention it to Baba.

After Ukpo died, I realised that he and Helen were the only friends I had ever had. I should have made other friends, to share stories and laughter with. It was obvious that in my class no one was older than me, not even SMG, though some were physically bigger. Aside from the age gap, I found it difficult to befriend them because they had fancy things I didn't. I was unable to forget Mama's advice: 'I'm not happy your proud father is putting you in a school where you will meet rich children. Don't covet their things in anyway. Remember the womb you've descended from.'

It was Sunday and I was very lonely. Because Mama was not around, I did not go to church. Baba went to church once in a while, when he felt like it, and sat in the last pew, right at the back. He would return home with a litany of criticisms. Our church had a tradition he hated: multiple offering times. He once asked Mama, 'What does that reverend do with the money? Each Sunday service people give offerings three or four times, and yet he looks as poor as the rats in his church.'

Mama took this as an insult, an assault on the anointed one of God.

'So you want to fight for your reverend?' Baba asked her.
'You're driving yourself to hellfire!' Mama fumed.

Baba laughed. 'I'm sorry for you. Your reverend makes you poorer and instils in you the fear of hellfire.'

'It's because you don't give an offering to God that you're poor. Examine yourself, Father-of-my-children.'

I decided to take a walk to the Muslim cemetery. The cemetery was unfenced even though there were relics of a fence. The concrete walls supposed to support the barbed wire had fallen in some places and bent elsewhere. The barbed wire itself was either nonexistent or hung loosely.

To the east of the cemetery lay fresh, rectangular ridges. They must have been new graves. I walked towards the ridges slowly, my sandalled feet brushing the dry, hard, thorny undergrowth. I counted the ridges: fifty-six. I wondered who were buried there and what had sent them to their graves. I walked on, to the southern border of the cemetery, surrounded by mango and *dogonyaro* trees. I saw some men lounging around beneath them. I stood at a distance and watched. Occasionally, their half- closed palms moved stealthily to their lips.

I was surprised to see Omodiale swaying towards me in stylised steps, his left palm half-closed. A ring of smoke trailed from his head, the heavy odour of marijuana. I made to turn back when he called, 'M-Boy.'

I looked at him. He took a long drag and threw away the stub. He stood in front of me, the odour all over him, and I gave a quiet snort of disgust. He threw his right arm round my shoulders and I stood rigid, annoyed, unable to push him away.

'Y'know, you're too young to enter this kingdom,' he said, a smile on the right of his mouth.

'I'm only taking a walk,' I snapped.

'Sure. Y'know, from taking a walk to having the baptism that lands you in the kingdom.'

'I want to go home.' My voice was tinged with anger.

'Where else will you go, but home? Y'know, someday you'll get to know that this kingdom is greater than home. Not now.' He took his arm away and swayed off.

I liked the way Omodiale spoke English. He had a nice accent. As I walked home slowly, I thought of Mama and my siblings.

Before I took the last turn to our house, I saw two children, a boy and a girl, half-naked, throwing stones at a hen and her new brood of chicks. The hen was helpless. She moved back and forth squawking loudly, charging towards the children, her wings half-opened, then hurrying back to her chicks.

'Hey, leave that hen alone!' I shouted at the boy, who was apparently the leader.

He cast a look at me and then took to his heels. The girl followed him.

I was back at school on the day it resumed for the third term, eager to see Millicent and Ola who had become friendly with me. Neither was there. We were not many at school. After the ritual of songs and prayers on the assembly ground, I lounged around in the school compound. Other students were also walking around aimlessly. Our teachers were in a meeting.

I moved to the cashew tree near the gate, attracted by the

Press Club board. Handwritten essays, old and dirty, were pasted on it. They must have been there since the previous term. I had begun to read one of them when a girl walked up.

'Hello,' she said.

'Good morning.'

I turned and could not remove my eyes from her. I stepped back and took in a full view of her: her long face; her fresh, boyish sideburns; pert breasts; fleshy, bandy legs; and her downy skin. Even her height. The girl turned to me, surprised at my behaviour. But it was not her I was seeing. Was this mere resemblance? Why had Helen come to me in this spitting image? And Helen's voice, full of panic and death, filled my mind.

'Are you all right?' the girl asked, staring back at me.

'Yes, thank you.'

I walked off to class, sad.

The next day Ola resumed school. He was a marvel: a new uniform, a new pair of sneakers, a bought-from-America baseball cap, a bought-from-London school bag and a golden wristwatch. As soon as we left the assembly ground for our class, he started hovering around me, carrying wrapped parcels and tins of corned beef.

'Hey Murtala, I've got a gift for you,' he said, sitting on my desk, having said hello to Millicent.

'Thanks, Ola.'

He handed it to me. I slipped the wrapped gift inside my school bag as our English teacher came in. Her dress style amazed me. She must have been very rich, wearing all those fine clothes. Her lessons were my favourite and her accent was an inspiration. Each day, each night, I yearned to speak like her. In my loneliness at home, I would lock myself in the inner room and imitate her.

During the break, when most students had left the class, Ola watched me unwrap the gift. I sprang up and almost danced. 'So kind of you, Ola. Many thanks.' It was a beautiful pair of sneakers, the type he wore.

'Would be nice for us to wear the same kind of sneakers.' He pointed at his.

I sat down, pulled off my worn rubber sandal from my left foot and tried one on. It fitted well.

'I took the size of your foot; you didn't know,' Ola said.

I stared at him in my exceeding happiness. I felt redeemed. I was no longer the only one in the class to have nothing new.

'Do you like them?' Ola asked.

'Very much.' I wished I knew a better way of saying it.

'Let's go out,' Ola said.

I put the shoes back into their packet. As I was about to put it into my black polythene bag, Ola said I should keep it locked in his leather bag so it would be safe.

'Congrats, Murtala.'

It was Millicent, smiling sweetly. I had congratulated her earlier on her new uniform.

'Thank you. Thank Ola for me, please.'

She did.

Ola smiled shyly. 'It's nothing. I told my dad about Murtala and he decided to buy the pair along with mine.'

We ate the chocolate bars that Ola had brought.

* * *

As I was returning home, my attention was caught by a poster on the left of the mosque in front of our house: George Bush's screaming mouth facing Saddam Hussein's stony stare. War raged in their eyes. Written close to George Bush's head was *In God We Trust*. Close to Saddam Hussein's head read *Insh'Allah We Shall Win the War*. This was superimposed on multi-coloured figures of soldiers, armoured tanks and machine-guns. A flame splashed at the bottom of the poster. In the flame were mangled bodies of people.

Ola had told me about the Gulf War. 'My dad says the US wants to stop Iraq from taking over Kuwait.'

'Why is Iraq taking over Kuwait?' I asked.

'Iraq is greedy. Kuwait is an oil-rich country.'

'They want to take what doesn't belong to them?'

'Yes. Bigger countries always bully smaller countries. My dad says the US is helping Kuwait so that later it can turn around and take over Kuwait's oil.'

'I think that's what our social studies master calls imperialism.'

'Exactly, Murtala. My mom says human beings like using their power to conquer their fellow human beings.'

'Like the killings in Kano.'

Ola nodded. We were silent for a while.

'The US is also afraid that one day Iraq will become a superpower,' Ola said.

'What's a superpower?' I asked.

'A country that's powerful, like the US, is called a superpower.'

I was confused. 'If the US is already a superpower, why be afraid of another country becoming a superpower?'

'Still the greed. They call Saddam a dictator.'

'My father calls our president a dictator, too,' I said.

'Most military leaders are dictators. My dad says they rule by issuing orders.'

Ola went on to tell me about Saddam Hussein's stubbornness. He said the war might snowball into another world war. I did not know he knew so much about other parts of the world. When I asked him how he and his parents knew that much, he told me that they had a satellite dish on their house.

I stepped into our room and found something surprising: Baba in the sitting room, gleefully watching a *tokunbo* black and white TV. It was on top of the cupboard in a corner of the room. Baba looked at me and grinned broadly, like a child who has won a game.

At last, a TV set. I was excited, though deep inside, I wondered why he only bought used things. Could Baba not buy a new TV?

My younger ones and I had engaged Baba on the issue of having a family TV before. Baba had been frank with us. 'My children, if you think I don't need a TV and other electronics in my house, you're wrong. I need them more than you do, but I don't have the money to buy them.'

'Baba, we need a TV more than you do. You're always sleeping or going to work,' Ajara had said.

'Do you think I would sleep the way I do with a TV here?'

'Mama says you're lazy; that's why you sleep always,' Yakubu blurted out.

'She's a foolish woman. And don't give me that kind of report from your mother. If you say so again, I'll spank you.'

Yakubu had sulked.

Baba had gone on to tell us that if he wanted to watch a football match, he would go to a beer parlour where it was mandatory to buy a drink. His problem was the money to acquire electronics. Could we not see that his salary barely fed us? If it were not for Mama who often brought home foodstuffs from her income, we would have been malnourished.

We thought Baba was prone to exaggerating. Imatum had made a long face and asked me, 'Don't you think Baba as a policeman earns more money than Helen's father who is a mere messenger? Yet Helen's father has a colour TV and a fridge.'

'But Helen's father is a messenger for the Central Bank. The government pays them well. Baba is just a corporal in the police,' I had told her.

'But why does Baba have only two stripes?'

'Go ask him.'

'Me?'

'Why not? You're his friend.'

'Only when he quarrels with Mama and wants me to side with him.'

When we had sought Mama's opinion, she condemned our thinking and gave us a standing command: 'You should all advise your father and support him to save money, go to the village and build a house. Then we'll return home and live an honourable life. Do you like the *efulefu* life we're living here? I keep telling you, being a farmer in the village is far better than being a policeman like your father.' At this, she clamped her lips shut.

Undressed, still enthusiastic about the TV, I sat opposite the small screen. The station was CTV. Three men, wearing *babanriga*, were seated at a round table, talking.

Baba was dozing. I focused on his face: it was wrinkling. Was Baba becoming old so soon? In Mama's presence he had once bragged that his black, gleaming skin used to dazzle women. 'That was when the world still had some sanity and I fed on chicken and milk,' he intoned. Ukpo and I used to take Baba's old album and discuss the photos that showed him in his youthful majesty. In one photo, he was tall, his hair in Afro. He wore a tight-fitting T-shirt over trousers that were tight around his thighs and very baggy around his feet, swallowing the platform shoes he wore below. We amused ourselves at the shape of the trousers. 'The baggy part can swallow a human being,' Ukpo said.

'Mama said they used to call it *bongo*,' I told him.

When we showed the photo to Imatum, she told us that it had always fascinated her. 'Baba is right after all,' she had said. 'Mama is the problem. She has reduced him from being so handsome to being so ugly.'

* * *

We got a letter from Mama. A man with a long jaw and a tiny beard on his wide chin delivered it. As soon as I saw him, I had the urge to burst into laughter. He sat on the chair close to the door. He held his head stiffly, twitched his nose periodically and pressed his handkerchief against his nostrils as though the air in our room was foul. He was in the kind of uniform that security men in banks wore and his skin was smooth and fresh.

Baba came out of the inner room to meet him.

They had barely exchanged greetings when the man said, 'You've stopped coming to the tribal gathering.' His tone was flat.

'Not so, Musa,' Baba answered.

'Then why don't we see you again?'

'Have you people stopped hating one another? Have you stopped sleeping with one another's wives? And that chairman whose belly is fattening daily with people's money, have you thrown him out of the group?'

Musa focused his eyes on a wall, smiling. In his smile was something like mockery. 'Well, if you don't like our group, fine. You should, I suppose, belong to any group you like. But I suspect you're the type who sees fault in every good thing. You've chosen to be a recluse. Is it good for you and your family in this time of violence?'

'I don't join a bad group because I'm afraid of violence.'

'You sound crazy, Odula. In this time of violence, you should learn to associate with people.' There was a tic beside his right eye.

'Every age has its violence,' Baba said, his voice gentle but hard. 'Half of life is violence: open, clear violence. And the other half is peacefulness, but hidden and elusive. The chairman who steals the group's money is also violent.'

Musa gave Baba a sharp look. Then his face split into that mocking smile again. 'I see. A policeman with great wisdom.'

'Wisdom doesn't belong to bankers alone, not to talk of those among them who wear security uniforms.'

Musa left, after urging Baba to do something about his family in the village.

'He's the chairman. Didn't you see the burden he carries as a stomach?' Baba told me.

I opened my mouth, astonished. I did not know Baba could be up to such mischief.

Baba read the letter slowly. He became pensive. I sat opposite him, shifting uncomfortably to remind him that I was in the room with him. He did not raise his head. I became worried. What could it be that Baba had read to turn him so sullen? I stood up and walked out, heading straight for the crumbling building held together by sticks that housed our bathroom, passing the children playing soccer in the compound. My urine shot out forcefully.

As I returned to the room, Baba raised his head. His eyes were flushed and moist. I recoiled into a chair. Baba gave me the letter, stood up and walked into the inner room. The wooden bed creaked.

I read the letter slowly. It was written in a bad hand. In it, Mama said that Imatum and Oyigwu had fallen seriously ill. She complained bitterly that Baba had not sent money to her. She said Baba was an irresponsible husband and father.

* * *

A few days later, Uncle Tony came to our house. He had gone to the police station to look for Baba because he did not know where to find our new house. Baba was not there and one of the policemen on duty had described to him the place we lived. Uncle Tony looked weak and sad. He was recovering from a fever. Baba told him about Mama's stubborn attitude. He listened to Baba without interest.

My loneliness disappeared during the few days Uncle Tony spent with us. I told him everything that had happened to us during the crisis. He also told me how the killers had murdered Christian students on the university campus.

He and Omodiale became friends.

6 | *Baba Tells Me His Life Story*

Baba told me his life story:

'Murtala, I was a bright boy like you and anything in print charmed me. In my primary school, I was one of the best pupils and my teachers liked me. We did not start school early in life the way you do these days. They used to tease my father that the book juju he gave his son was superlative. My successes came in dreams; dreams that disarmed imagination, unlocked the hidden doors of the mindscape. Have you ever dreamt you're reading something and when you wake up, behold what you read in the dream was the accurate answer to your examination question? I belong to our ancestral dreamworld, like you.

'But I don't dream answers that solve my problems anymore. Oh yes, I still see things when I sleep, but what I see are bad things and perhaps that's why we're condemned to nightmares.

'I was my father's favourite, because I learned fast. I was the inquisitive monkey ahead of others. "Come, come see what I've discovered," I would call to my mates. While they watched, astonished, I would solve arithmetic problems too advanced for our level. I moved ahead of my mates from class one to class three; then it was called double-promotion.

As you already know, I was in class five when fate flung me out of the school.

'My father was indeed proud of me, praising me openly, not a habit found among our people. He wanted to see me become a great man and didn't believe that only a child who went to farm, who was powerful in tilling the ground, was great. My father wanted me to be great in the magical ways of words.

'"I want you to study hard and be like Ijamani," my father would tell me in privacy, whispering the words as if he didn't want the world to hear him. 'Ijamani' was a mispronunciation of 'Germany', our headmaster's nickname. He dazzled my father with his knowledge.

'I'd nod my head. And my eyes would sparkle with a promise he understood; my mind would leap to the next level of epiphany. I didn't go to the farm except on weekends; he was careful not to burden me with much work. While many tongues wagged that my father was spoiling me, my mother understood his vision and didn't complain that he was misdirecting her first son.

'"Son of the Wind," she called me one day. "As fast as the wind are your wings. No witch, male or female, can touch you. Go ahead of them; you are from my brave hips." I was grateful to her for sharing my father's perception. I vowed I would never let them down.

'Then my grandfather died suddenly. He had a large family and had instituted a hierarchy-by-eldest-son. My father, being his eldest son, took over the affairs of the family. That was the beginning of my problems. His siblings, who were now working for him, pried into my future. They became envious, assailing my father with their crooked reasoning. They were working for a man whose first son didn't work because he was 'special', even though the same boy would benefit from their labour. They put the issue to him in such a way that it gnawed at his conscience. My father was caught in the dilemma of either letting me continue my schooling or withdrawing me to join his younger brothers in farm work. Now, Murtala, these uncles of mine were grown-ups and I was still a teenager.

'One day, my father sent for me. I met him in his *uponu*.

'"I have been having sleepless nights over my brothers' murmurs. You'll stop going to school."

'My eyes dimmed and my stomach tightened. Tears welled up in my eyes. "But I want…"

'"I have spoken."

'That was final. He was a man of few words. Like every old man in our village, my father regarded words as sacred. "Words," he once told me, "are seeds that grow. If you plant good words, they will yield goodness; if you plant bad words, they will yield evil." I knew it would be futile to make him change his mind.

'I was devastated. I plunged into a hunger strike until I was close to death but realised that death was the worst option. I sought solace in the Catholic Church that had just started in our village. The church leader was interested in me. He did his best to change my father's mind, although my father insisted on his decision, pointing out that I was a child of the family and should gladly accept the decision of the family. I was forced to follow my uncles to my father's farm. They taunted me and created opportunities to beat me up each time I followed them there.

'The church leader, a Tiv man, tried to assuage my depression. One day he told me, "I'll bring you up in a spiritual way. If you behave well, I'll recommend you to the church to train." Encouraged by that promise, I toiled for him. For a full year I toiled, waited eagerly, but was not shown the way to school. I became worried.

'"Be patient, time will come. There's a time for everything," the church leader kept consoling me when he noticed my worry.

'"I pray every day, Master," I told him.

'"The Lord answers prayers."

'My father did not like my closeness to the church leader and he accosted me. I saw him as Satan obstructing my future. My mother confronted me one day: "Son of the Wind, we are worried that you have become a slave to that stranger, who is himself a slave to one *Ijisos*."

'"Let no one be bothered that I choose to slave. I have my life."

'"But you are a descendant of the Wind. The Wind does not know slavery. Haven't I told you of how we fled our original land and crossed the river because of the slave trade? We eluded the Hausa slave traders. And when they came here, we resisted them squarely. Now, we cannot watch you turn into a slave."

'"I'm slaving for Jesus Christ."

'"Is that sickly-looking stranger your *Ijisos*?"

'"I say Jesus Christ, not the church leader."

'"The whole village sees you washing, fetching water and

cooking for him. When did you become a woman to cook for a man, ehn, tell me? Do you not know shame?"

'My parents didn't have to worry for long.

'It all crashed one afternoon when I stood by the window of the church leader's room and watched as he pounded away on Ikende, one of the beautiful girls in the church. I left, disappointed. Shattered. All his overtures to make me return to his house and church failed. I could not reconcile the piety of the revered church leader with such a common sin of the flesh. I convinced myself that his promise to me was false; he lived a life of falsehood.

'I hit utter frustration. My spirit was drunk on rebellion: confrontational, disrespectful, implacable. I became a recluse. Then, I simply packed my clothes and left the village. I was the first boy in the village to be disgruntled with his father's decision and to set his own vision abroad. At the stream you cross before entering our village, I took water in my right palm and vowed: *I'll only return when I have the triumph of my soul*.

'I went straight to a recruitment ground: I wanted to join the army to fight in the civil war, to vent the self-righteous anger I carried. The first man I met in army uniform told me that the war was over. He was amused that I didn't know.

'I reluctantly settled as a labourer in Nasarawa, not far from our village. I carried blocks and mixed sand and cement for the first storey building in Nasarawa. Traders from our village, on their way to Kaduna, saw me and told me how my disappearance had inspired moonlight songs. When the traders saw me again, they gave me my father's greetings. I felt uncomfortable, being so close to home.

'I hitchhiked to Illorin and walked into Talatu's arms. A great woman, Talatu. She rescued me from the hunger and harshness of the street. She was a slim, tall woman with bleached skin. Her laughter revealed the allure of gapped teeth.

'On my fifth day in Illorin, I still had nothing to do, so I lounged around and carried loads to earn some coins. I slept on the veranda of the brothel where she lived.

'"Wetin you dey do here?" she asked me in a serious tone the first day she saw me.

'"I have no place to sleep."

'"Where you come from?"

'"Plateau State."

'"Ei! Plateau? You mean Benue Plateau?"

'Astounded, she drew closer to me. Her lively eyeballs arrested my shy look.

'"From Plateau? Who bring you here?"

'"I'm alone. I'm looking for work."

'"E be like say you go school, *abi*?"

'"Yes, primary school."

'"So wetin you dey do here, fine boy?"

'"I'm no longer in school. I want to work."

'"You come alone? Na master dey bring boys like you to work for farm for money. Where your master dey?"

'"I don't have a master and I don't know how to farm."

'She cackled, clapping her hands. "Hey I don see sometin today. Na *oyinbo* pikin you be wey you no know how to farm?" She turned towards the door and shouted,

"Imeri and Matta, a beg make una come see wetin I dey see o."

'In a moment, five women, half-naked, rushed out of the brothel. They had wiggly buttocks and bleached skins, their bodies smelling of unwashed flesh.

'I became shyer as they crowded around me, throwing questions at me:

'"Where you come from, han'some boy?"

'"You wan rape Talatu?"

'"Wetin bring you here dis morning?"

'"Talatu, wetin de boy do you?"

'I could not answer their questions.

'"Na shy boy e be, make una leave am," Talatu said.

'She took me to her room.

'I lived with her, running errands for her. She fed and even gave me pocket money. She introduced me to her *babalawo* as her small husband and sent me to him now and then to collect incense and concoctions for her. She taught me how to cook *jollof* rice. She taught me how to speak Pidgin English well.

'"Why you comot from school, fine boy?" she asked me one day.

'"My father no want make I continue."

'"Your father?"

'"Yes."

'"Why e be say all dose village old men dey so wicked. Na my papa make me be *ashawo* today. Him and his brodas tie my leg and hand, carry me go give one old man wey dem say I must marry. I run comot from de old man house."

'I became popular in the brothel.

"'Talatu's husband, abeg go buy me tomato."

"'Make you help me fetch water abeg."

"'Talatu, I wan send your husband."

"'Hhm, Talatu dis ya husband fine well well o; you fit do *ojoro* marry am."

"'Talatu, if you make *iyanga* too much I go snatch dis boy from you."

'In the evenings, when she attended to her customers, I would wander around silently – I had no friends – and return to the brothel at midnight. She insisted I sleep with her. Talatu instinctively knew that I was a virgin, even though I was in my late teens.

'Half-drunk one night, Talatu decided to give me a lesson. Touching her crotch, she said, "*Toto* sweet well well," her lips widening to a toothy smile. "No mind people wey say na sin. No be God make am? I go teach you how to fuck, you hear?"

'I stared at her.

'The next day I disappeared from Talatu's arms. With one menial job after the other, I roamed the town of Illorin. After a year, Talatu got me in the main market of Illorin where I did not expect to see her.

"'Hey! See my Benue broda wey run comot from me because e dey fear to fuck," she said cheerfully.

'I was amazed that she was not angry with me. "Good afternoon," I greeted her.

"'Where you dey now?"

"'I dey with one man."

"'Come, you like police work? One of my customer be police officer and dem dey recruit."

'"Yes I like am," I said excitedly.

'I followed the tall goddess home. For the three days we waited for the police officer to come – for that was what she said – she ushered me into the world of flesh.

'I trained and became a policeman. I've spent about eighteen years in the police.'

I stared at Baba as he coughed and became silent. Then I asked, 'Baba, if you've spent eighteen years, why are you still a corporal?'

'Oppression, my boy, oppression. Have you heard of an embargo on promotion? We're in a country where embargoes are placed on all positive things by the military dictators. Each dictator came with his baggage of embargoes. When they don't promote us, they save a lot of money which would have been spent on salaries. Only for themselves. Let me tell you, Murtala, the police force is the most fertile ground for oppression. Or let's say the entire military and paramilitary force. Have you heard Fela's *Shuffering and Shmiling*?'

I nodded. I always heard that song from Omodiale's room.

That's our condition. With a loud *yessa*, we salute those who oppress us. Then we smile and return home to the hostility of our wives and children.'

I kept watching Baba keenly, my palms cradling my cheeks, my head tilted sideways.

'But I had my ill luck too, Murtala. It was perhaps my bad uncles who bewitched me. As a young policeman, I was to attend a promotion interview, the only promotion interview that ever came my way. I prepared for it. But on the day of the interview, I overslept. Your foolish mother was there; she went to the market early in the morning without waking me up.'

Baba did not have any reason for calling Mama foolish. She had told us the story. She told us how it was Baba's habit to sleep any time he was home. 'At one point, I thought sleeping was a sickness that all policemen had,' Mama told us. 'But I found out that it was only my husband who slept without control.'

Later in the evening at about six, I took a walk to Kwana Hudu. I walked leisurely along the main street. I did not follow the shortcuts. I did not want somebody lurking in a corner somewhere to attack and kill me. That fear had always been in my mind since Baba told me that people were still killing people in hiding.

In front of one large house I saw a heap of burnt kerosene stoves, water-heating coils, clothes, pans, plastic buckets, small radios, books and other small household items. Rains had washed away the ashes and the burnt objects were scattered around. I saw such heaps in front of many burnt houses. I noticed that men did not sit under roadside trees, playing cards or draughts, laughing loudly as they used to do. I did not see women, sitting under trees, often beside the men, plaiting hair, talking and occasionally bursting into gossipy laughter. I did not see those kiosks under trees, owned by housewives who sat and played ludo. I did not see little children, naked, bathed in sand, seated on the ground under trees, playing. The main street, though not deserted, was quiet. Hausa girls moved around, hawking oranges, bananas and spices. I saw a few non-Hausa people alighting from buses and entering houses. I tried to see if I could recognise anybody. I did not.

I met the barber who saved our lives sitting on a wooden bench in front of the zinc stall he used as a salon. He was excited when he saw me. 'How are your parents?'

'They're fine.'

He offered me a seat. I declined politely.

'Where do you live now?'

'Kwanar Jabba.'

'It's not far from here.'

'My mother and my younger ones have gone to our village. It's only my father and me.'

'Well, that's good. Most people have run away. The killers behaved as if the strangers didn't have their own hometowns.'

'Most people haven't returned.'

'How will they return?' He looked into my eyes. 'If they have things to do in their places, will they return to a place where they'll be killed?'

'Certainly not.'

'And yet Prophet Muhammadu *sallalahu alaihum wasallam* enjoins us to welcome strangers and live with them. It's the strangers that bring the things we need that we don't have.'

I looked at the door of our former house intently. 'Has anybody occupied our former house?'

'Who will occupy it? No Hausa man will pay Hajiya Halima what your father was paying her. The crisis has impoverished many landlords and landladies here.'

After a moment of silence I told him, 'I'm leaving.'

'Thank you for coming. Greet your father for me.'

I took a turn towards Helen's house. It was a huge house, burnt. The part of it to my right, as I stood in front of the house, had collapsed. I saw a dog, two cats and a few hens amongst the debris, foraging. Helen's apartment was in the part that had not fallen. I saw the metal door of the apartment hanging on a loose hinge, slashed at the middle. I saw the curtain, dark blue with white stripes, dirty, dancing in the evening breeze. My eyes were riveted to the curtain, willing them to penetrate and see what was inside the room. Would the remains of Helen be there? Had anybody buried Helen the way we buried Ukpo? Did anybody tell her, 'May your soul rest in peace'? Had anybody prayed for her?

Sweet Helen, why don't you simply walk out of that room? Where are you? Are you in the marketplace, where Ukpo is, homeless, hanging in the air? I'm standing here, waiting for you. Please walk out of that room, Helen.

Darkness enveloped me suddenly. Even the sun, my companion, did not wait for me. I wiped tears from my eyes and hurried home, afraid that I might meet my own death.

7 | *Father is Christian, Mother Muslim*

'My father is a Christian and my mother a Muslim,' Ola said, a smile on his neat lips.

'How can that be?'

'Oh, that's how it is, Murtala.'

I looked into Ola's eyes. I thought I might see something strange in them. There was nothing. I wondered how a Christian and a Muslim could be in one house as husband and wife. How would they pray? How would they put up with each other?

'How did they come to like each other? Christians and Muslims always hate each other. '

'My dad says it's love. They really love each other.'

'What about you and your siblings?'

'We are free to be in any religion.'

'It's amazing, Ola. I can't imagine my family being like that. My mother quarrels if any of us doesn't go to church on Sundays. She doesn't like us having Muslim friends.'

Our classmates had all left. Ola and I were always the last to leave the class after school. Sometimes, his father's driver came to take him home. In most cases, however, he preferred to go home by public transport, because of me. We often stayed back in class to chat and do our assignments together. I was better than him in maths and integrated science. He was better than me in social studies and English.

'Hey Murtala, let's go have a snapshot.'

'Why? This hot afternoon?'

'We'll go to a photo studio. Want to see how our sneakers look in the photo.'

He persuaded me.

We met Millicent on the way. 'Your father's car hasn't come for you?' I joked.

She always smiled sweetly before replying. 'I don't have a father's car.'

'But you look like someone whose father has a car,' I teased.

A mate of ours waved at us from his father's car.

'I guess you were too late to catch your own father's car,' she said as she walked beside me.

We all laughed.

We reached a crossroad at which Ola and I said goodbye to Millicent. She beamed at me, 'Goodnight and sweet dreams.'

Ola insisted we have lunch before the snapshot. If we had eaten, we would look more relaxed and the photo would be better. Since he had money and was given to impressing me, he took me to a fancy restaurant. I felt very uneasy when I saw that all the people inside were adults. Their faces gleamed. Their necks were fat. The image of Baba with his thin neck crossed my mind.

'Take your seat.' Ola pointed to a seat. He sat down opposite me. He picked up the laminated piece of paper that was the price list and called out the menu for me.

'I'll eat fried rice,' I said.

I had heard some of my classmates, especially Jennifer's clique, talking much about fried rice, but I did not know what it was. This was an opportunity to taste it. Ola stood up and walked to the buffet. I took the price list and looked at it. I was shocked to see the price of fried rice: a hundred naira! Quietly, I stood up and walked towards Ola. I met him halfway, returning.

'What's it, Murtala?'

'Don't order the fried rice.'

'Why? I've already ordered it.'

'The price is too high.'

Ola laughed quietly, patted my shoulder and walked me to my seat. I was ashamed. Most of the people who were eating turned to look at us.

When the food was brought, I stared at it. How could I eat a plate of food worth one hundred naira? The money Baba and I fed on for a week was not even that much. How did Ola get the money to pay for my plate and his?

'Murtala, what are you thinking? Eat your food.'

'I can't eat.'

'What do you mean? You said you'd eat fried rice.'

'Yes, but…' I could not speak further.

Embarrassed, Ola stared at me.

When I came home in the evening, I found Imatum. I could not believe my eyes. Her neck, arms and legs had grown longer and thinner. Her skin had grown darker, her face gravely pimpled. I stood staring at her, first from shock, then to tease her.

'Why are you staring at me like that? Am I a ghost?' She blinked rapidly and turned away, her lips pursed.

'I think you're a ghost of Imatum from the village. They said you were too sick and we thought you'd die,' I said.

She turned her eyes back to me, widening them. 'It's you that will die!'

'Who showed you here?'

'Sergeant Abu brought me.'

I took a good look at her. 'You're not the Imatum I used to know.'

'How can you still know me when you're in the city enjoying life?'

'Enjoying life? Didn't Mama say life in the village was a lot better?'

'Ha! Don't mind Mama o! She is there with her *wahala*.'

'How are they?'

'They're there. Why don't you go to the village?'

I dropped my school bag, walked into the inner room and undressed. I came out of the room, eager to tease Imatum some more.

'Thought you'd not return to Kano. You should have been married off to a farmer.'

'God forbid! Me? I'll marry a rich city man, not a poor man, like you and Baba.'

I had a good laugh. 'I'm not going to be as poor as Baba. I'll go to university and become a medical doctor.'

'If you don't behave like Baba and Mama.'

'What do you mean?'

'Baba, always sleeping and doing nothing. Mama, always thinking of the village and poverty. Don't you think something is wrong with them?'

I laughed heartily again. I moved towards the TV and switched it on. I sat down opposite her. She was sitting where Baba always sat.

Imatum drew down the corners of her lips, stood up and walked to the TV. She felt it with her right hand and hissed. 'Better not to have a TV than to have this small black and white box. You should've told him.'

'You'll tell him yourself. You're his friend.'

'Haven't you become his friend, after staying together for this long?'

'I'm his good friend only when he's talking about his suffering and SAP.'

'What's that?'

'Structural Adjustment Programme. The government is adjusting our lives.'

'Is that why he bought this kind of TV?' Imatum hissed again, sat down and crossed her legs.

Our door, always ajar, opened wider as Baba stepped into the room. I greeted him, turned to Imatum and winked at her: *Baba almost caught you talking unkindly about him.*

Baba stood in surprise as Imatum bent her knees to greet him.

'Where is your mother? Where are your siblings?' He looked around expectantly.

'They're still in the village.'

'Why?' Baba's hands were on his waist and the unique smell of his uniform spread through the room.

'But Baba you should know why.'

'Don't be stupid, Imatum,' Baba said, walking into the inner room.

I listened to him as he undressed, sat on the bed and unfolded his naira notes.

Imatum moved towards my bed. Her eyes focused intently on the picture of the malnourished child I had cut out of *Triumph*. She crossed her arms.

'I pasted it,' I said.

'To bring you more nightmares?'

'Isn't the picture fascinating?'

'It's ugly. The boy is dying.'

'Dying of hunger. Should remind you the world is a place of hunger for many,' I said.

Imatum returned to her seat. 'Why must you keep things that remind you of the ugliness of the world? What do you have to remind you of the beauty of the world? You see what I mean when I say…'

Baba interrupted her from the inner room. 'Imatum!'

'Yes, Baba.'

'What beauty of the world did you see in the village?'

Imatum did not answer.

8 | *Imatum Tells Us Her Story*

Baba and I sat in rapt attention as Imatum told ns her story:

'Grandmama said she wept so much that, as our people say, she didn't have any more tears. The village mourned with her. Uncle Audu laid out the real horror before her: "The whole city of Kano is aflame." She had borrowed money and was about to leave for Kano when we got to the village.

'"My daughter, the cowards in the village said, Ene you can't go to Kano, you'll be killed. I told them, I, daughter of the Wind, shall go look for my children and return unscathed. Watch and see."

'Audu would bring Grandmama to Kaduna and put her in a bus to Kano. "He said he wouldn't go into Kano with me and I said, just put me in a vehicle that would take me to anywhere in Kano. The Wind would lead me to my children. They thought I was joking, but I showed them that a woman does not joke with the seeds of her womb. If you were still alive and I found you, I would bring you home. But if you were dead, I would follow you to the grave," said Grandmama. So she was extremely happy when she saw us, but she wondered why Baba and Murtala and Ukpo hadn't come. Mama told her that Baba would not come home. Grandmama said she was only worried about Ukpo her father and Murtala her husband. She knew she had lost her son, Baba, to the wider world the day he vanished from the village because he was forced to drop out of school. Veteran seers had confirmed this to her, but she had not worried about it. "He will come," she told Mama. "One day, the gods will come in a whirl, lift him off the ground and fling him home."

'Mama told her that we had lost Ukpo. Grandmama and other people in the house did not know how Ukpo looked. They remembered seeing him when Mama breastfed him. But they all wept.'

I looked at Baba. His gaze was bland. His mien was cool.

'The day we arrived in the village, we all, except Mama, sat in Grandbaba's *uponu*. He stared at us in a mystical way, not removing his catlike eyes from us. He would occasionally shake his head slowly and sigh loudly. Oyigwu and Emayabo stole looks at Grandbaba with fear. When he wanted to touch them, they screamed and held me tight. At one point, he looked at me and said, "My daughter, I told your father to abandon his police work and come home, but he would not listen. If only he were as sensible as your mother." I simply turned my face away. I wasn't in a mood to talk with him. He ordered that a goat be slaughtered and pounded yam prepared for us. While we were still mystified by Grandbaba's undivided attention to us, the pounded yam was brought. We did not eat much. I watched Oyigwu, Anyaosu and Emayabo fiddle with it. Yakubu ate well though. Grandmama asked Mama why we did not eat well. She told her that we were not used to pounded yam, because yam was too expensive in the city.

'"Why do you keep my children in a land where yam is unaffordable? Don't people farm there? Are you not a farmer?" Grandmama asked.

'"Their land is not good for growing yam," answered Mama.

'"And that fool will not find his way home. O Wind, I invoke you to fling him home."

'We stared at her, confused. It was disconcerting to hear her insult Baba with such ease.

'We moved into a room close to Enegaladi's. There was only a slim metal bed with a tattered mattress on it. Everything looked strange. I asked Mama to show me the big houses she said Grandbaba had which would make life in the village better than in the city. She told me to stop asking stupid questions. I pressed her. "I want to be convinced."

'She shouted, "Why are you so senseless, Imatum the courageous one? Can't you see the peace and the abundant food the village is blessed with? Did you eat pounded yam and goat meat in the city?"'

'"We're not moving to the village because of pounded yam and goat meat, are we?"

'"That's just one: good food. You would see other advantages if you used your head."

'"What I want to see is the big houses in your big stories about the village."

'Then she said there were free plots of land. With a small amount of money, Baba could build the house of his dream if he decided to return home. I finally told Mama that, for me, the village was a disappointment.'

Baba was nodding and smiling. He said, 'I've always known you to be a wise and courageous daughter.'

'But Mama thought I was foolish. She berated me when I asked questions.

'Something however worried her. Her age-mates whom she thought would come to her help – and some of them were really doing well with their farms – disappointed her. One day, Mama and I went to see Ladi, one of her friends. Mama sought a favour from her: a loan to start a business.

'"Ijaguwa, my friend," Ladi said. "Have you hidden the money you brought from the city? Do you want to finish ours with us before you bring yours out? Or is your husband bringing the money later on?"

'"Ladi, I don't understand you," Mama said, confused.

'"It's I, and other people in the village, who don't understand you. For several years you've been in the city making money and now you return with your children, feigning wretchedness. Isn't it for money and a better life that people leave the village for the city? We didn't hear that your wealth was burnt in the crisis. The other time you visited home, you flaunted your riches before our eyes."

'Mama was shocked. Her expression became pained. "I'm sorry for coming to disturb you, my friend. I thought you would understand my case. The city has many faces and the face I've seen is what makes me what I am. I'll try another person."

'As we were about to leave, Ladi said, "Nobody will give you what you're asking for. People are expecting to see what you've brought from the city for them. I advise you to think of something else."

'Mama thought aloud on our way home. She didn't understand why people reacted that way when they knew what had driven her from the city. "Imatum the courageous one, if your father had listened to me, if I had stayed in the village, none of these women could have competed with me. Before I got married, they used to borrow my clothes to wear. They used my make-up."

'Mama took the challenge to fend for herself. Since it was harvest time, she took us to the farms of rice farmers who needed farm hands. After we had worked for the day, they gave us a share of the harvested rice. My problem was that no matter how long we stayed on the farm – we always stayed from morning till evening – it was only one basin of rice we earned. And you know, they told us contemptuously that we were no-good-for-farm city children. A basin of rice was sold for five naira. All of us: Mama, Ajara, Yakubu, Anyaosu, Emayabo and Oyigwu went to the farm only to earn five naira.

'One day I confronted her again. "Mama, I want you to explain the wisdom in this hard labour we do just to earn five naira."

'"It's better than sitting at home, Imatum the courageous one."

'"How?"

'"In any case, the five naira you see as a pittance is big money here."

'I didn't understand her logic and had told her straight. "Mama, you've put us into slavery."

'Mama was enraged. She screamed about my inconsiderate attitude. She raged about my senselessness. She railed against the killings in the city. Then she burst into tears about the death of Ukpo. After that I stopped arguing with Mama. I noticed that during our arguments, my younger ones stared at us, confused and sad. She reported me to Grandbaba. He called me twice and urged me not to think like my father who was already lost to the misery of the city.'

I looked at Baba. He was very attentive.

'I followed Mama sheepishly, doing whatever she wanted. I also hoped for freedom. I thanked God that I was a woman and would soon be away from her.

'Then one day, while the sun was high, I think at midday when we were working on the farm, I suddenly caught a cold. I shivered. My temperature ran high. I told Mama that I had a fever. At first, she was sceptical but, on second thoughts, told me to go home. At home, I met Oyigwu struggling with Grandmama who was still in her farm cloth. Her veins swelled as she tried to drag Oyigwu into her room.

'I intervened. "What's happening, Ene?"

'"Bless my ancestors that you are here. I returned from the farm and met this small husband of mine under the sun. I implored him to leave the sun, but he will not. He has a fever I am sure."

'I felt Oyigwu's temperature by placing my palm on his forehead. It was high. Oyigwu and I entered our room. That was the beginning of our illness. Grandmama was never tired of bringing a new herb, even when we had not known the potency or otherwise of the previous one. I was always inhaling the steam from some herbal concoction, drinking it and bathing with it. At some point, my health would improve. But, continually, I would have the urge to go sit under the sun. Sporadic shivers would grip me. I would lose my appetite. I would hate the village and myself. Oyigwu's health declined. He had convulsions that really terrified Mama. I advised her, "Mama, take Oyigwu to the village nurse instead of relying on these herbs." For the first time she listened to me. She sold two basins of rice and took Oyigwu to the nurse and his health improved.

'Then it was Ajara's turn. Hers began with retching. Anything she ate she vomited. She grew weak. Again, Grandmama brought different herbs. When Yakubu started, it was coughing. In short, all of us fell ill within a few days. Even Grandbaba was upset. But people kept consoling us that it was the change of environment, that it was natural we should experience it. Mama sold all the basins of rice she earned. She couldn't go to farm because she had to attend to us. Any day my health improved, I would look after the children while she went to the farm. She had to earn money by any means. Nobody gave us money, although our relations brought us food and fruits. Grandbaba made sure that we got an adequate share of the foodstuffs he gave out.

'In the night at bedtime, we would all kneel down while Mama prayed, helplessly gasping: "God, are you there? Do you see what's happening to my children? Do you want to disgrace me, God? Come to our aid, Almighty God, you who led the children of Israel through turbulent times, you who saved us from the killers in Kano. Come to my aid. If it is witches that are after us, let the fire from above consume them. If it is the spirit of sickness that is after my children, God prove that you exist for me as you do for others."

'After the prayer she would not sleep. Ajara, Anyaosu and I slept on the bed while Mama and the others slept on mats. Because I didn't sleep either, I would hear Mama murmuring, "God Almighty, are you there? Ijenebu, my mother, Adanu, my father, are you there in the land of the dead? Did I do any wrong by bringing my children to our ancestral home? Are you watching what is happening to me? Why would you put me to shame, my God? My God and my ancestors, this is the time I need your help. Come to my aid. My children and I want to live. We must live."

'At a point Mama wanted to move to her father's village, but was discouraged because she had no parents anymore.

'The village Methodist church reverend, lanky and soft-spoken, added his generous prayers and charity. He frequently came and prayed for us in our room. He always advised Mama after praying: "Mama Imatum, take heart, God Almighty will see you through. You're going through a temptation and you should be careful not to give up your faith to the calls of the pagan god. If your father- or mother-in-law asks you to offer sacrifices or do any unchristian thing because of your problems, don't listen to them. Remember, the Lord will not forsake His own.'

'I noticed that each time the reverend came to the house, Grandbaba would come out of his *uponu* and skulk around in the compound. One day, he called Mama and me to his *uponu*. Sitting up on his reclining chair with his eyes on the floor, his index finger drawing something on the ground, he said, "Wife-of-my-son, it is because I do not want to hurt you that I allow that scoundrel to enter my house."

'"Scoundrel? Who are you referring to, Ada?"

'"Your *ichochi* leader, of course."

'"Oh the reverend. I'm sorry, Ada. I'll tell him to stop coming. Why do you call him a scoundrel, Ada?"

'"Tell him to stop coming to my house. We have heard stories about him sleeping with people's wives. They sent him away from Ogwufa village because of that habit. And we will drive him out of here soon."

'"But he's supposed to be working for God."

'Grandbaba raised his head and looked at us. "Can he not work for his god in his village? He is just a vagabond. That religion of yours turns people into vagabonds."

'Mama stopped the man from coming to our house.

'I made a few friends among our relations who sympathised a lot with me. They were young girls like me, eager to come to the city. They wondered why I should leave the city, a place of pleasure, to live in the village. They said my mother was old-fashioned and it was unfair of her to deny us the pleasure of the city. "After all, we know the story of how your mother left the village when she was young. All her mates envied her," Ajumi, my friend, told me. They said when Mama visited home, in those days, she was a delight to everyone and they composed songs with her name. My friends helped by contributing money for me to return to Kano. They told me to look for opportunities to help them come to the city.'

'Did you tell her you were coming?' Baba asked.

'I told her once and she objected to it. To her, all I needed was a little more patience and things would get better. When the rainy season came, she would have her own farms and things would improve. I disagreed with her. I hadn't seen anything that made the lives of the village farmers better. I wouldn't remain in the village even if we had our own farms. "You've been infected with the city disease like your father," she told me. I didn't inform her I was leaving. But I told my friends to tell her that I was gone.'

'We're all children of violence, at least by the religions we practice,' Omodiale said. He was bouncy and lively. He wore a white undershirt over a pair of jeans. His hands in his pockets, a gleaming necklace dangling on his chest, he looked like those broad-chested American film stars on our TV. 'Y'know, the graves are multiplying at the cemetery. Go there now.' He pointed towards the cemetery behind our house. 'You'll see many more new ones.'

I stood watching, engrossed. I held my school bag under my arm. My sneakers were dirty from trekking. I was thirsty.

Baba Fatima sat in his chair, staring at Omodiale. Baba Peter, bare-chested, stood facing Baba Fatima. Baba Peter's worn trousers dropped below his waist, revealing the waistline of his white underpants, coloured with dirt. His buttocks were bigger than his wife's.

'But dat cemetery na for only Muslims; why dem dey die like dat?' Baba Eddy asked, his large stomach bobbing up and down as he spoke. He seemed to be suffering from what my integrated science teacher called obesity.

Baba Fatima said, 'You don go Christian cemetery to see how dem dey die? Na both sides dem dey kill each other. Anytin pass nine o'clock in de night, dey fit kill you for any corner.'

'Hey! God forbid,' Baba Eddy said, making the sign of the cross.

'Hhm na for Allah's hand I dey o,' said Baba Fatima, opening his palms skyward.

Baba Peter asked Baba Fatima, 'Na true say you become Muslim dat time wey dem de kill people?'

'Ah, my dear, I for don die if I no join dem dat time o.'

'Me I no fit do like dat. Man no suppose to be coward.' It was Baba Eddy.

'Y'know, Baba Eddy, I disagree with you,' Omodiale said. 'That cool, ageing man sitting there would've been *kpai* if he hadn't Islamised. Really, it's not cowardice but wisdom. Y'know, the only problem is that the old man has refused to return to his original religion.'

'Wetin you mean, Omo? Make I go back to Christianity? I go do so when I retire go my village,' Baba Fatima said.

Baba Peter laughed. Baba Eddy sneered.

I saw Zubairu and another Hausa man walk past to the mosque. He greeted us in Hausa. We answered in a chorus.

'But I no dey see you enter mosque to pray,' Baba Peter told Baba Fatima.

'I dey do am small small. Na…'

A voice interrupted Baba Fatima: 'Excuse me, Sir!'

We turned towards the thin, feminine voice. Only her head was out of the door. Omodiale walked to her in his room.

Lowering his voice, his eyes still on Omodiale's room,

Baba Peter said, 'Every day na so so different girls dey come here. Which work he dey do sef?'

'Ask am na,' Baba Fatima said, smiling.

'Na wa o,' Baba Eddy said.

'No be teacher him be?' Baba Peter asked Baba Fatima. 'Since I know am, he dey do many things. E fit tell you say him be contractor.'

His eyes darting to Omodiale's room, Baba Eddy said almost in a whisper, 'He fit be four-one-nine man.'

Omodiale bounced out of the room. The girl followed him. She was petite, innocent-looking and wore a school uniform. Obviously shy that we were looking at her, she turned her face away as she hurried past. They walked out of the gate.

'Hey! *Chineke!*' Baba Peter burst into laughter, clapping. 'Dis one no be small enjoyment o. Under thirteen!'

Squinting towards the gate, Baba Eddy said, 'Which kin' enjoyment? Na children abuse.'

Baba Fatima said, 'Make una tell am *jare.*'

'Who go tell am?' Baba Eddy said. 'Talk make you see how he go scatter your head with grammar.'

'Me and him don live for dis house for long, before crisis. He no take anything serious at all. Na so so girls. And he get degree from Ambrose Alli University,' Baba Fatima said.

Omodiale walked into the compound, beaming at us, his steps those of a proud cockerel.

Baba Eddy, his squint splitting to a smile, told Omodiale, 'Na so you dey cool for barracks dat time of crisis, Omo.'

'O yes, brother. Y'know, I don't understand why people are so serious about violence and killing.'

'Wetin you mean?' asked Baba Peter.

'What happened was not new. And, in any case, it was bound to happen. Y'know, the number of people killed is so tiny in the history of violent killing. Violent killing has been there since the beginning of the world. Y'know, we'll all die, violently or not, and leave the violence behind. What do your religions tell you? A simple act of offering to God brought violence between brothers: Cain and Abel. Look at it this way: Christianity and Islam are rooted in violence. When a…'

Baba Eddy interrupted him. 'Na lie, Omo. God command us say: Thou shalt not kill.'

'No argument about that, brother. Y'know, if you read your Bible or your Koran well, you'll see several incidents where the same God ordered killings and destructions. Don't get me wrong, brothers, I'm not saying God is a liar.' Omodiale looked into Baba Fatima's eyes, into Baba Eddy's, then into Baba Peter's. He seemed to be seeking consent to proceed. We were attentive, like students before a teacher.

Then he launched into a spiel:

'And the Lord commanded the children of Israel to go and claim the Promised Land. That land wasn't unoccupied; it wasn't fallow waiting for the children of Israel. So what happened? They went, equipped with a holy instruction to kill other people and take the land. Brothers, the tradition of killing people and taking their lands, rooted in Christianity and Islam, has continued throughout all ages. And Saul and David and Samson and other biblical warriors continued to kill other people with holy instructions. And the last messenger of God came with the power to kill, to conquer. And his conquest spilled from Arabia to other parts of the world, to poor Africa, where the sword was placed on our fathers' necks: they either accepted the religion or *kpai*. And the children of Cain filled the world. Brothers, don't you know that the makers of eloquent weapons of mass destruction are children of Cain? And from conquest to conquest, from empire to empire, a lot of blood was shed. And for flimsy excuses, which were not more than the urge to obey that holy instruction, the world rose against itself in what are now called First and Second World Wars. Do you know how many people died in the First World War? Britain lost about eight hundred thousand men; Germany lost about one point eight million; France lost one point six million; the USA lost one hundred and sixteen thousand men. Those were men in some of the active countries who died fighting the war. You can't count people like you and me, innocent and vulnerable, who died in the remote ravages of war. Figures for the Second World War were even worse. Brothers, have you heard of Hiroshima and Nagasaki?' Omodiale burst into a song, swaying rhythmically:

'Remember Hiroshima
Many, many years ago
Mama and Papa are crying
For the plight of their posterity
Hey, come away Rastaman
Are you sure we're in human race?
Hey, come away Rastaman,
Are you sure this is human race?'

I recognised the song by Maxwell Udoh.
Omodiale continued. 'Two cities: human beings, their

properties, their wealth, turned into the debris of violence with atomic bombs. Those bombs were manufactured with one prayer in mind: *In God we trust*. Brothers, do you know of the Warsaw uprising where two hundred thousand people were massacred? Do you know of the Great Purge of the Soviet Union between 1957 and 1938 when about one point three million people were *kpai*? Do you know that when Hitler got his own inspiration, let's call it an unholy instruction, he descended on the Jews and, through a systematic design, about six million of them were *kpai* in cold blood? And the violence was brought to Africa, with pillage and thievery. I mean, brothers, from the slave trade to colonialism. Continental violence.

'Do you know of the massacre in Sharpeville, South Africa, in 1960? Do you know of the lives of black people wasted in Kenya before her independence? And the children of Cain, in order to keep the trend of violence, killed all our *Jesuses* so that they could use their Jesus to rob us. They slew our black saviours: Patrice Lumumba, Amílcar Cabral, Martin Luther King Junior, Walter Rodney and Steve Biko. Look brothers, the violence you see today has a history. The first blunder of creation was the holy instruction to kill people and take their lands. There lie the roots of all violence. Now let's ask ourselves, are those being killed human beings like those killing them? Why are some people created only to be killed? Why are some people created only to have the pleasure of killing other people?' Omodiale looked at the other men, a grin on his lips. Beads of sweat stood on his forehead.

'Hhm, Omodiale, dis your talk don make piss dey worry

me sef. Make I go piss first,' Baba Eddy said, as he grabbed his crotch and waddled to the bathroom.

'Omo, dat na dangerous talk,' Baba Peter said.

'Omodiale, if you talk like dis for outside dem go kill you fast fast,' Baba Fatima said.

'Y'know, I'm not afraid of violent death, Baba Fatima. That's why every day, every hour, I live my life to the fullest. I indulge in all the pleasures I approve for myself, knowing that in a twinkle of an eye, the club, the rope, the sword, the dagger, or the gun will come for my life. Or the ultra-modern parcel bomb with which they quenched Dele Giwa. Unlike you, I accept that violence is bound to happen. The foundation of the world and its religions is laid on violence. Even our primitive societies were founded on violence.'

'Wetin yon mean?' asked Baba Peter.

'Well, Baba Peter, the empires, the kingdoms, the blood-thirsty monarchs. Have you heard of Oba Nogbaisi and Usman dan Fodio?'

Baba Peter scratched his head.

'No mind am, Baba Peter,' Baba Fatima said, 'wetin him know about Oba Nogbaisi? Dem never born im papa dat time sef.'

Omodiale laughed.

I left them and walked into our room, thirsty and hungry. I kept wondering how Omodiale had acquired all that knowledge.

9 | I Freeze, Gaping at Her

I froze, gaping at her. My school bag fell from under my arm. Mama was sitting on a small stool in front of our room, her right palm cuddling her cheek, her eyes staring blankly. She was emaciated and yellow-eyed. She smiled at me and looked away. I could not utter a word. *Is this my Mama: that courageous woman whose voice rang out so confidently against our delinquencies and Baba's misbehaviour? Is this my Mama, averting her eyes, subdued, like a famished beggar?*

Her voice was low and sad. 'I've grown sickly, haven't I? And you're so shocked you can't even tell me welcome. I meant well for everyone.'

My head grew heavy and my stomach tightened. I blinked and felt drops of tears on my cheeks. I was dumbstruck.

Mama ignored my tears. 'Enter the room, your wife has been waiting to see you.'

I wiped my tears, picked up my bag and entered the room, wondering who she could be referring to. There was Grandmama, all bony, veins conspicuous, staring at me with her beady eyes. She was really old and I wondered why she had bothered to make such a journey.

'Is this my husband grown so big?'

'That's your husband,' Mama answered, stepping into the room.

'Eeeeeh!' she shouted, standing up and grabbing me in embrace. I felt the bones of her body as she held me tight. Crushed by sadness, I merely opened my arms in order not to embarrass her. Then she moved her body away, squinting at me, her hands on my shoulders. 'My husband, you're becoming a man, a handsome man. Can you fight now?'

I essayed a smile and managed to say, 'And you're becoming a beautiful girl. I'll fight for you.' Grandmama broke into a song, dancing in an amusing way.

Gun ne gun ne	*My own, my own*
Ingi loba de	*When I will marry,*
I lai gini de	*Where will I marry from?*
I lai g'Usha lo	*I will many from Usha.*
Oji w'ohi guwa	*What makes them great?*
Ijebe n'onu	*They are great wrestlers*
Anu ga byun g'ebe g'uwa	*That is what takes me to them.*
Gun ne gun ne.	*My own, my own.*

She laughed, revealing her toothless gums. 'I am happy that you are still alive for me.'

Mama was also laughing. I grinned as best I could. Grandmama returned to her seat.

Ajara and Anyaosu curtsied before me.

'Welcome, Murtala,' Ajara greeted me.

'Thank you. How are you?'

'I'm fine.'

'Welcome, brother Murtala.'

'Anyaosu, how are you?'
'I'm fine.'
'And you, Yakubu?'
'I'm fine. Welcome, brother Murtala.'

Though they were not looking so healthy, they were not as emaciated as Mama. Ajara still had her slender build, but had grown hollow-eyed. Anyaosu had lost some weight and looked sad. Yakubu had sores at both ends of his mouth. Oyigwu and Emayabo were on the bed, asleep. I wobbled into the inner room, undressed and ate my lunch silently. It was *jollof* rice with smoked fish. The way it tasted, I was sure Mama had prepared it.

Baba returned from work an hour later. As soon as he entered, he halted, surprised. Oyigwu shouted 'Baba!' and rushed to him. Baba lifted him up. Emayabo clasped her arms around Baba's right leg. In awhile, she disengaged herself from Baba and came and sat on my lap. Her eyes glittering, she asked, 'Brother Murtala, where is brother Ukpo?'

I did not expect her question. 'I'll tell you later.'

'I want to know. Tell me now.'

'I'll tell you later. Just stay calm.'

'You promise?'

I nodded.

Ajara, Anyaosu and Yakubu greeted Baba quietly. He responded by uttering their names. Baba and Mama did not exchange greetings.

Baba greeted Grandmama who replied by saying, 'I have come to confirm that you are still alive and normal!'

Baba did not say anything. His mood was that of pained

humility. He pouted his thick lips in a sullen silence. He withdrew to the inner room, still carrying Oyigwu. I prayed that no quarrel would erupt. But Mama looked too weak to quarrel and Baba was too depressed to bother.

We were all indoors except Imatum who had recently developed a habit of spending her days out. 'I can't continue to sit in this oven you call a room,' she had told me one day.

'Where will you go then?' I had asked.

'Into the world. I can't remain in the heat of an oven when there is air out there.'

Baba had told her to wait until he received that month's salary before she returned to school. There was no alternative.

'*Kpan kpan* here. Madam, welcome o.' It was Mama Umoru, one of the wives of the limping man from the mid-west of the country.

'Tank you, Madam,' Mama answered her.

'How road?'

'We tank God o.'

Still standing in the doorway, she turned her face to Grandmama and spoke louder, 'Old Mama, welcome o.'

Grandmama's attention was on the TV. I told her that the woman was greeting her. She turned to her and said, in our language, 'Thank you, my daughter.' She quickly turned her eyes back to the TV. It had occupied her attention ever since I had put it on.

Mama Umoru laughed and left. Mama Tindele came next. Mama Eddy also came; she entered the room but, like Mama Umoru, did not sit down. 'We tan' God for safe jorni for una,' Mama Eddy said.

'Tank you, Madam,' Mama replied.

Baba came out of the inner room, wearing his favourite safari suit, the one he always wore to Sabon Gari. Oyigwu bounced happily behind him and together they went out. After some minutes, Oyigwu returned with a packet of biscuits. Baba did not.

I saw shock in Imatum's eyes when she sneaked into the room. It was already dark outside.

She had taken to using make-up in an excessive manner. She was becoming healthy, in fact, well fed. Tall and beautiful. She did not eat food at home even if she cooked. She had complained that her hair was lice-infested from the village and had had it cut. She used a perfumed moisturizing cream, not the Vaseline we used.

Mama's reply to Imatum's greeting was, 'Since we came in the afternoon, I'm just seeing you. Where have you been? Is this the freedom you ran away from the village for?'

'I've been with my friends.'

Imatum sat down beside Grandmama. 'Ene, welcome.'

'My daughter, I have been asking after you,' Grandmama said without removing her eyes from the TV.

'That's not an excuse, Imatum,' Mama continued, her voice low, almost tender. 'A woman who tells lies is totally irresponsible.'

'I saw her with a man in a corner yesterday,' I intruded.

She retorted, 'It's a lie!' She turned to me, stamped her foot and shouted, 'Don't blackmail me, Murtala.' She sucked her teeth at me.

'What blackmail? I saw you with Omodiale yesterday.' I pointed towards his room.

'I was only greeting him. Is he not our neighbour?'

Mama's sunken eyes thrashed Imatum.

Disturbed by our loud voices and removing her eyes from the TV reluctantly, Grandmama threw a contemptuous look at Imatum and said, 'My daughter, have you returned here to become wayward? If it is a man you need, follow me to the village and I will get you the best of men. At your age, I was already married with a child.'

Imatum swelled with anger. She stamped into the inner room, grumbling.

'Murtala, why are there so many rat holes in the room?' Mama asked.

'The compound before this one was better. I told Baba that we should stay there, but the rent was higher and Baba said he couldn't afford it.'

'The same old song. But I expected that houses would be cheaper as people have fled the city.'

'Houses in Kwana Hudu are cheap but not here. People who return prefer to live close to Sabon Gari.'

'I can see people have returned. They are so many, as if there wasn't any crisis.'

Grandmama said, 'Do you think they are all human beings? Many of them are ghosts. I am convinced that people who die in the villages come to the city where nobody knows them.'

We laughed.

'How do you know?' I asked.

Grandmama said, 'Those tall buildings can only be built by ghosts. No human being would want to live so high above the ground.'

'Ene, they're built by human beings. They are called storey buildings.'

She stared at me, disbelieving. 'No, my husband. You're deceived. Ghosts can take the shape of human beings if they choose to.' As an afterthought she said, shading her eyes with her palm and pointing at the electric bulb, 'And why do you bring this bright sun into the room? Is it good for you?'

'Can't you see clearly with it?'

'No. Too much brightness is not good for the night.'

Baba slipped into the room late in the night when everyone had fallen asleep. I was peering into my book, using the kerosene lamp. There was a power cut. I raised my head and greeted him. He stood, looking round the room. Grandmama was sleeping on my bed. Sprawled on the mat were Yakubu, Oyigwu and Emayabo. Imatum, Ajara and Anyaosu occupied the metal bed in the inner room. I had figured out how I would sleep: there was a blanket to spread on the floor near the mat.

After a while, Baba walked noiselessly into the inner room. He reeked of alcohol. I heard him undress. I heard him fumble with dishes. I heard his quiet slurps as he ate. Later I heard his voice and Mama's voice. They kept whispering, disturbing my reading.

After some time, Baba called me.

'Yes, Baba.'

'I think you should go to bed now. It's late. Do you understand me?'

Of course I did not understand but I said, 'Yes.' I lowered the lamp a bit, kept it near my head and carried on reading, pretending to be asleep.

Their voices petered out. After a brief silence I heard the wooden bed in the inner room creaking gently.

I could not read anymore.

The next day I woke up at my usual time, took the buckets and went to collect water. When I returned, I met Baba, Mama and Grandmama seated, facing one another.

'My husband, you must join us. You are already a man.'

I sat close to Grandmama.

Grandmama continued what she was saying before I came in. 'It is distressing the way you have abandoned your father and me. Are you still punishing us for making you drop out of school? And for how long? Do you know people laugh behind me, saying "Look at her, she has a son in the city but suffers from poverty?"'

Baba suffers from poverty. Doesn't Grandmama know? My attention drifted to the chirps of the weaverbirds on the *dogonyaro* tree in the compound.

'Since you have refused to come and see us at home, I have come to see you in the city. I am a responsible mother. A mother's bitterness against her child ends on the tongue; it does not descend to the belly. If it does, our people take it as witchcraft. Your father wishes you a good life and prosperity, praying that one day you will understand why he took the decision that has provoked your unending hatred towards him. It is not that a child has no right to be resentful of his parent's decision. But such resentment ought not to move beyond the tongue to the belly. My son, you have let your resentment settle in your belly.

'If today, may my ancestors forbid, you drop dead here, will your wife and children bury you here? Do you not have roots?'

Grandmama paused, but Baba did not answer. He held his head in his hands.

'I come to you with the empathy of a mother. The message I have brought from your father is that you should prepare and return home.'

Baba said nothing.

'I am happy that your wife understands this thing. Most women keep our sons tied to the city because of their greed for material things, but your wife is different. I am proud of her, because she is a brave and courageous woman.'

Silence followed.

I heard sounds of people opening doors in the compound. My attention lay on Baba whose arms were folded across his chest.

He raised his head and began. 'Our mother, thank you for taking the pains to bring this message. If anybody tells you that I don't appreciate your coming, the person is lying. It's true that I've not been to the village for a long time now, but it's not true that it's out of hostility towards you and our father. It isn't easy for me to come home, because of two things: one, the police work does not give me holidays. The second thing is that I don't earn enough money to spare any cash for travelling.

'I agree with you that my wife is courageous, but she is

also very unreasonable. Even when she sees how I suffer, denying myself what men like me wear or go out to do, just to make sure that our children have something to eat and go to school, she doesn't appreciate my efforts. She dismisses me as a no-good policeman, compares me with her friends' husbands and regales her children with tales of my weaknesses. If I leave the police force, what do I do, where do I go?'

Imatum walked out of the inner room. Without greeting anyone, she negotiated her way through, jumping over the mat, and left.

'To the fuss about returning to the village. My thinking is that before I move to the village, I should have saved some money with which to settle down. My retirement benefit will not be enough. I know of retired policemen who died because they didn't get their pensions. So I need to save money.

'Our mother, when you go home, tell our father that I've received his message and I understand his feelings.'

Silence. I was eager to prepare for school. I shifted uncomfortably. Grandmama turned to me. 'My husband, what do you have to contribute to this?'

'I don't have anything,' I said quickly. I wondered what I would contribute here. As far as I could see, Baba and Mama had reasons for how they acted. The problem I had with both of them was that they were dismally inclined to magnify issues that seemed minor to me. Were there any families I knew that were not poor? Except Ola's family. Even Millicent's family, as ravishing as she looked, was poor. The day she told me that they often ate *garri* and *kulikuli* for lunch in their house, I was shocked.

Grandmama asked Mama if she had anything to say.

'Let me defend myself against the charge of unreasonableness,' Mama began. 'I don't have the mind to tell my husband a lie. I can't tell my children that their father is a hero when they themselves know he isn't one. The joy of every mother is to create harmony and happiness in her family, based on truth. Each day I wake up I set my hands to work, just to make my house happy. But here we are, everybody torn between the city and the village, between sickness and health, between hunger and nourishment. They deride me as the old-fashioned one, eager to return to the village. But die village is our home. Don't our people say that no matter how sweet a strange land is and no matter how sour your homeland, it is better to be in your homeland? The hardship at home is the type you can deal with. Look at these little ones and me in this strange land. If hunger comes, we confine ourselves to this room and eat the unspeakable. Is it to the strangers in this compound that I will go for help? At worst, I'll even pretend that my children and I are not hungry, while we're actually starving. But if it's my homeland, I can go to my sisters because my children are theirs and I can go to my husband's brothers and sisters, because my children are theirs.'

Oyigwu woke up, sat up on the mat, rubbed his eyes and looked at each of us. He stood up and moved towards Mama, his wet pants smelling of urine. He leant on her lap, yawning.

'I have every reason to detest his police work, Mother-of-my-husband. He was in the police before I married him. Since I joined him, we have been living in Kano; all his transfers have been within Kano. I once advised that he should seek transfer to a place near home; he said it was not possible. But I knew it was possible for others. I advised him to look for a trade aside from his police work, because his monthly salary is too small. He said it was impossible. He prefers to sleep. But I know that there are policemen who engage in other trades because their salaries are meagre.

'Didn't you wish me ill luck when I was leaving? Yes, I suffered with my children in the village. We've come back to you, and to the city of violence. So do whatever you want to do with us.'

10 | *Ola Insists I Visit*

Ola insisted I visit him. 'I spoke to my parents about yon and they want to meet you.'

I wondered what Ola had told his parents about me. That his parents were interested in meeting me was fascinating.

I went in the afternoon on a Sunday. By 1 p.m. I had left our church and headed for school. I sat out front for about five minutes before Ola arrived in a large Mercedes Benz. The car had barely halted when Ola opened the front door and hopped out. He beamed at me.

'Happy Sunday, Murtala.'

'Same to you.'

'So, we go?'

I nodded. He opened the back door for me. I entered and he climbed in beside me. The smell inside the car was pleasant and the air was cool. I marvelled at the milk-coloured seats. I greeted the driver and he grunted a reply. Ola and I chatted on as the driver concentrated on the busy roads. People were driving back from church. We drove past burnt and collapsed buildings.

'Would you like to eat ice cream?' Ola asked.

I did not want to spoil an otherwise memorable day with a no. I said, 'Yes, please.'

'Where do you want us to go get it? Alheri?'

I didn't know what Alheri was, but I nodded.

He ordered the driver to take us to Alheri.

After a while, we found ourselves in front of a glass building with 'Alheri' boldly advertised on it. There was a huge neon signboard in front. Inside the rectangular building, I was careful to stay behind Ola, who confidently walked ahead, giving me a reassuring look from time to time. There were many children of Emayabo's age there. Some were hugging their parents, some were straying to empty seats, while others were eating and talking. A boy who had turned a plastic can into a football was running after it, defying his mother's soft call.

Ola collected two cups of ice cream. He brought out crisp notes from his wallet, paid, and we walked out. Once we had closed the car doors on either side, the driver drove away. We started eating our ice cream.

We passed many houses, passed Yarkura Market, negotiated more roundabouts and flowed from one road to the other. I saw Bata, a superstore where shoes were sold. Opposite it was another huge glass building with the word 'Leventis', in blue, inscribed at the top. We took a corner and flowed into a broad street called Bank Road. Keeping my eyes on the signboards, I saw 'Gamji Bank', 'Kabo Air', 'First Bank', 'Union Bank' and 'Alheri Travels'.

Ola's house was a huge building. I had seen such mansions on our TV and in the magazines he brought to school, but I had never been this close to one of them. Not only Ola's house, but the whole neighbourhood was made up of such mansions. Each had its own fence, the gate firmly locked.

Ola held my hand jovially as we stepped into the big house, not through the main, wide, glass and curtained entrance, but through a small door to the side.

I found myself in a large kitchen, tiled in gleaming cream. I smelt fried chicken.

'It must be a new house,' I told Ola.

'No. We've been occupying it for… well, I was born here.'

'And it's looking so new.'

I thought of our house with its fading, peeling paint and hole-infested walls.

Shiny shelves housed shiny dishes and pans. The pots were not sooty like ours. There were also closed drawers with golden handles. The water sink had a loop-shaped tap. A compartment for kitchen knives hung on the wall.

A buxom woman wearing an apron stood facing an object that looked to me like a small fridge. But there were two big pots on it, blue flames under them. Was it a different kind of stove?

The woman turned to us, a dimpled smile on her cherubic face. Her eyes were bright and her skin shone. I bowed and said, 'Good afternoon, Ma.' I was convinced she was Ola's mother.

'Don't bow to greet me, boy,' she said, laughing. 'I'm not Queen Elizabeth.'

'Hello Aunt Becky, meet Murtala, my friend. Murtala, Aunt Becky is our cook,' Ola said.

She was bursting with life. 'Oh nice to meet you, such a handsome boy. And respectful, too.' Then she asked Ola, 'Is Murtala having lunch with us?'

'Yeah, Aunt Becky. Thanks.'

We went through another door and stood in a smaller, narrow room with a rectangular table on which stood water flasks and other containers.

'Our dining room.'

'Dining room?'

'Yes, where we eat.'

I nodded.

The dining room opened to a much wider parlour with decorations that seemed superfluous. The floor gleamed with tiles. On one side, a sky-blue set of chairs was arranged. Farther away, next to a wall, sat another set of ash-coloured chairs. Opposite the first set was a tall, golden cabinet housing a huge TV set and several unfamiliar electronic devices. I looked up and saw three ceiling fans, brown in colour, with many things like plastic flowers pasted on the blades. They spun slowly. There were four large glass windows with curtains. Each curtain was packed and held tight at the middle, letting sunlight into the spacious room. I saw large framed pictures on the wall. I looked at one closely and saw that it was a painting of a woman.

'Feel at home, Murtala. Welcome to my house,' Ola said.

'Thanks, Ola.'

'Sit down. I'll go get my parents.'

He took a flight of stairs up and I watched him disappear. As I sat on one of the ash-coloured chairs, I let out a puff of air, clenched my fists and relaxed my body. I loosened the uppermost button of my jeans, which were tight at the waist. They were the best I had for a visit to an important place like Ola's house, but were undersized and so short that the gap between the cuffs and my feet was disturbing.

When Mama had bought them, long ago, her thinking had been that since I was growing up, I needed oversized clothes to grow into. I had outgrown this pair, but did not have another.

I raised my head to see the amazing sight of the people coming down the staircase. Two small girls of about eight followed each other. They must be the twin sisters Ola had spoken to me about. Behind them was an older boy, followed by Ola. I knew Ola was the eldest, like me, so this was his younger brother. Behind Ola was a light-skinned, plump woman with wide lips. Ola's resemblance to her was in the almond-shaped eyes. The father brought up the rear with a bearded, calm and smiling face. He was as handsome and tall as a film star.

I stood up as they came down the staircase. Ola rushed and took up a position beside me, his right arm across my shoulders.

'Hello Murtala, welcome to our house.' The voice was a baritone.

'That's my father,' Ola said.

'Good afternoon, Sir,' I said, bowing my head as I saw people do on TV.

Ola went through the ritual of introduction with joy. Not that I was nervous, not that I flushed, not that my vision blurred, but I wished it all away. My behaviour pleased them. The twins were Mary and Martha, also called Hassana and Husseina. The boy was Ayo.

After they shook hands with me, the parents returned upstairs. As they walked towards the staircase, Ola's father turned back and asked, 'How are your parents, Murtala?'

'They're fine, Sir.'

'Make sure you enjoy yourself in our house,' Ola's mother said.

'Thank you, Ma.'

I looked at her as she ascended the staircase. I tried to figure out what in her appearance was Islamic. She did not cover her hair with a veil, not even with a scarf. She wore a tight, knee-length skirt. Her top was also tight. Even her accent did not betray her as a Hausa woman. And she looked so young that had Ola not introduced her as his mother, I would have sworn she did not give birth to him.

Ola and I sat on a sofa. The twins sat on separate seats opposite us, staring at me. Now and then they whispered to each other. Ola took two objects that looked like calculators from the centre table. These he pointed at the huge electronics whereupon they groaned and blinked to life. The image on the TV screen was large. A slender white woman was singing, her movement suggestive. The song that boomed in the room did not seem to come from her thin lips.

'That's Celine Dion,' Ola said to me.

'Okay.'

Not wanting to betray my ignorance before his siblings, I was careful with the kind of answers I gave.

'Excuse me, just a minute,' Ola said, standing up. He walked towards the stairs.

The twins came and sat on the sofa, sandwiching me. They became giggly. 'Your jeans are too small for you,' Martha said, looking into my eyes.

I was amused. Really, I had the urge to burst into laughter.

Mary sat straight and measured herself against me. 'I will be taller than you soon,' she said.

'That'll be nice,' I replied, chuckling.

My attention was divided. I looked from one to the other, admiring their satiny skin.

Mary said, 'You look like Mel Gibson.'

'Really?' I tried to match her citified accent. Of course, I did not know who Mel Gibson was.

'Which of his movies do you like?' It was Martha who asked.

'Ehm… ehm… well, many of his movies.'

Mel Gibson was either a moviemaker or an actor, I figured out. I readied myself for their next assault.

'Name one of his movies for us; maybe we've not watched it,' Mary said.

'Okay, let me remember the latest one. I'm sure you've not watched it.'

They were eager but allowed me to think.

Ola walked down the staircase, carrying some huge photo albums. I was relieved when he started opening one of them, ignoring the attention I was paying his sisters. Mary and Martha returned to their seats.

We went through the photos slowly. Ola had an explanation for each photo.

'Dad and Mum at the London School of Economics.'

'Your parents studied in London?'

'Yes. They met there.'

He flipped the page. 'That's me, when I was a baby. I was born in London.' It was a plump, smiling baby.

The next was a picture of a fat man in *agbada*. 'My

paternal grandfather, Chief Adebayo. Heard of him? Former Minister of Finance.'

'No.'

'Was popular. He's dead now.'

We were on the twenty-fourth photo when we heard a certain pleasant sound. The twins jumped up at the same time, shouting, 'It's lunchtime.'

When we moved to the dining room, I noticed its beauty. The chairs were soft. The table was covered with a fabric on which were woven patterns. Ola sat directly opposite me. The twins faced each other. The older boy, Ayo, who had all the while been by himself in a corner of the sitting room, reading a book, sat facing no one. Ola's parents did not come down. Before me lay a china plate, a knife, a fork and a glass. The glass and the plate were facing down. Beside the glass sat a folded hand towel. Three big food containers occupied the centre of the table. Ola opened one, revealing steaming rice. Another contained chicken stew. Ola used a big plastic spoon to dish out the rice for himself and served some for me too. Then he pushed it towards his siblings. He pulled the third big food container and spooned out some stew for himself and for me. A large piece of chicken, so large that it looked like the complete chicken Mama had brought home one day, lay across my plate.

Aunt Becky walked dancingly into the dining room. Posing with her left hand on her waist, she tilted her head to the right, made a face, and said liltingly, 'I hope I'll get compliments after the meal.'

The twins, as though well-rehearsed, craned their necks, made faces and said, 'Yeees, Aunt Becky.' Then they giggled.

She said, 'Bon appétit!'

'Thank you,' they chorused and started eating.

I became uncomfortable when I realised there was no spoon. I looked at them. They were eating with knives and forks! I took the fork with my left hand and the knife with my right. I moved the fork to my right hand, the knife to my left. Then I returned the knife to my right, the fork to my left. I looked at Ola's hands. The knife was in his right hand while the fork was in the left. He took the food to his mouth holding the fork in his left hand. I noticed that others did the same. When I tried it, my hand trembled. I caught Martha staring at me, so I returned the fork back to my right hand and fetched the food gingerly.

'Hhm, my sister, they poured petrol on me and set me ablaze,' Hadiza said in our language, sitting on a sack of *alubo*.

Mama was in tears, staring at her. She sat on one of the sacks. I stood beside her.

She tried to raise her voice above the din around us, but her mouth would not open any wider. The lips were charred, crushed to one side. 'That day, I came to the market earlier than my usual time. A lorry had arrived the previous night with supplies of *alubo* and, as usual, I rushed to get the best sacks for both of us. I did. Look at them.' She pointed at four sacks of the cassava flour leaning against the wall.

'Thank you, Hadiza. If you knew, you wouldn't have come.'

'I moved out to my stall,' Hadiza continued. 'I was even lucky to have a morning buyer and was attending to him when we suddenly heard the loud voices of people shouting that Muslims were killing Christians. Religious riot again? There were gunshots. I hurriedly brought my basin of *alubo* here. I met Madam Well-Well on the floor, frightened, shivering, urine trickling along her stretched-out legs. "Stand up, let's go home," I told her, pulling her up. She wouldn't move.'

'Did she want to die inside here?' Mama asked.

A figure filled the doorway. We turned. It was a woman whose mascara had smudged onto her eyelids. 'Hey Mama Murtala, you don come? Ha, why you tay too much for village na?'

'Mama Bonboy, tank you o. I no even wan come back sef.'

'You see wetin happun to Hadiza?'

'Na so I dey see am o.'

She exchanged greetings with Hadiza, told Mama that she was hurrying to see one of her village women and left.

Hadiza continued: 'Madam Well-Well kept weeping. We heard loud chanting, but I couldn't make out what the chanters were saying. I heard people banging and locking their stores in a frenzy. Convinced that death was coming, Madam Well-Well scrambled to her feet. We moved out and I managed to lock the door. We…'

A loud song drowned Hadiza's voice. We waited to see the singers. Five beggars clad in tattered *babanriga*. Three of them were blind, led by two small boys of Ajara's age. They carried small bowls. The remaining two beggars looked very ugly. Their deformed, brittle palms lacked fingers. Their lips were chopped off and their eyeballs bulged. They stood by the door and raised their voices high. The leading singer's lips opened in an exaggerated way as he tilted his head backward.

'May Allah give you good luck,' I told them.

Disappointed, they lowered their voices, turned and walked away.

I turned and saw a scowl on Mama's face.

'I'm listening to you, Hadiza,' she said.

'Hhm my sister, we ran through the narrow streets in the market. In Balewa Street, we came upon young men carrying clubs, knives and swords. They had broken into stores. Some of them loaded electronics into a small truck while others stood on guard. We turned immediately.'

'Must be Hausas, looting.'

'They were Igbos. I held Madam Well-Well's hand, pulling her along. One of them ran after us. "*Oya*, make una stand there!" His voice sounded like thunder. We froze. He raised his right hand which held a huge club and stretched his left hand towards us. "*Oya*, bring money quick quick." I felt relieved that it was money he needed. I turned out my pouch, turned out Madam Well-Well's and gave him all we had. He swaggered away.'

'And why did they pour petrol on…'

'Don't be in a hurry, my sister. Let me finish.'

'I'm…'

Another beggars' song broke out: children's voices. I

turned to the door, waiting. In a minute, six children filled the doorway, all carrying small bowls. Mama cast a glance at them, angry. In Hausa, she shouted, 'Leave the doorway and allow air in.'

I was shocked at her hostility. I walked to the door and told them, 'May Allah give you good luck.'

'*Amin*,' they chorused and left.

Hadiza continued: 'We trekked through Sabon Gari. Madam Well-Well was sure we couldn't survive it. I told her Allah would see us through. To cut a long story short, my sister, we had almost moved out of Sabon Gari when we heard chanting voices again.'

'Muslims or Christians?'

'Christians. We dodged behind a building and hid. The chanters came close but didn't see us. Then a small boy, much younger than Murtala, shouted, pointing at us, "Here are two Hausa women! Here are two Hausa women!"'

'Oh the little devil!' Mama exclaimed.

'Fear gripped me. The killers stopped; they listened to what the little imp was telling them. "Let's run!" I told Madam Well-Well but I knew we couldn't run anywhere; they were so close to us. "Where do we run to?" was the last thing Madam Well-Well said. She collapsed. I tried to pull her up. The killers were upon us. Hhm my sister, so in one's life there is a time one comes face to face with death. I thought I had met my end.'

'Hadiza, I saw death too and I'm still seeing death.'

'I was screaming, "We no be Hausas! We no be Hausas! Na Plateau we come from!" They circled around us. The leader of the killers, a hulk of a man I had never seen in my life, said, "Na Christian you be?"

'"Yes." I lied to save my life. If only lies could save life, my sister.

'"Say Our Lord's Prayer make we hear," he thundered.

'Allaaahu akbar! I exclaimed in my mind, *Allah the Great, is this the end of me?* I stood there blank and hollow like a useless thing.

'"I say, say Our Lord's Prayer!" he barked.

'I only stared, teary and felt myself leaking from my anus and vagina. I dropped to my knees, my arms splayed out in utter supplication.

'"Pour petrol on her!"

'I sprang up, screaming. One of them began to pin me down. I squirmed, turning my head. The man with the container started pouring the petrol.

'Then we heard the sound of tyres squealing. I heard gunshots. "Police! Police! Police!" The killers took to their heels, but a matchstick had hit my left breast. At the same time, Madam Well-Well's body was aflame. I collapsed, screaming. A policeman flung me into a big gutter. He poured sand on me and quenched the flame.'

Mama was sniffling now. 'So that was the end of Madam Well-Well?'

Hadiza's voice suddenly became weepy. 'My sister, I wish it were my end too.'

We were silent for a while. I moved to the wall and leant on it, still staring at Hadiza.

Mama asked, 'What about your husband?'

'He survived. He got me in the General Hospital.'

I had met Hadiza once, when she had visited us the previous year. Then she was plump and dark, newly married. Her homeland was a village near ours, but she grew up in Keffi with her aunt. Her husband was a driver at Kano Airport. Now she looked like a monster to me. Her left ear was burnt, only a lump remained. Her legs, arms, neck and face were charred. Was her whole body like that? A bump, like a huge blister, was visible on her chest, above the breasts. I wondered how her breasts looked.

'May her soul rest in peace, Madam Well-Well,' Mama said in a shaky voice.

'Hhm, only one of her children survived. Hassana.'

Madam Well-Well was richer than most women in the trade, Mama told me. Mama, Hadiza and other women kept their sacks of *alubo* in her store and paid her for storage. Each morning they came to the store and fetched the flour in basins for their open stalls.

Mama said, 'Hadiza, you can't remain in this trade. You can't sit in the sun anymore.'

'So my husband says. He doesn't even want me to come out. But I told him that I couldn't remain at home. I'm healthy now. I can work. Though my life is now half, I'll live it.'

'I agree with your husband.'

'The other reason he wants me to remain at home is that I'm a sour sight to people. But is it my fault that I'm looking like this?'

'No, it's the killers' fault.'

'It's Allah's destiny, my sister.'

I could not stop looking at her and I imagined many things. She could have been Mama. She had seen death, but did not die. If Helen had survived, looking like Hadiza, how would I regard her? How would her beautiful bandy legs be? Would her attractive skin still be the same? It gave me the creeps to think that Helen might have ended up looking like Hadiza, burnt and wasted.

Mama and I pushed through people as we headed towards her stall. People were milling around. I wondered why there were so many people. Ola was right, after all, when he said that Kano was the largest city in our country after Lagos. He said most of the people in the streets and in the markets were immigrants from Niger and Chad.

'Mama Murtala, good morning o,' a Hausa man in *riga* greeted Mama.

Mama stopped and turned. One of the beggars stepped on Mama's foot. She pushed him. 'Don't step on me, you wicked child,' she said in Hausa.

'Mama Murtala,' the Hausa man called again.

'Mallam Gambo.'

We moved into Mallam Gambo's store. It was stocked with general items such as milk, sugar, tea, canned tomato, corned beef, detergent, spaghetti and rice.

'The market is still overflowing with people. I thought there would be fewer people, because of the crisis,' Mama told the man in Hausa.

'There will not be, Mama Murtala. There are hundreds of men and boys in the market, like that one who stepped on your foot, doing nothing.'

'They carry loads for people and beg for money,' I explained.

The man looked at me. His eyes were bright with kohl.

'Must be your young man, Mama Murtala. Is he the Murtala?'

'Yes.'

'Welcome, Murtala.' Without moving from where he sat, he picked up a tin of condensed milk and handed it to me. 'Here. You'll like it.'

'Thank you,' I said, happy.

'They are bad, those boys,' Mallam Gambo said. 'They pray for riots in order to loot.'

'Not only them,' Mama said. 'Adults looted, too.'

'Oh yes. The Hausas sent these boys to loot. But the Igbos, especially our fellow traders, came here armed. They protected their own stores while they looted stores owned by non-Igbos.'

'Is that so?'

'They looted my store, Mama Murtala. I found my store as empty as a mosque in an unholy hour. And I was told who did it.'

'Hhm. A bad time for all of us; I lost my son.'

'*Innalilahi!* Sorry, Mama Murtala.'

'He's Murtala's immediate younger brother.'

'Accept my condolences, Murtala.'

'Thank you.'

We left Mallam Gambo. Mama's stall was not really a stall but an open space where she would sit. A plump woman was sitting on the very spot, a basin of *garri* in front of her. At first Mama was confused, thinking she had not found the right place. So we moved forward a bit. Then she returned and pointed at the basin of *garri*. 'This is my space.'

The woman sprang up, 'Madam, welekom, you wan buy garri?'

Mama was amused. 'No. Na my place be dis.'

The woman did not understand. Or pretended not to. 'Wetin you dey talk?'

Mama was calm, looking straight into the woman's eyes. 'I say na here I dey sell *alubo* before fight come.'

The woman smirked and rolled her eyes, looking Mama up and down. 'Wetin you mean sef?'

'I wan my place.'

She mimicked Mama in the most contemptuous way I had ever seen. Then she sucked her teeth loudly. 'Abeg comot for my face!'

My heart beat faster.

Without raising her voice, Mama asked, 'Your head dey correct so?'

The woman flew into rage. She was shouting, 'Make you no insult me, you hear? Make you no insult me, you hear?' She repeated, her voice growing louder.

Other market women who had been looking intervened, shrieking:

'Wetin happen?'

'Madam, na wedn?'

'Why una dey quarrel?'

The woman was throwing up her hands. 'Abeg make una see dis *yeye* woman for me. She jus come here say make I comot from here, say na her place. She dey craze!'

Mama raised her voice higher. 'Na you dey craze! Mad woman.'

'God punish you! You know wetin I come meet here? Na

tyres dey burn put here wey I come sweep am put my seat. And you jus comot from sky tell me say na ya place. Dem write ya name put? *Onye oshi!*' She started speaking Igbo rapidly to the other women around her. She took off her scarf and tied it round her waist.

Many people were watching us. I wished I could vanish. Two women came to Mama and one said, 'Mama Murtala, welcome o.'

'Tank you, Mama Adejo. Why una no dey here? Where una dey now?'

'Hhm na so we come meet dis Igbo women. If you talk, dem go gather fight you. And if you go report dem for market office dem go go bribe de people wey dey dere.'

'So I go jus leave am make e cany my place?'

'No worry, come, we go make place for you.' Mama Adejo held Mama's hand and pulled her away.

I followed them.

11 | *Grandmama Intends to Return*

Grandmama had intended to return to the village two days after arriving, but Baba told her he did not have money for her transport fare. She had to wait till pay day, still ten days away.

'How can I remain in this land of ghosts for ten days? I smell death all over. I can't stay,' she protested.

'There's nothing I can do to get money, our mother,' Baba said matter-of-factly.

'Odula, you want to keep me away from my farms? What will I be doing here?' she wailed.

Baba did not say a word. He stood up and entered the inner room.

When Ajara told her, I heard Imatum say that it served Grandmama right, that it was her *I-too-know* that had brought her to Kano, and that Grandmama boasted too much about things she could not do.

When Grandmama took her grievance to Mama, the latter said, 'Same old story, Mother-of-my-husband. You've seen it yourself.'

'I will be dead if I spend ten days here doing nothing, eating this dog's food you people eat. Won't you cook pounded yam for me at least one day?'

'Ask your son,' Mama replied.

When she asked Baba, he chuckled and said, 'Our mother, you should thank God that we have *tuwo* to eat. That's what I can afford. '

Grandmama pursed her lips, whipping herself into a childish fury. Then she burst out in an authoritative tone: 'And why do you insist on living here? Do you want the children to die of hunger? Since I came here, I have not eaten any real food. I see that you have lost your senses, my son.'

Baba ignored her.

Grandmama ate what we ate. The TV set, when there was power, helped relieve the boredom of her stay at home. When I returned from school, I sometimes took her out for a walk.

'If you're not careful, you'll pick juju from the ground,' I said when I noticed her habit of picking things up from the ground.

She stopped walking, laughed heartily and told me, 'What will the ghosts in this city do with the blood of an old woman?'

On her last Saturday with us, Grandmama called me after our usual breakfast of pap. We went out of the room, as she did not want anybody to hear what she had to tell me.

'My husband,' she started, looking into my eyes as we stood outside the stunted fence. 'You and I will go out today. I'm going to be a young girl, walking by your side.'

'But you're not a young girl.'

'Oho! Do you mean these smelly girls around are better than me?'

We laughed over her joke. Then her laughter stopped

abruptly and she stared at me intently. 'You are going to show me where my father is buried.'

'Where we buried Ukpo?'

'Yes, my husband.'

'I don't think I can still…'

'Son of the Wind, don't go that way!' She brought her face closer to mine. 'That is foolish talk. Two brothers were walking on the road and death snatched one away. And you don't know where he is buried? You should know. And you must take me there now.'

Along the Kwanar Jabba road, we walked side by side. I was surprised at the unusual clarity of Grandmama's sight. She saw everything and asked many questions. Each time she saw the remains of burnt cars and buildings, she cursed the killers.

'If you were here during the crisis, what would you have done?' I asked her.

'Do you think those beasts would have got me?' she asked instead of answering my question.

'You're old. You wouldn't have been able to run.'

'Me? Daughter of the Wind?' She cackled. 'Have you seen anybody catching the Wind? Your foolish father has refused to bring you home. A day spent in your grandfather's *uponu* will make you a proper son of the Wind. Your brother wouldn't have died if your father had connected him to his roots. And that is why,' Grandmama stopped and turned to me, taking my hand, 'you must come to the village with me so that we connect you to the Wind and the Wind will be your eternal companion and protector.

You're overdue for the initiation. Do you hear me? Will you come with me?'

'I'm going to school.'

'It will not take much time.'

'I can't go now. Maybe during holidays.'

She began to walk again. I walked alongside her.

'You talk like your foolish father, my husband.'

I tried to avoid arguments with Grandmama. When we were close to Airport Road, I looked sideways at the heap of debris where a bad smell used to hang in the air. All of a sudden, I heard a car brake, screeching. A harsh honk sounded. Other oncoming cars braked and honked. I spun around. Grandmama had strayed onto the road. I rushed after her, grabbed her arm and pulled. She squirmed her arm free from my hands and looked at the honking cars, unconcerned, as if it was not for her they had stopped. She walked away from the road unhurriedly. The agitated drivers were shouting:

'Get out of the road!'

'Witch!'

'Which kin' old woman be dis?'

'O boy, why have you brought this witch to the road to cause accident?'

'Young man, what are you doing with this old woman on the main road?' a concerned passer-by asked.

I did not answer. As the cars drove off, people stuck out their hands, their fingers splayed in insults.

'See what you've caused,' I said, infuriated.

'What did I cause, my husband?'

'Why did you move into the road? The cars would have knocked you down.'

'Shut your mouth up. Do you know what you are saying?'

'You heard them shouting.'

'Oho! They are shouting at themselves, not me. Did they want me to jump? Are there no old women where they come from?'

'You strayed to the road!'

'The road is for all of us.'

'I think we should return home.'

'No. You must take me to see my father.'

I was so angry that I did not answer her questions and we walked on in silence.

We reached the cemetery. We trod on the undergrowth, moving slowly, conscious of the eerie atmosphere. I went ahead of Grandmama, my senses alert, anxious to prove myself a descendant of the Wind. I did not falter until I led her to the spot. Grandmama was pleased.

She circled the ridged grave and stood on the eastern side of it. Her back was against the half-risen sun. She started an incomprehensible incantation. I watched her keenly and was ready to scream should anything unnatural happen.

As she turned to the sun and began to sway sideways, her utterance became intelligible:

'Son of my son,
I am your grandmother,
Daughter of the Wind, come to you.
Ukpo, our father, *Zaaaaaki*.

Did you not leave our spiritland,
Enter the womb of my son's wife,
Emerge in the world with gallantry
As you promised us?
Did you not elude, defy
The fickle emotions of the earth
And all its little illnesses,
Son of the Wind that you are?
And you allowed the violent one
To seize you at a tender incarnation!
You puzzle us, Ukpo,
Our father, son of my son.
You choose to melt
In the violence of mere metal
When you have fathered
Sons and daughters of the Wind
Who can bear you across
The stings of death.
Come back again, Ukpo,
For you are the real, rare offspring of the Wind,
The tough being that should
Inhabit this terrible world.
Do our people not say
The world needs the tough ones?
Return, return, I say return
To the choice wombs
Of our daughters and daughters-in-law.
I, Anyalewa,
The toughest of your daughters,
Daughter of the Wind herself,

Stand before you
With a promise of a pure white he-goat
Today in this sunrise.
But I have caught the leprosy of
A strange land here.
When I return to the roots,
The blood of your he-goat
Shall reach the spiritland.
And having declared for you
What the mortal can offer the immortal,
My supplication is this:
Set the glare of your lion eyes on
The family of Odula,
My son, your son.
He whom you so loved that
You obliged entry into his wife's womb,
Do not abandon him.
We are worried that
He has chosen the misery of
The city in the rags of the police,
But he is our son, our own blood.
Hold his hand and lead him
Out of his self-damaging blindness.
No, not even a single needle
Should touch the flesh of
His wife and children.
They shall neither feel
Headache nor stomachache,
Nor the heat of fever.
Save them, hold them in your arms,

Let your mane protect them.
Shield them from the violence of
The evil ones feasting, gloating
In the death-dance of violent religions.
That's my supplication, Father Ukpo.'

The lilting flow of her voice ceased. Her swaying body stilled. The sunlike radiance on her face dimmed. She looked at me, blinked and smiled.

'My husband, you'll live long.'

'Amen.'

'You're the tough light that will explode in the darkness that clouds your father's vision.'

'Amen.'

'You're the regenerative spirit our ancestors have sent to Odula in spite of his misguided hostility.'

'Amen.'

'But my husband, you have to connect to your past; you must know why you are a dreamer.'

'But my dreams are nightmares.'

Grandmama laughed. 'Dreams are dreams. Among our people, dreamers are great people.'

I did not say anything.

'My husband, let's go home. But we have to go to the main market first.'

Trek to the main market? As we walked out of the cemetery, I told her, 'The market is far from here. We can't walk to the place.'

'Are we crippled?'

'Don't you understand when I say the place is far? Well, let's go. It's you who will be tired.'

'Me, daughter of the Wind?' Grandmama laughed. We were now out of the cemetery, on the road. 'Not me, my husband. Is the place farther than my upper farm? You know my upper farm, don't you?'

'No, it's not.'

'So why can't I go? I go to my upper farm every day.'

We walked from one street to the other, taking a few turns. When we reached Yarkura Market, Grandmama, who had been behind me, took the lead. She wanted to buy clothes and plates because she had heard they were cheap in Kano. In the first shop we entered, Grandmama spoke our language to the trader. I intervened.

In the second shop, when the language Grandmama spoke confused the trader, I told her, 'Can't you see they don't understand our language? They only speak Hausa here.'

Grandmama snapped, 'There you go again, fool! Is it my problem if they only understand Hausa? Is that not their language? Let them speak their language; I'll speak mine.'

I stared at Grandmama, exasperated. 'It means you don't want to buy anything in this market.'

She fired back, 'No, it means they don't want to sell anything in this market. And who will lose? I'll return to my village with my money, but they can't return to their houses with their merchandise.'

12 | *Baba Changes*

Baba changed when Mama and my siblings returned from the village. Perhaps it was because Mama too had changed. Physically weak, she had lost the charms of motherhood. The silence and resignation she brought from the village festered and turned into a disturbing fury. She found fault with us, shouted at us, insulted us whenever she insulted Baba and often wished to be left alone.

The day before, she had returned from the market very angry. Oyigwu ran to her, chanting 'Mama *oyoyo*.' She almost did not notice him when he clung to her. She had a faraway look as though it was not a market but a place of mourning she had come from. She entered the room with Oyigwu still holding on to her cloth. 'Leave me alone!' she barked at him. He recoiled and burst into tears.

'Mama, why shout at Oyigwu?' I asked, worried.

'You shut up over there!' she snapped back.

Unlike Baba, Mama often shouted at us. She even beat us, but always with good reason. Did she have any good reasons to shout at us now? Had Oyigwu done any wrong in welcoming her as a child welcomes its mother?

'I didn't buy anything for you, if that's why you're shouting "Mama *oyoyo*",' she said brusquely.

Oyigwu looked at her fearfully, then turned his teary

eyes to me. He drew closer and I picked him up. 'Stop crying. Let's go out. I'll buy you biscuits.'

Mama complained aloud about how the market had changed. People only stared with sunken eyes, wanting a lot of *alubo* for little money. Adults would go on their knees to beg for extras. She could sit for hours without a single person coming to buy her *alubo*. At home she did not count money as before, but sat brooding and lamenting, her eyes turned away from the TV. She accused Baba of causing her depression, sang sad songs and read her Eloyi Bible silently. With a heavy sigh, she retired to bed.

In the evening we were eating our supper when Imatum returned from an outing, clutching a small polythene bag. The weather was hot and there was no electricity. Unlike other families who ate dinner outside, we ate ours inside no matter the heat. The room was filled with the smell of our sweat and the aroma of the food. Imatum stood by the door and sniffed as if she had suddenly found herself in a smelly latrine. She asked Yakubu, who was sitting on the floor, to make way for her so she could move into the inner room. Mama and the girls were eating in the inner room, which was even hotter than the outer room.

'Good evening, Mama,' Imatum greeted her.

Mama exploded. 'Where are you coming from?'

Imatum shouted her answer. 'I'm coming from my friend's house. Shouldn't I go to my friend?'

'Every day you go to your friends. Your friends don't ever come to your house. Imatum, what a stupid liar you have become!'

'I'm not a liar!'

'You talk to me with a raised voice!'

'You just leave me alone!'

Mama sprang up and came after her. Imatum turned and rushed towards the door, stumbling through the *tuwo* Yakubu was eating. Yakubu shrieked. Imatum was gone. She did not return until Mama had gone to bed.

Baba returned from Sabon Gari, bleary-eyed and belching an offensive odour of beer. He carried an old copy of *Newswatch*. He addressed Mama, 'Look here, woman, we're dying of SAP.'

'What's that?'

'There you are, poor uneducated woman who makes trouble for her husband. Structural Adjustment Programme is…'

Mama interrupted him, raising an arm. 'Don't take me there, Father-of-my-children. You look elsewhere for the causes of your problems while they are here with you.'

'That's incorrect. I'll tell you what you don't know,' Baba drawled, belching.

'Not while you're drunk.'

'I'll take that as an insult.'

'Do something about the mouse holes in this room.'

'Mouse holes?' Baba asked as if something grave was being brought to his notice for the first time.

'Don't you see the huge mice that live with us in this house?' Baba laughed, throwing his head backward. 'Ija-guwa, you amuse me. If the mice didn't live in the room with us, where else would they live? How would they survive?'

Mama smiled, in spite of herself. 'I can see that something is wrong with you, Father-of-my-children.'

'No,' Baba retorted, 'It's you something is wrong with. You complain of holes in our tiny rooms when the whole world is infested with holes.'

'I don't understand you.'

'The mice come out in the night to steal and destroy our things. Highly-placed human beings crawl out of their holes in big cars and aeroplanes in the secret of the night to steal and destroy common people's wealth.'

'I still don't get you.'

'Dullard!' Baba shouted, saliva spurting from his mouth. 'The mansion, hidden from public view, surrounded by a fence and tall trees, where the rich *oga* hides his thieving hands, is a hole. So is he not a big mouse?'

'God gives and takes. He makes a man rich or poor...'

'When he likes!' Baba belched again, levelling a look at Mama.

'You also have to ask.'

'You don't need to ask, Ijaguwa. And when he likes, he tells Muslims, "Hey, rise and kill the Christians". And then turns to the Christians. "Hey, rise and kill the Muslims". Is that not what the human mice have reduced God to?'

'You didn't go to church today, Father-of-my-children.'

'Church?' Baba sprang up, grasping his crotch and staggered out of the room, heading for the bathroom.

* * *

I accosted Imatum. 'Where do you get money to buy these things and play Father Christmas always?'

'What's your business?' she retorted. 'Yes, I'm a Father Christmas. I know how to make money and help my brothers and sisters.' She sucked her teeth, rolling her eyes in contempt.

'Oh yes, I know you're born to help others, but you make your money by following men about.'

'I use my talent to make money. If you think I get money from men and you're envious of that, you can go hit your head on a tree. I don't use your body to follow men anyway.' She gave me a sidelong glance, rolling her eyes again.

It was a hot afternoon. The air in our room was stuffy. Anger welled up in me. We were sweating, glaring into each other's eyes spitefully. Her impudence maddened me. Our sisters were staring at us, unable to intervene. My body was growing stiff and hot. I dropped the book I was reading.

'Don't tell me nonsense when I'm trying to call you to order.' I was wagging my finger at her.

Imatum burst into a mocking laughter, clapping her hands. 'May God have mercy on Baba, the patient one. Baba has not roared to call me to order. But you, you want to kill yourself with the task of calling me to order. If I were you, I'd mind my own business. No use being envious of each other.'

'Envious? Well, I'm not envious of a prostitute like you!'

She flared up. 'Don't call me a prostitute. I warn you, don't call me a prostitute again. You're the one who is a prostitute! Kill yourself with envy. That's why this house will remain poor forever!' She stormed into the inner room.

I restrained myself from raging after her. 'I'll let Mama know of your fucking around to bring money home,' I railed.

She rushed to the door of the inner room, almost screaming, 'Tell her. Let her kill me. When she kills me, every envious mouth will be shut. Mama knows that I'm bound to be rich and nobody can stop me. Am I responsible for your condition? Book-reading poor boy like you! Your mates are making money outside. You imprison yourself in this oven, hunched over books, pretending to be an important person. Poor...'

In her outburst, she did not realise that I had drawn close to her. The blow caught her by surprise. She yelped and came after me. Her wild fingers went for my neck. I dodged and hit her left ear. She gripped the neckline of my shirt. I hit her repeatedly. She scratched me furiously with her long fingers. Ajara and Anyaosu tried to pull us apart.

Mama Tindele, fat and round, suddenly appeared in our room, yelling, 'Leave her alone, Murtala! Leave her. You, take your hands off his shirt.'

But her fingers had dug into my shirt, madly tearing it. Enraged, I kicked her repeatedly, harder, more harshly. Her screaming voice rose to a pitch.

I heard Omodiale's voice: 'M-Boy! Unbelievable...'

I heard the voices of other neighbours in our room. I ignored them, ignored my siblings, but Baba's sudden voice pierced through to me: 'Murtala!' I let her go and raised my head to see Baba's face. 'Do you want to kill her?'

I did not answer him.

It was night. Our door flew open and Baba, stark naked, hurried out of the room. Mama sprang up, alarmed. I stood up too. Mama made to grab him, but Baba trotted off, headed for the bathroom.

The children, women and men sitting in front of their doors, under the moonlight, watched in dismay. Some of them rose with exclamations.

'Wetin be dis?!'

'Jesus Christ!'

'Who be dat?!'

'Na Baba Murtala!'

Mama stood motionless in front of our room. I knew her feet would be too heavy to carry her. *Why has the moon chosen to be bright this hour? Why?* The neighbours were staring. *No, don't ask me for an explanation. Don't ask me anything about this bizarre sight.* I followed Baba, walking gently, bravely, making sure that I remained calm. The silence from everyone spoke of sympathy. Before he reached the bathroom, Baba grabbed his penis, his urine splashing around. He did not go inside. I stood beside him, unable to say a word. His urine gushed forth. I thought the world stood still as the gushing sound of Baba's urine filled the compound.

'*Chei!* Dis na piss?' It was Baba Peter.

'Na wa o. I for like am if to say we get tap wey dey rush like dat.'

Some people burst into laughter. I did not hear Omodiale's voice.

I grew cold with shame. I looked at Baba's face. He was rheumy-eyed, swaying as the urine flowed. He seemed to relish the way he held his penis, the way his crotch thrust forward. Still I could not talk. *Why can't something awful, more awful than this, happen now?*

His penis still dripping, Baba turned sideways, staggering and knocking me out of the way. If I had wanted to keep pace with him, I would have had to trot. But I allowed him to go. It was a costly mistake.

Baba plunged into Baba Eddy's room.

Mama Eddy screamed, 'No enter my room! No enter my room!'

Other people shrieked along. Baba Eddy was not home. I rushed into Baba Eddy's room where I found Baba standing and muttering in the centre of the outer room, turning round, confused by the shouting. I grabbed his arm and shouted: 'Baba, this is not our room! You're naked! In somebody's room!'

He levelled his look at me and belched, rocking his head drunkenly. I was glad there was a power outage. I repeated what I had said, louder. Then widening his blurry eyes, he said, belching, 'Mur-ri-ta-la, what are you saying?'

By now I was pulling him with all my strength. He yielded. His legs hit the doorstep and he collapsed, filling the doorway. I was helpless. I looked towards the others for assistance, unable to say a word. Omodiale promptly came to my aid.

'M-Boy, let me raise him up. I can.' He fixed his hands in Baba's armpits and, biting his lower lip, struggled to raise him, staggering backwards. 'Y'know, I underestimated his weight, M-Boy.'

No other neighbour came to help.

Omodiale succeeded in pulling Baba up. 'Now to your room.'

I led the way.

'For our place, dem say na quiet people dey dangerous pass people wey dey talk.' It was Baba Peter.

Baba Fatima answered him, 'Abeg, keep quiet, na wetin you get to talk be dat?'

'Wetin I for talk? Dis policeman dey dis compound, even to greet, e no fit greet. E tink say na him get sense pass everybody. See wetin e don do now.'

'Dat na *yeye* talk.'

Baba Peter raised his voice, 'Wetin you…'

An angry female voice howled, 'Abeg make una shut up!' It must have been Mama Peter. Of all the women in our compound, only she could openly shout at a man.

Omodiale and I were struggling with Baba at our door. The neighbours crowded around, now silent as though in worship. They moved out of the way for us. Omodiale dragged Baba into our room. Mama had hidden herself inside the inner room, weeping. A number of children followed us.

'Keep him on the floor,' I told Omodiale. I pushed away the wobbly centre table.

Baba lay on the floor, in a sprawl, muttering something.

'Thank you, brother Omodiale.'

'Don't mention it, M-Boy. Y'know, this thing happens

from time to time. It's part of the life we're condemned to. Take it easy.'

Imatum suddenly appeared, shooing the children away. Some neighbours stood by the door, looking into our room, saying:

'Murtala, sorry, you hear.'

'Madam, sorry oh.'

'Make una take am easy.'

'Na so man wey dey drink dey do.'

I thanked the people for their concern and closed and bolted our door.

Baba was fast asleep, snoring. Oyigwu, awakened by the noise, took Baba's hand, attempting to drag him. 'Baba, shtand up. Baba, shtand up.' Emayabo and others stood, watching in amazement.

Mama came out of the inner room, weeping, cursing and praying at the same time: 'Jehovah my Lord, why am I fated to be with such a man? Tell me why all this is happening to me. Murtala, your father has lost his honour to beer. Tell me, when did this habit start?'

I could only stare at her. It occurred to me that Baba was never this disgracefully drunk when Mama and my siblings were away in the village. I did not bother to tell Mama that this habit was just as strange and off-putting as her own habit of being hostile towards us.

13 | *Somebody Knocks at Our Door*

Somebody knocked at our door. 'De Father-of-dis-house dey?'

It was Baba Fatima.

'Yes, I dey,' Baba answered. Baba was dressed for work. His head had grown too thin for his beret. It used to fit him and make him look handsome.

'Good morning. De landlord don come o.'

'Good morning. I hear you.'

I followed Baba outside. I took a deep breath. The air felt healthier than the stuffy, urine-smelling air in our room. A gentle breeze was ruffling the leaves of the tree in our compound. It was a bright day and light clouds moved gently in the sky.

The compound was fully awake. Mama Peter was shouting at Peter to finish shitting quickly. He was sitting on a potty. Ado was also sitting on a potty in front of his father's room, one of his small legs stretched, the other bent at the knee. His head rested on his left palm and he seemed to be dozing. I saw Rekiya, smart in school uniform, a little bag strapped on her back. Mama Tindele sat in front of her room, her fat legs stretched out. Turaki, her youngest child, sucked at one of her large breasts while standing. Mama Eddy had lit the stove beside her door and was warming something that looked like leftover food. Her daughter, Julie, Anyaosu's mate, who was dressed in school uniform, squatted beside her. The stove exuded dark smoke. I saw Ramatu, the daughter of Baba Rafatu's first wife, tugging at her mother's wrapper, whining. The mother was breastfeeding her new baby. Loud music boomed from Omodiale's room. Always, it was Fela Kuti. Always, it was *Suffering and Smiling*.

Near the latrines, I saw six people standing, four carrying crumpled paper in their hands. Zubairu, gripping his kettle, his face twisted, was nearest to the second latrine. Inna, the old Hausa woman, leant on the wall and placed her kettle on the ground beside her. Five buckets filled with water, three of them without handles and sponge cases dancing in two of them, stood near the bathroom. Aminatu, one of Baba Rafatu's adolescent daughters, was bathing her siblings. 'Kneel down well!' she shouted at the one she was washing, spanking her buttocks. There were three others waiting their turn. Beside her was also Fatima, Imatum's friend, bathing her younger brother.

Under the tree stood the landlord, much younger than Omodiale. Our house was his share of the inheritance his father had left. He was smoking. He had a funny way of exhaling smoke: his thick, dark lips pouted leftwards, his entire face slightly inclined in that direction. The smoke came out of the gaping mouth and his large nostrils in jets. He was in a *riga* and a pair of sandals, his long toenails conspicuous.

Baba Peter, Omodiale, Baba Fatima, Baba Tindele and Baba stood around him.

'Yes, yes, I don come, make ebrybody bring za money.'

The landlord stuck a cigarette, which was a mere stub, between his lips and stretched out his hands, demanding. He was talking to no one in particular. The authority in his voice was unmistakable. He tapped his chest now and then, when he spoke.

Baba spoke Hausa to him. 'Yahaya, I've not got my salary.'

He answered Baba in Hausa, smiling. 'Officer, every time you complain of salary. Are you working free for the government?'

'Most of us in the government service are donkeys, Yahaya. To survive, you have to be a donkey.'

Baba left abruptly, not looking back. The other men stared at him. Yahaya was not disturbed by Baba's discourteous action. He took his time to light another cigarette. He inhaled deeply, then exhaled the smoke towards Baba Peter.

'Come, why you dey smoke put for my face? You well so?'

Yahaya turned to him, '*Oya*, bring ya money.'

'Na because I no be policeman, you dey ask me for money?'

'Za rent! You're occupy my house. You fay ya rent!'

'No shout on me, Yahaya. You know say you be small boy.'

'Who be small boy?' He turned to Baba Fatima. 'You hear am too? You be caretaker, you bring zese mad feofle to my house...'

'Nobody is mad here!' Omodiale shouted. He had been staring at Yahaya with indignation.

'You, bring ya money. I don tell you say you can't stay in zis house pree op charge.'

Zubairu caught our attention. He was walking from the

latrines back to his room, his countenance downcast, his slippers making a loud *slap-slap* noise. He seemed inwardly agitated. Looking towards the latrines, I saw his kettle on the ground.

Omodiale was talking to Yahaya. 'Do I look to you like someone who will stay in your house free of charge? You should be happy that I'm living here, by the way. Y'know, I've warned you to be careful the way you talk to us here.'

Yahaya ignored Omodiale and turned to Baba Tindele. 'And you, *Mallam*, ya own is two mons only.'

Baba Tindele gave him a withering look. 'I tell you say my roof dey leak. Rain don dey come. If you no repair de roof, I no go pay any money. I go use de money repair am. *Shikenan*.'

That did not seem to bother Yahaya. He exhaled his smoke with a relish, his eyes half-closing. Then he chuckled, shaking his head, exclaiming, 'Zese feofle por my house!'

'Ehm you, Mr Caretaker,' Baba Peter turned to Baba Fatima. 'Tell am say make he see,' he pointed his finger in the direction, 'our bafroom dey fall. One day person go dey baf and the room go fall for him head. Why e never repair am? We don complain since.'

Baba Fatima stared at him, mutely.

Baba Tindele added, 'And our latrines don dey full. De second one, shit don reach de mout of de hole sef.'

Yahaya was shifting from one leg to the other, inhaling smoke and exhaling it towards Baba Peter and Baba Tindele. The smoke irritated Baba Peter. He kept waving it away with his open hand. Yahaya momentarily folded his arms across his chest. His eyes were on Baba Fatima.

Very uneasy, Zubairu emerged from his room, half-trotting. Omodiale burst into laughter as he saw him. Zubairu went for his kettle on the floor, near the latrine. I heard one of the people standing there tell him that Inna, very pressed, had taken his turn in the latrine. Zubairu exploded with anger, shouting that he was also pressed, so much so that he could not even stay in one place. He was shouting in Hausa, 'And who is inside the second latrine? Does the person want to spend the whole day inside? Is the person eating or shitting inside?'

They were begging him to calm down. He stiffened his body, contorting his face, then relaxed and leant on the dusty wall facing the latrines.

I turned to the men under the tree who were also watching Zubairu, amused.

Omodiale started. 'Y'know, the real problem is that the two latrines and one bathroom are not enough for us. See how people line up to shit,' he pointed. 'Yahaya, listen to me, see the population of us in this compound; see what you have for us as latrines and bathroom. Y'know, this is unreasonable.'

Yahaya retorted, 'Don't tell me nonsense! You feofle has flenty flenty wives and children. So you shit flenty. Is my pault? Gonment say do structural adjusmen frogramme, marry small, born small children, but see za froblem you cause por yourself.'

'God punish you with your govment!' Baba Tindele burst out. 'How many children your papa born?'

'Thirty-five!' Omodiale shouted, laughing. 'Is that not what you told me, Baba Fatima?'

Yahaya was cowed into silence. He exhaled his smoke, staring at Baba Fatima.

'You be small boy, you no get sense...'

Yahaya interrupted Baba Tindele, pointing at him, the cigarette stuck in the fingers. 'Don't insult me because you no get money to fay. But you must to fay. You hear me? All op you must to fay. Two mons, three mons, five mons, and you, Omodiale, seven mons!' He turned to Omodiale.

Omodiale had opened his mouth to reply when, again, the loud *slap-slap* of Zubairu's slippers drew our attention. He looked really agitated.

In a tone full of mockery, Yahaya asked in Hausa, 'Ehm Mallam Zubairu, can I have your rent?'

Zubairu stopped suddenly. He turned to the men under the tree. Shooting his index finger towards Yahaya, Zubairu blurted out, 'May Allah's curse be upon you for bringing such discomfort on me!'

The other men burst into laughter.

Yahaya had a good laugh and said, 'May more of Allah's curse be upon you for...'

The remaining words stuck in his throat. Zubairu rushed straight for Yahaya's throat. Though taken unawares, Yahaya managed with one hand to free his neck from the furious hands. He was not entirely lucky. Some fingernails had dug into his neck. The hands settled for the neckline of his *riga*, squeezing it, dragging it, tearing it. Yahaya's free hand let the cigarette go, finally. He used it judiciously, landing a heavy blow on Zubairu's jaw. Zubairu slapped

Yahaya hard across the face. Baba Fatima, suddenly realising that he needed to separate the fighters, tried to throw himself between Zubairu and Yahaya. He held Zubairu by the arm, yanking him. 'Zubairu, leave Yahaya's cloth. Leave de cloth na.'

'I'll kill this bastard!' Zubairu swore in Hausa.

'You want to kill me? You want to kill me?'

'Hey, no killing here,' Omodiale shouted, lending a hand to Baba Fatima.

Baba Peter stepped back, saying, 'Abeg leave dem make dem fight. Na him Hausa broda fit fight am.'

Omodiale succeeded in holding Zubairu by the waist and pulling him.

Zubairu was shouting, 'I'll kill that bastard, I swear by Allah.'

Baba Fatima let out a loud shout, stepping back from Yahaya. I turned to see. Yahaya was charging towards Zubairu, wielding a pointed dagger.

'Knife! Knife!' Baba Peter shouted.

Yahaya moved fast. Zubairu dodged to the left. The dagger struck Omodiale's right arm. Letting go of Zubairu completely, Omodiale gave a sharp whimper. He squatted, then sat down on the floor, his legs splayed.

For a moment, everybody stood frozen, staring at Omodiale.

In that instant, a slender woman emerged from the second latrine. Zubairu rushed in, shit dropping from his shorts.

* * *

The beginning of March brought some luck to Baba. He was liberated from constant morning duty. Now he had three shifts: 6 a.m. to 3 p.m., 3 p.m. to 9 p.m. and 9 p.m. to 6 a.m. Also, he had been posted to Yarkura Market.

Baba had just returned from work. He sat down and began to remove crumpled bank notes from his bulging socks.

Ajara asked, 'Baba, why are you always hiding money in your socks?'

Baba smiled at her and sat up. 'Ajara, will you understand if I explain to you? Since you've asked, listen carefully. The police force is a place where there are layers of corruption…'

I was surprised that Baba was in the mood to talk. Only Ajara and I were in the room with him. Since there was a power cut, the air in the room had become quite hot.

'It's a hierarchy of corruption from the officers to the rank and file. The peak is the IG of police. Ajara, do you know what IG of police means?'

Ajara shook her head.

Baba looked at me. 'Murtala knows it. Tell her.'

I turned to Ajara and said, 'Inspector General of police.'

'He's the biggest criminal among the police,' Baba continued. 'Of course he doesn't go through the stress of putting money in his socks the way I do. Poor me. We try to outsmart one another in corruption.' Pointing to his half-empty socks, he continued. 'This is my own way of outsmarting them. People tip me without the knowledge of others and I slip the naira into my socks, protected by my trousers. No one has got the sense to do this. So, clap for your father.' He chuckled smugly.

We burst into laughter, clapping hands.

Ajara was not done yet. 'Baba, our Sunday school mistress says corruption and bribery are sins.'

Baba twisted his lips in disdain and said, 'Ajara, next time your Sunday school teacher says so, be brave enough and tell her that corruption and bribery are the only ways of surviving in our country. Human beings must survive.'

I pondered over Baba's answer. The advantages of Baba's corruption were everywhere. Since he had begun to bring sock-hidden money home again, we had resumed buying sugar for the pap we ate for breakfast. We no longer occasionally skipped lunch because there was really nothing to eat. We no longer ate mushy *tuwo* to make the flour last longer. We now had meagre scraps of fish in our soup. We no longer quarrelled over who had used the last piece of toilet soap, nor had to gravely resort to Omo detergent to bath. We no longer woke up looking for chewing sticks to clean our mouths. Most important of all, my siblings, all except Imatum, had returned to school. Baba gave Mama money to buy new uniforms, books and pencils.

Imatum said she was thinking over whether to return to school or not. I was shocked that Baba let her be.

A week later, when Baba had switched to night duty, he returned from Sabon Gari drunk and went straight to bed. It was 7 p.m. and he instructed me to wake him up before 9 p.m. for his duty. I woke him up at 8.30 p.m. He raised his head, grumbled, his eyes glassy, and returned his head to the pillow. I tapped him again. 'Baba, it's time for you to go to work.'

Baba raised his head higher this time, his eyes agitated, and yelled, 'Gerrout of here, *oya*!'

I recoiled, scared, and left the inner room.

Mama looked at me pityingly and said, 'Leave him alone. Maybe he won't go to work today.'

At a quarter past ten, Baba woke up and went out to pee. When he returned he stood in the outer room, looked down at me and asked, 'Murtala, what's the time now?'

I told him.

'And you didn't wake me up?'

Mama, who had been peering at her Bible, intervened. 'He woke you, but you refused to get out of bed. Didn't you know?'

Baba glanced at her angrily and hurried into the inner room. He dressed hurriedly. He came out of the inner room, yawned loudly and grunted that he was going to work. We bade him goodnight.

Baba did not return at six the next day. At times it was usual of him not to return home.

Mama left for the market.

I could not go to school because I had been driven out for not paying my tuition fees, so I kept the home, sat inside and read my books. I helped Ajara prepare our lunch and played with my younger ones when I was in the mood. If I got bored, I strolled to the quiet area of the cemetery, pondering events.

Imatum came home occasionally. She displayed what she called riches: a fair, glowing skin; a Bob Marley hairdo; a long pair of earrings; long nails; a blouse that exposed the upper parts of her small breasts; a pair of tight-fitting jeans or miniskirt; a strange pair of shoes and a most disturbing catwalk. Added to those were her condescending looks. It was the day Yakubu told me that he saw one fat Hausa man bring her home in a big car that I knew how far she had gone. Until then I thought she still followed those Hausa hawkers who lived behind our house and spent their daily earnings on cigarettes and girls. I thought she still followed the labourers in the next street who liked to show off with girls. I thought she still lingered with Omodiale who, at one time, had also wooed me with his generosity. One day he had bounced over to me, taken out money from his pocket and offered it to me: 'M-Boy, you need this for your break time in school, y'know.'

'I don't need your money!'

He had simply smiled and left me.

I had resolved not to tell Imatum another word about the life she had chosen.

She had started going to a new church. 'I've found my church; I won't go to your church anymore,' she announced to Mama one Sunday morning as Mama berated her for being in bed when she ought to be preparing for church.

'Imatum the courageous one, what are you telling me?'

'I've found a church I like.'

'Has your rebellion reached that?'

'It's not rebellion, Mama. Church is church and God is God.'

'Then why seek him in another church?'

'I seek God wherever I like, Mama. My church is a church of prosperity.'

Imatum was unrelenting in her stance. Mama reported

Imatum to Baba, something she had never done before. Baba grabbed the opportunity. 'I don't intervene in such trivial issues as church problems.'

Mama was hurt.

That night, I dreamt that Imatum had travelled to London. She wrote us a letter to say she would never return to Nigeria and that she wished us good luck in our poverty. My younger ones rejoiced over the news, but I felt sad because it occurred to me that she might have gone to London to become a prostitute. The dream was so real that when I woke up and saw her I was surprised and relieved.

14 | *Baba Does Not Return*

Baba had not returned from night duty. Could something have happened to him on his way back? Where had he gone afterwards?

By 3 p.m. I was really worried, not knowing what to do, when Sergeant Abu came. His appearance alone conveyed his message. I greeted him. He did not sit down. Rather, he asked me to follow him outside. Standing by his Vespa, he looked into my eyes and spoke to me in our language. 'Your father is in trouble.'

'What's it?' I heard myself exclaim.

'Yesterday, he was late to work. Our DPO went to his outpost on patrol, searching for policemen who couldn't do their job well. A new DPO who thinks he knows discipline better than anybody in the world. He didn't see your father and there was no excuse. He ordered that your father be locked up.'

'Oh my God.'

'He said to inform you. Tell your mother.'

'Thank you.'

I watched his Vespa disappear.

I told my siblings. They wondered how Baba, himself a policeman, could have been locked up by a policeman.

Ajara giggled and said, 'That man is telling a lie. Baba is drinking beer in Sabon Gari.'

Imatum hissed loudly when she returned from her outing. 'We'll rest from the disease of poverty in this house.'

I told Mama what had happened to Baba. She remained calm, as if used to hearing such news. She sat down opposite me and said, 'It's nice the police can discipline him.'

'Not a kind thing to say, Mama.'

'There's a consequence for every sin. Did he not drink and forget to go to work?'

I heard Imatum giggling from the inner room. Emayabo and Oyigwu were engrossed in the TV. Ajara and Anyaosu were inside the inner room, eating. Yakubu was not at home. Perhaps he was at his best friend Denis's house.

I implored, 'Mama, I want to go see Baba. Please help me with the fare.'

'I can't waste the little money I earn by sitting under the sun on a man who has lost his senses to beer.'

Mama kept her word.

I went to bed sad. Now and then I awoke, pushing Yakubu's legs away from mine. He slept heavily and moved restlessly on the bed. I heard the faraway howling of dogs and crickets chirping nearby. An owl was hooting somewhere in our compound. I stopped my mind from wandering as I wanted to think. Then I became conscious of the movements of the mice in our room. I heard their rushing motions, right on the springs of my bed. They were racing, fighting, shrieking. They scratched the plates on the floor. In the quiet of the night the noise was incredibly loud.

* * *

The next day, Saturday, at about 11.30 a.m., I was contemplating trekking to Yarkura Police Outpost when Ola appeared at our house.

'Hey, Murtala!' He was right by our door, about to step in.
'Ola!'

I jumped up with a mixed feeling of joy and sadness. I had been evasive each time Ola asked me to invite him to our house. I did not want to bring him into our poverty, to make myself an even greater object of pity. We knew of the social divide between us and treated it with a delicate silence. I had been wary of exposing the extent of my destitution to Ola.

Ola wore a pair of sky-blue jeans, a new white Nike T-shirt, a Nike baseball cap and a pair of Timberland boots. He had a bag strapped to his back. He was bustling with life. He sat down even before I offered him a seat, but chose the worst chair. It wobbled and he drew his buttocks to the edge, carefully holding the arms.

'Be careful with that chair, Ola. Come to this one.'
'Thanks.'

He stepped on a drop of pap. I saw other drops lying where Oyigwu was sitting and eating his breakfast.

Our room still stank of urine, as Emayabo and Oyigwu would not stop wetting themselves. I tried to look happy for his sake, but it was difficult.

'My dad hasn't got his salary. I can't come to school.'
'I know. I missed you. The whole class misses you.'
'I miss all of you too.'

'How are your parents?'

'They're fine. My dad is at work and my mum in the market. What about your parents and the lovely twins?'

'They all said to greet you. Always want you to visit again. The twins say they must pay you a visit one day.'

'All! I'd be happy to have them,' I lied.

'Your house isn't far from the school.'

'How did you find your way?'

'Hauwa, our classmate, described it for me. She lives close to you.'

'I know.'

'Our maths master is worried that you came first in the class, but don't have the money to pay the school fees.'

'How did he know of my problem?'

'Don't know.'

'Is Millicent fine?'

'Very worried.' Ola grinned. 'She begged me to… Well, if she had the money, she would have paid for you.'

Ola removed his bag from his back, unzipped it and dipped his hand inside. He brought out a small, folded paper and handed it to me. It was a receipt.

'My dad gave me money to pay for you when I told him.'

I stared at him, astonished, open-mouthed.

'Yeah, he likes you.'

'Thank you, Ola. I'm really grateful. But you didn't have to tell him about me.'

'I had to, Murtala. They're happy that I'm doing well in school. You've been helping me.'

'That's not enough for this kindness, Ola.'

Ola was quiet, looking round the room. Then he said, 'I also got some books for you.'

I grabbed the books with joy. It was the first time I had been given books as a present. 'Wao! They're beautiful.'

They were wide hardcovers. The bigger one was blue, with tall letters at the top: *Wild Animals*. Its glossy pages contained the pictures, names and habits of wild animals. I stopped at the picture of an animal that looked like a goat, but was thinner and more beautiful. Under it was written 'gazelle'. The explanation said it was a small slender antelope, found in Africa and Asia, with curved horns and a yellow-brown coat with white underparts.

'One of the prettiest animals in the world,' Ola said.

'It's really beautiful.'

The other was brown, with *Senegal Photographed* splashed on the middle of the front cover. I flipped through the book. The glossy pages contained fantastic pictures of cities, mansions, seas, villages and peoples in traditional attire. I stopped on a page that showed a young man and woman, scantily dressed, with strands of cloth round their heads, their arms open and their heels raised in a torrid dance. Beside them were four men, beating drums. Two of the drums were long, one was large and the fourth was quite small.

'Fantastic, isn't it?' Ola said.

'Oh yes.'

'Senegal is in West Africa, not far from here.'

'Must be a small country. Our social studies master says most of the countries in West Africa are small.'

'It's francophone.'

'French-speaking?'

'Yes. Let me show you something.' Ola took the book from me and turned the pages. He stopped at a particular page and gave it to me. It showed an ancient stone building with a small, low door, lower than the doors to our rooms in Kwana Hudu, that opened onto the sea. The water was so close that one could step from the door right into the water. There were small rocks at the foot of the building. Under the picture was written 'The gate of no return'. I read that the location was Goree Island, where African captives bound for Europe and America were kept before final transportation. Every captive who passed through that door never returned to Africa.

'It's so small. The people had to bend to pass through it,' I said.

'Yes, Murtala. My dad says in those days if you were taken as a slave, you became short and bent, no matter how tall you were. You could never walk tall. Everything made for you was short to make you bend and look short.'

'Interesting.'

'When we were there on holiday, we saw that the rooms in which captives were kept were low and small. People squeezed themselves into the rooms.'

I stared at the picture.

Ola continued. 'My dad says it is one of the reasons why Africa finds it difficult to grow tall.'

I pondered over what Ola said. I would discuss the issue with Uncle Tony, who studied history at Kano University, when next he visited us.

Suddenly, I realised I had not offered Ola a drink,

although I had no money to buy him anything. I thought of offering him water, but ours was dirty. When the water was collected in a cup, it had particles dancing in it.

Frankly, I said to him, 'Ola, I'm sorry I don't have anything to offer you.'

Ola smiled at me. 'Why don't you take me around this area? My first time. It's called Kwanar Jabba, no?'

Glad for the option he had offered, I said, 'Yes.'

I put on my shirt and we went out.

The sky was bright, but not without light and straying clouds. We walked through the nameless, untarred streets which stank of gutters, freshly shovelled. Heaps of slime from the gutters lined the streets. It was a national sanitation day.

'I notice that there is one wall between houses. No house has its own space,' Ola said.

'See the sizes of the windows.'

'So small. And Kano is a very hot city.'

'Imatum, my sister, calls our room an oven.'

'It's not healthy,' Ola said, his eyes on the squat houses.

We came to the main road of Kwanar Jabba, its only tarred road. Bus conductors were calling out: 'Sabon Gari', 'Yarkura', 'Bata', and the blaring of car horns filled the air. Wheelbarrow pushers jostled us. A man, pushing a small bicycle, an ice cream cooler fixed in front of it, was singing loudly in Hausa. Children followed him. Yoruba women, carrying large basins filled with plastic household items, with babies strapped on their backs, walked along the road.

We came upon a crowd in a circle. Inside the circle was a wiry man, holding a long rope that encircled the tiny waist of a monkey. The monkey, dressed in trousers and a T-shirt, was dancing to drumbeats. At one point, the drumming stopped. The wiry man asked the monkey to walk like a prostitute. It catwalked. Then he asked the monkey to lie down as a whore does, satisfied with her pay. The monkey briskly lay on its back, threw its legs wide apart and, with his tiny palms, beckoned the imaginary male to mount it. The man told the monkey to imagine itself as the goalkeeper of the national team. The onlookers would want a glimpse of his stamina. The monkey hopped about, diving to the left and to the right. People cheered and applauded. Ola was fascinated. At the top of his voice, the man implored the spectators to be quiet. Then he said, 'In the name of Allah, we seek kind donations for our intelligent friend here.'

Ola was one of the onlookers who gave him some coins. Thereafter we went to the biggest provision shop at Kwanarjabba. Ola bought Coca-Cola and egg rolls for us. We sat on a bench in front of the supermarket and watched people coming and going.

'So many people,' Ola said.

'Yes.'

'I'd like to come here frequently to watch these goings-on.'

'Really?'

'You don't see such things in my place.'

'I know.'

All of a sudden, Imatum appeared in front of us, accompanied by a young Hausa man. I recognised him from the cemetery, where I'd seen him smoking marijuana. I was embarrassed, but remained calm, pretending not to know her. She did not acknowledge my presence either, though she saw me. She took the boy's hand in hers and wiggled her buttocks as they walked into the shop. My body tensed up and tears stung my eyes. Was it anger? Was it pain? Was it frustration?

'Do you want some more to drink?' Ola's voice jolted me back to the reality that he was there beside me.

'No, thanks.'

'I would really love to come here often to see people.'

'It would be nice to have you around all the time.'

Before Ola left he gave my siblings some coins. He wanted me to promise him that I would be in school on Monday. He did not need my promise. Already bored at home, I was very eager to return to school.

15 | *I Go to See Baba*

I went to see Baba at the police station. The police sergeant on duty took one look at me and said, 'You're Odula's son, are you not?' I told him yes. He said I resembled Baba.

Baba came out of the cell, half-dressed. He looked sad, his forehead creased.

'Murtala, did you come alone?'

'Yes.'

'How are your younger ones and your mother?'

'They're fine.'

He caught sight of the polythene bag hanging from my hand.

'What's that you're carrying?'

'It's food for you.'

He took it and put it on the counter. He was on the other side of it. In a friendly tone, the sergeant told Baba, 'Odula, you know say you no go pass dis counter o.'

Baba cast a spiteful look at him. Then he looked back at me. I looked away.

'You can go home now. Thank you. Tell them that I'm all right. I'll come home as soon as they release me.'

Three policemen were dragging a tall, dark man into the office. The man's hands gripped the door frame. He grimaced, his teeth biting his lower lip, as he struggled to withstand the pressure from the policemen.

'Wetin be dat?' the sergeant yelled. 'You no wan come inside, you bloody criminal!' He rushed to the door and kicked the man in die crotch with his boot. The man collapsed, yelping.

'Bastard! Pull am comot from dere!'

I left, downcast. What kind of reprimand could keep Baba in a cell as if he were a criminal? Why would he – who had been coming to work every day with no holidays, for as long as I knew – suffer such a disgrace because he was late for work? For once, I agreed with Mama that Baba was wasting his life in the police force.

Baba returned home in the evening, when it was dark. He looked morose and sulky. His brow was knotted, his lips pursed. His sunken eyes roved restlessly.

'Welcome,' Mama greeted him coldly. She was mending her blouse with a needle and did not look up. He did not react.

'Baba, where did you go?' Emayabo cried, elated.

'Sabon Gari.'

Oyigwu, who would have gleefully shouted 'Baba *oyoyo*,' had fallen asleep.

Anyaosu said, 'Baba, I prayed for you.'

'Thank you.'

It was hot. There was a heavy odour of sweat in the room. The window was closed in order to keep mosquitoes away. Gentle music wafted to the outer room from the inner room. Imatum had bought a small radio. 'Aunt Deborah gave me money and I bought what I liked,' she told Mama when confronted.

I told Yakubu to take water in a bucket to the bathroom for Baba to bath. He did. When Baba returned from the bathroom, I served him food. Now Mama was studying her Bible. When Baba started eating, she closed the Bible and began to sing a Christian song: *My Redeemer Liveth*. She hummed it, then she sang it with some spirit, clapping.

Baba ate his food slowly, silently, his eyes darting around. I detected rage in them.

Yakubu took the plates away after Baba had eaten.

'What kind of a wife are you?' Baba began abruptly. 'I slept in a cell two nights and you can't even welcome me home, ehm.' His tone was serious.

Mama's tone was also serious. 'What kind of a husband are you that you find yourself in a cell of all places, Father-of-my-children?'

Silence, ominous silence. I looked across to Mama. Her lips were firmly locked. The music from the inner room grew louder.

Baba said in a raised voice, 'You're so wicked! And you carry the Bible…'

Mama retorted, also shouting, 'I choose to be wicked to someone who can't cure himself of the evil of beer. I have seen that alcohol is a thing of your family. Your mother…'

Baba raged. 'Leave my parents out of it! What makes you think it is right to insult my parents right under my nose? Have I ever insulted your parents?'

Mama did not apologise. 'Don't shout at me. I'm stating a fact!'

Baba sprang up and hit Mama hard across her face. Mama tumbled down from the chair, screaming. She was scrambling to her knees when another blow sent her across the floor, to the mat, startling Oyigwu from sleep.

'Baba, please, leave her alone. Please, leave her.'

I was pulling him. He pushed me aside. He kicked Mama repeatedly. She twisted on the floor, her shouts for help decreasing with every kick. I sensed that her breath would cease. I was helpless.

'Do you want to kill our mother? Do you want to kill our mother?' It was Imatum in the doorway.

'Shut up there!' Baba shouted at her, breathing heavily. He moved back from Mama.

Imatum shouted back. 'Kill her then! Kill her and kill all of us! Did she send you to drink? If you touch her again, I'll go report you to the police. They will lock you up again!' Imatum was dead serious, furious.

Baba rushed after her, but she had already dashed back to the inner room and banged the door shut. She bolted it.

Mama lay still. I knelt beside her. A thought occurred to me and I stood up and locked our door.

'Emayabo and Oyigwu, stop crying,' I told them. They stared at me with teary eyes. I heard shuffling legs outside, near the door. I heard knocking at our door. I did not answer. My siblings continued to stare at me.

I knelt down and called softly, 'Mama.'

She did not respond. Blood oozed from her nose and her left eye was swollen. I looked at Baba. He was surprisingly calm, mute. Ashamed, perhaps. I vividly remembered the day Baba had told me that only cowards beat their wives, that he would rather divorce Mama than beat her.

I boiled water and cleaned Mama's wounds, while Imatum comforted our younger ones.

Next day, Baba woke up quite remorseful. 'I'll take her to a private hospital,' he told me, as if I had asked him.

Imatum did not say good morning to him. Behind him, she made an insulting gesture by opening her left palm and splaying her fingers, muttering inaudibly, 'God punish you!'

We took Mama to Castle Clinic, close to Sabon Gari Divisional Police Station. As we paid for the registration card and sat down, I watched with fascination the quick movements of the nurses. They appeared very neat. Their faces, arms and legs glowed. I heard a baby screaming. A nurse walked briskly to where we sat, looked into the file she was carrying and called out: 'Ruth Okundayo.' A lady answered, 'Yes.'

'Follow me,' the nurse said.

The lady who followed her wore expensive clothes made of a cream lace material. I looked round at the people seated and saw that they all looked neat, rich and sophisticated. Only Mama, Baba and I looked poor.

A man of Baba's age entered the hall. His receding hairline was grey. He wore glasses which neatly framed his eyes. He was clad in a long-sleeved shirt, a tie and a pair of trousers. Almost half of the people seated rose to greet him.

'Good morning, Dr Hassan.'

'Morning, Doctor.'

'Welcome, Dr Hassan.'

'Good morning, Doctor.'

He answered 'Morning.' His voice was soft; he nodded along. A much younger man, in uniform, carried his bag and some books. They climbed the stairs to our left.

'That's the medical director,' a man told a woman sitting beside him.

Soon Mama was called. Baba followed her. For the next fifteen minutes I did not see them. I got lost in a world in which I imagined myself as a doctor, a medical director, with my own hospital. I imagined myself coming into my hospital, the patients standing to greet me. I shook hands with them and asked them about their work and their families, about SAP and the activities of the military president. I imagined myself treating Mama and Baba and my siblings. I pictured myself making money and lifting Mama and Baba out of poverty.

Mama opted strongly to return home when a bill of five thousand naira was issued to us after two hours. '*Chaakokoo!*' she shouted, berating Baba. 'Why did you bring me here? Can't you see why I say you don't know how to go for what is fit for you, Father-of-my-children?'

Some patients stared at us, surprised.

Baba was sober, indeed happy at the thought that he was compensating for battering Mama by spending such a huge amount of money. 'They did X-ray and other tests. There is also the consultation fee, the drugs. I'll pay, don't worry. Thank God my salary has been paid.'

'I must worry. Did you beat me up so that you'll spend the money that should be used to buy food for my children? Murtala, let's go home.'

Though there was no internal injury, Baba insisted that

Mama stay in the hospital for full medical attention. She dismissed this as unreasonable and we returned home.

When we returned from the hospital, we met Uncle Tony. It was quite some time since he had last visited us. He did not like coming to our house since we had moved to Kwanar Jabba, because our two small rooms were too crammed for comfort. I told him that Baba Rafatu occupied the same size double room with his two wives and fifteen children. He smiled and said it was stupid of a man as poor as Baba Rafatu to have two wives and that number of children. It was because of such people that the government, through SAP, was making noises about birth control.

'Really, the issue is not about birth control alone,' Uncle Tony said. 'Africa is a spacious continent, but many people are crammed into tiny rooms.'

Uncle Tony's eyes had grown redder and his lips darker. I noticed a bruise on his right cheek, towards his ear. The short-sleeved shirt and trousers he wore were faded, almost threadbare. His long hair was dishevelled. He looked sad. He stood up to greet Mama and Baba.

'My dear in-law, when did you come?' Baba asked.

'About half an hour ago.'

Mama was quiet, her eyes still swollen. She covered her head with a veil. Uncle Tony looked at her and then turned his face away. One of my siblings must have told him. Mama did not sit down in the outer room. My siblings followed her into the inner room.

'Welcome, Uncle Tony,' I greeted him.

'Thank you, Murtala.'

Baba first sat down and then stood up. His eyes roved round the ceiling, taking note of the cobwebs. He seemed restless, even nervous. He switched on the TV. Thereafter, his hand reached for the switch of the ceiling fan. It started with a sharp noise, rolling lazily. Baba moved to my bed and sat on it, looking at Uncle Tony. 'I can see some bruises on your face. Did you fight?'

'Another religious riot on the campus.'

'Oh yes, I heard of it. Are you seriously injured?'

Uncle Tony pulled up the left leg of his trousers, revealing a swollen ankle. He touched it, grimacing. 'I scaled a fence and landed badly.'

'Too bad. You need some drugs.' Baba dipped his hand inside the pocket of his trousers and pulled out some bank notes. He gave Uncle Tony twenty naira. 'Go get some drugs for yourself. '

'Thank you,' Uncle Tony said, taking the money.

'Don't mention it. When you've taken the drugs, you'll tell us what happened.'

I followed Uncle Tony to the drugstore. He limped, grimacing now and then. 'I heard your dad didn't sleep at home two nights and returned to beat up his wife.'

'He was locked up in the police station.'

I saw Emayabo and her friends, seated on the ground playing, their unclothed bodies dusty.

'For what crime?'

'He went to work late.'

Uncle Tony said, 'That's strange. Is there such discipline in the police today?'

'They have a new DPO who is a disciplinarian.'

Uncle Tony smiled wordlessly.

We got to the drugstore. I watched silently as he explained his condition to the man in charge. My eyes caught a large poster above a shelf. Two images of Saddam Hussein, adjacent to each other, were on it. On the left, he wore a *riga*, his head hugely turbaned, and looked pious. On the right, he was in a military uniform and looked aggressive. Splashed above the images ran the words: ALLAHU AKBAR! WE HAVE WON A JUST WAR.

The man selling the drugs suggested that Uncle Tony take injections. He refused. Instead, he collected some drugs, paid and we left.

As we entered the compound, I saw Omodiale, his arm bandaged, sitting in front of his room, reading a newspaper. Some children were playing soccer even though the sun was high and the day was hot.

'Hello Omodiale,' greeted Uncle Tony, moving towards him.

He raised his head. 'Ah brother! Thought I heard your voice a while ago. When did you come?'

'Not long ago.'

'You're limping.'

'Same story. Rioting. Fleeing. Jumping. And sustaining injuries.'

Instead of expressing concern, Omodiale was bristling with laughter, saying, 'You're the metaphor, brother. Isn't that what the world is today? Rioting. Fleeing. Sustaining injuries. Limping. Y'know, I see why the faithful yearn for the peace of paradise. When you live in a world filled with violence, the alternative is to console yourself with the belief in a world devoid of violence.'

Omodiale's bandaged arm caught Uncle Tony's attention. 'That bandage, is it a joke?'

'Ha! Didn't M-Boy tell you? Well, let's accept that some violence comes as a joke. This,' he pointed at his bandaged arm, 'came as a big joke from my dagger-wielding landlord.'

'Your landlord?'

Omodiale ignored the question, turned to me and said, 'M-Boy, kindly bring that bench for your uncle to sit.'

I looked into Uncle Tony's eyes. I thought he would turn down the offer, because he was supposed to take his drugs, but he did not. I brought the bench and he sat down, facing Omodiale.

'Get me some water for my drugs, Murtala.'

I had turned to go when Omodiale told me to fetch the water from his room instead. The tall water container was in his inner room. On the other side of it, a girl was sleeping on a huge mattress on the floor, her face to the wall. She was stark naked. I moved gently so as not to wake her, fetching the water in one of the stainless cups neatly arranged on a plastic tray.

Omodiale was narrating what had happened to him. I gave the water to Uncle Tony who had already unwrapped the drugs. He swallowed them quickly, eager to listen to Omodiale. I took the cup back. I stood, shocked, when I saw that the girl lying down was Fatima, Omodiale's next-door neighbour's daughter. She had turned her face towards the door. I hurried back out.

Omodiale had taken Uncle Tony to the climax of his story.

It did not sound like a sad story. They laughed and shouted. I sat down with them because I liked the way they spoke English. I liked their many-referenced chat. They did not talk like Baba Fatima, Baba Peter, Baba Eddy and Baba Tindele who mostly expressed anger, referring only to their present conditions and quarrelling with one another over trivial points. The depth of their reasoning fascinated me.

'Y'know, as is the tradition in the world, when someone inflicts violence on you, he brings you relief materials. I…'

Uncle Tony cut in. 'That's positive violence. There was nothing like relief incentive for those butchered by Samuel Doe in Liberia.'

'Ah, positive violence and negative violence. A nice classification there. Brother, I took advantage. Y'know, I insisted on my seven-month rent debt being written off as a relief incentive for the violence committed against me.'

'Was it done?'

'He had no option. Y'know, whatever is your demand, once it's backed up by the almighty police, it must be granted.'

'Next time he will treat his tenants with some respect, I suppose.'

'Sure.'

It was Uncle Tony's turn to tell Omodiale what had happened at the university. He was asleep in the night when a commotion awoke him. His two roommates and he were confused, at first. The commotion was on the same floor as their room. It was, in fact, only two doors away. They heard a heavy footfall in front of their room. Then a voice shouted that everybody should come out of his room. Everybody!

Every damn *kafiri*! The urgency of the voice, its fierceness and its deathly tone made frightened students fling the doors of their rooms open. The corridor was jam-packed. Uncle Tony was alarmed that the people he saw, those who had caused the commotion, were turbaned, wearing traditional Arab kaftans, their waists girdled. They spoke Hausa fluently, harshly.

Everybody was instructed to leave his room, to go down the stairs and out to the courtyard. Some people were shouting, asking what had gone wrong. The students, some in pyjamas, some in shorts, some simply with large towels round their waists, lurched down the staircase. They scurried out like cockroaches, terrified, knowing that whenever Muslim students unleashed their wrath, the consequences were overwhelming. People would be killed. People would be wounded. People would lose property. The university would be closed down.

Uncle Tony, among the last to get down, met the crowd, fluttering, murmuring in a silent rage. Inside the large circle, on the floor, lay two bodies, a man and a woman, stark naked, freshly mangled. The male lay on his back, arms straight apart. The whitish pulp of a smashed brain was part of his head above his arms, tilted as a result of a broken neck. Below the arms was a plump, handsome torso, stabbed in two places, one of his legs straight and the other bent. His severed penis lay on his hairy stomach. The woman was inches away, her head also smashed. She must have been flung furiously against a wall. She lay on her stomach, the smooth mounds of her buttocks lustrous under the bright fluorescent light. Her thighs were slightly apart. Blood oozed out of her gaping vagina, trickling along the edges of a dagger that was stuck inside it.

A chill coursed through Uncle Tony's veins. The bodies were those of Dayo, the ebullient Yoruba guy on their floor, and Jessica, his Calabar-born girlfriend. Dayo was an advanced student of economics, with just a semester left before graduation. He was known across campus by all for his vivacity, for the music that boomed in his room, for his famous brokering of peace among feuding student politicians, and for his terrific oratory. Dayo found Jessica last year and promptly broke the hearts of his four, well-manoeuvred girlfriends. Why? She took him, through her lusty lap, into what he called the nth paradise of the flesh. He also boasted that Jessica cooked the best food he had ever eaten. He once called Uncle Tony and his roommates to eat *edikaikon*, a traditional Efik soup, prepared by Jessica. She was a second-year student of mass communication. She was ravishing and intelligent. Dayo and Jessica were a pair, inseparable, enviable, almost legendary. She loved his politics. He took her around with pride. His verve and robust laughter overwhelmed his jealous erstwhile girlfriends and envious guys.

And in their delirious affair, they forgot that Kano University had a rule binding all students, that no female student should enter a male hostel and vice versa. The male and female hostels had well-furnished common rooms where a student could receive a visitor of the opposite sex.

'My guy knew this rule quite well and had been obeying it before he met Jessica with the sweetest lap,' Uncle Tony said.

'Don't blame him, brother. Y'know, if I were there I would have been *kpai* too.'

Uncle Tony cackled. 'Yon mean it?'

'Oh sure,' Omodiale said, hunching forward. 'Y'know, religious crises are killing our young ones, thinkers of tomorrow. I suppose this Dayo was a great guy.'

Sure, he was. And that was why the Yoruba community on the campus rose up in rage. Other ethnic groups and the Fellowship of Christian Students exploded against the Muslim students. Why should the Muslim students take precious lives, simply because they appreciated each other's flesh? The Muslim students waxed stronger with their holy swords, asserting their will to kill any student who defiled the holy campus with sins of the flesh. Non-Muslim and Christian students grew more furious. Would the president of the Muslim Students Society come out and swear by the Koran that he had not fucked any girl on the campus? Or that his deputy had not fucked any boy, as he was rumoured to be a homosexual? While the argument raged on, the university authorities tried helplessly to intervene and calm the situation, but within twenty-four hours, four Muslim students, two men and two women, were found dead in the same manner at the back of the huge library building. A group of non-Muslim students, most of them cult boys, owned up to the killing, formed a mob and broke into a Bob Marley song: *How Long shall they Kill our Prophets, while we Stand Aside and Look…* The president of the Muslim Students Society, in a brief but grand event, recited the Koran and declared jihad. The campus was about to burst aflame. The vice chancellor, a bearded Marxist who had been trying his best to resolve the rift without the intervention of the army because he hated the military, gave up. Brutal soldiers were sent to flush the students out of the campus. Students took to their heels. While most of them scaled the fence unscathed, Uncle Tony did not.

Baba did not go out drinking that day. Perhaps he was still contrite about having beaten Mama. Perhaps he had learnt his lesson from the punishment the police had given him. He stayed at home, restless, doing nothing. After listening to Uncle Tony's story, he spent the day watching TV, dozing.

After supper, I brought out the receipt from Ola and handed it to Baba.

He asked, 'What's it?'

'It's a payment receipt. My friend paid my school fees.'

When Baba read the contents, he bowed his head and began to shake his legs. My mind leapt. I was inwardly happy that Uncle Tony was around. He was reading an old copy of the newspaper Baba bought occasionally.

'Mu-ri-ta-la,' Baba drawled, as if drunk.

Uncle Tony looked up at Baba.

'Yes, Baba.'

'Who is your father?'

Surprised at the question, I answered, 'You.'

Uncle Tony and I exchanged a knowing glance.

'Thank God your uncle who is more educated than you is here.' Then he addressed Uncle Tony, 'My in-law, listen to what I'm saying, please.'

'I hear you,' Uncle Tony said.

'Murtala, who has been paying your school fees since primary school?'

'You, Baba.'

'Where do I get money to pay your school fees?'

'Your salary.'

'And because the salary is delayed, you can't be patient?' For the first time, I felt really angry at Baba's reasoning. I gave it back to him. 'Have I not been at home for more than a month now, patiently waiting for your salary?'

'I asked you a question, you replied with a question. If we were in the police station, I could lock you up for that.'

Uncle Tony took it as a joke and had a good laugh.

I did not reply.

'And you begged your rich friend to pay your school fees. You want…'

I was so cross that I interrupted him. 'I did not beg anybody!' My voice was loud.

Uncle Tony looked at me, somewhat embarrassed.

Baba continued in a steady voice. 'This friend of yours just paid your school fees without your asking. Is that what you want me to believe?'

'Believe it or not, that's the truth.'

'Hhm. I can see you're becoming a man. Very assertive.'

I did not say anything.

'You will return this receipt to the owner, whoever he is! Thank God my salary has been paid,' Baba said with a tone of finality.

My stomach churned. My body tensed up. My eyes

misted. I stood up and left. Outside, hidden beside the mosque, I wept.

Uncle Tony found me seated on a stone in front of our compound.

'My young man,' he said in a friendly tone. 'Let's go for a walk.'

I stood up and joined him. As we made a turn, we saw a girl alight from a big black Mercedes. The car moved off in reverse. As we drew closer, we saw that it was Imatum. She and Uncle Tony exchanged greetings. She walked away, holding a polythene bag. 'She's not changed, I suppose,' Uncle Tony said.

'You can see it for yourself, Uncle. Her boyfriends bring her home in cars.'

He chuckled, shaking his head. 'Are you still being censorious? She must hate you now.'

'We fought the other day.'

Uncle Tony stopped and threw a quizzical look at me. Then he limped on. 'You fought her? Is that what you want to be doing?'

'She caused it.'

'I did advise you to ignore her, not to waste your precious time on her. Why don't you concentrate on your books?'

'I'm sorry. I regret fighting her.'

'You want to be a medical doctor. I haven't seen any medical doctor fighting. They're groomed to be gentle and caring.'

'I won't fight again.'

We took another turn and walked towards the main Kwanar Jabba road.

'Imatum has chosen her path. We all choose our paths. The point is, be wise when choosing your own path.'

'I agree with you, Uncle.'

We walked on in silence for a while.

'I'm sure your exam results are out.'

'Yes.'

'And you've maintained your position.'

'Yes.'

'You have great promise.'

16 | *I Behold Her Standing*

I beheld her standing there. I halted, then moved towards the wall. Her features were unmistakable: the downy sideburns, the narrow face, the bandy legs and light, hairy skin. It was Helen! I inched closer to her. She stood alone by the Press Club board. When she stepped away, I followed her.

'Rashida!' a girl called. She was beckoning to the Helen I was following. 'Hurry up and see.'

Rashida trotted off. She was holding a book to her breast and her head was tilted to one side. I stood watching as she disappeared into Class 2a.

I walked into my class. It looked new, enlarged by some newcomers.

'Alt, Murtala is here!' Ola shouted.

'Murtala is back!' shouted SMG.

Some students caught the frenzy, shouting. Others merely looked at me and turned their faces away.

'We'll celebrate your return,' Ola said.

'No!'

'Oh we must.'

'Please, don't.'

During the break hour, when many students had left, Shirley, a plump girl with an amazing toothy smile, brought a crate of Fanta to class. Obianuju, slim and tall, noted for bringing biscuits, shouted, 'Here is a packet of Cabin to go with the drinks!' She raised it up above her head.

SMG bounced up to us. Ola and some students who liked me had gathered around my seat. I had not expected him to join us.

Millicent was smiling sweetly. 'I missed you,' she said, blinking, when we settled down to eating and drinking. I liked the way she blinked at me.

'I missed you too. I was asking about you always.'

'You were sucking your mother's breasts. You didn't want to let go. Small boy like you,' she joked.

She drank from her bottle with elegance.

'If an infant like you…'

I was interrupted by Desmond, the only baritone in our class. 'Hey guy, nice to have you back.'

'Thanks.'

Ola moved closer to Obianuju. He liked her and wanted her to be his girlfriend, but she did not like him.

I turned to Millicent. 'Well, my mother doesn't have breast milk for children anymore.'

'Sure?'

'Sure. Will you let me copy from your notes?'

'Why not? When you're ready, tell me.'

'Thank you.'

'In your absence, I've been quite lonely. I love it when we work together.'

'Sorry about that.'

'Sometimes, Ola and I were helpless with our maths

problems. We realised how much we gained by working in a group.'

'I'm back. We'll continue to work together.'

She looked into my eyes. Then she became shy, tilting her head to the side.

That day, I saw a new female student in our class and overheard Obianuju and Millicent talking about her.

'She's not meant for this class,' Obianuju said.

'What do you mean?' Millicent asked.

'Can't you see she is far older than we? I guess she must be over twenty.'

Millicent giggled. 'No. How can you say such a thing?'

'Well, look at her face and fingers carefully. She told Desmond that she lived as a businesswoman in Lagos before coming here. Millicent, I think she is…' Obianuju moved closer to Millicent and whispered into her ear. Millicent giggled again.

Millicent discerned her motive the very first time the tall girl walked gracefully to my seat. She bent over me, her hands on my desk and confidently introduced herself. 'Hi, I'm Linda. I'd like us to be friends. Good friends.' I was so taken by surprise that I only stared at her. Her world and mine were so far apart.

Linda noticed that her presence disconcerted Millicent, and from then on she never again approached me when Millicent was present. Instead, Linda appeared in front of my house the next evening. She had connived with Ola to find out where I lived. Indeed, Ola was utterly amused by Linda's outburst of emotion. He even teased me. 'Aren't you lucky, Murtala. You can see I'm hunting for a girlfriend; but you've got two great girls without asking.'

I replied, 'You can have Linda, please.'

He chortled. 'Linda is not the type you seek; she seeks you. You're her choice. Good luck.'

Linda did not enter our house. She stood outside and sent for me. I was relieved that she did not see my poverty. She declared her intention immediately: 'I've come to take you out.'

I consented, not because I wanted to go out with her, but because if I had refused, she would have wanted to remain with me at home.

So out we went to Alheri where, with much caution, I tried to handle the cutlery with ease, sip the drink with ease and rock my head to the soft music. Then she took me to Kano City Amusement Park where, gingerly, I followed her as she led me from one flying sensation to the other. When we left I was dizzy.

Thereafter she led me into a photo studio.

'You'll look more handsome than me, sweetie,' she said after our second pose, giggling. I thought it was immoral of her to call me sweetie.

'No, it's you who will win.'

'You're such a handsome guy, sweetie.'

I wished I could get her to stop calling me sweetie.

She lay on her left side and asked me to do the same behind her. I did. She asked me to put my thigh across her hip. Because she was taller than me, I shifted up and did exactly as she said.

What kind of fun is this, Linda? Is this what you've brought from Lagos?

I saw surprise in the photographer's eyes as he trained his camera on us.

We stood up and faced each other. She put her arms on my shoulders. 'Do the same,' she said. I tried to do as she wished, but she was so tall that I had to be on my toes to put my arms on her shoulders. 'Okay, just let your arms go round my body, short boy.'

'*Nna* abeg make una do quick. My time dey go,' the photographer complained, scowling.

Linda snapped, 'Are we not paying you? Just mind your business.'

My anus went round Linda's body just above the waist and we held each other in an embrace. She brought her lips close to mine. I dodged. 'See you, shy boy. We won't kiss. Just pose as lovers in Indian films do.'

She told the photographer to snap only when her lips touched mine.

Ah Linda, what fun is this? But your verve reminds me of Helen.

She lay on her stomach and told me to do the same, opposite her. I did. 'Move closer. Like two snakes about to kiss. Don't you see it in Indian films, sweetie?' The man clicked the camera when our faces were so close that her pointed nose touched mine.

Then she pulled the armchair into the studio. 'Now, sweetie, strike a pose on this chair like a great guy.'

What am I doing? Where is this thing leading? What if I refused and walked out?

Linda looked elated. I tried to enjoy what we were doing.

I sat on the chair. She asked me to bend to the left and then sat on my lap. 'Let your hands go round me. Do it tenderly, like a lover.' I did. She held my hands and asked the photographer to snap.

In all, we had a dozen poses. The photographer kept stealing looks at me. Linda brought out crisp bank notes and paid the photographer a deposit. 'Just know that if the pics are not fine, we won't pay the balance,' she told him before we left.

When Linda put me in a cab to take me home, I was exhausted. Not even Ola learned about this heady outing.

Three days later, Linda insisted we go out again, on a different kind of outing. She would come for me at 7 p.m. Having not recovered from the amazement of suddenly having her in my life, I did not have the courage to say no. I could not eat when I returned home on the previous occasion. Our food looked exceptionally miserable. I could not even read. In any book I opened, I saw Linda holding me, pulling me playfully, crossing me with her arms and pecking my cheeks.

I was already dressed in my undersized pair of jeans and a not-so-old shirt when she arrived, a breathtaking marvel in a miniskirt. With a surprise. She handed me a paper bag as we stood outside our house. 'They're for you. I want you to appear in them.'

I gaped at her in astonishment. Inside the bag was a new pair of black jeans and a white T-shirt.

In that instant Imatum returned from her outing and

passed by, coughing loudly so I would see her. She giggled derisively. As much as I did not want to keep Linda standing outside, I also did not want to enter the room to put on the new clothes. But although I did not want to hear Imatum's mocking giggles, I had no option. So I returned inside, pulled off my clothes and dressed in the new ones. Emayabo, Oyigwu and Ajara looked at me in bemusement. Imatum alternated her giggles with a carefully chosen gospel song: *My God is Richer than Everyone.*

The cool evening breeze welcomed us to Sabon Gari as the cab took us to busy Aba Street. While some shop and supermarket owners were closing for the day, beer parlours and nightclubs were opening.

We were among the first to arrive at Bolingo Bar, where people were sitting outside under a large canopy, catching the best of life in the evening air. Men took a second look at Linda. I tried as much as possible to turn my nervousness into pleasure, so as not to let Linda know that this was my first time in such a place.

'Sweetie, what would you like to drink?' she asked.

'Maltina.'

She looked at me obliquely. 'You're a big boy, why Maltina?'

'I don't drink alcohol.'

'Why, sweetie? You're a guy.'

'I've not taken it before.'

She smiled. 'Oh that's nothing. You'll take it now.'

'It's not good for me.'

She giggled. 'You confuse me, sweetie. How do you know it's not good for you when you've never taken it?'

Baba's image, drunk, staggering into Baba Eddy's room, crossed my mind.

I shook my head. 'No, I won't.'

Gentle music wafted from inside the bar. I noticed people watching us, listening to us.

She ordered two bottles of Star beer, a seductive smile playing between her lips and eyeballs, calling me to calmness and letting me know she was in control. I smiled at her, now relaxing. She was making a man out of me, a great thing, I supposed.

Linda felt the bottles when they were brought. 'I give unto you the star of my life, sweetie.'

I smiled, touching the neck of the bottle. I was thinking of how to pour the drink into the glass. The bottle was larger than the ones I had handled before. I let go of the bottle. Better to watch Linda do it. She tilted the glass and poured the beer into it slowly. I did the same. Then she raised the glass towards me. 'Let's make a toast. '

We toasted. She sipped. I watched her and sipped.

'Sweetie, have you thought of writing love lyrics for me? I like them.'

I certainly knew what she meant by love lyrics, but I did not know how to write them. This was not the place to tell Linda so. I nodded and said, 'I'll write lyrics for you.'

'Can't you call me darling? You did promise me,' Linda said, feigning annoyance. She looked beautiful under the fluorescent light.

'I'm sorry. I'll keep my promise.'

I relaxed my back against the seat. The new jeans felt

tight at the waist, so I undid the button. In the rather large T-shirt, I felt small.

Linda ordered two plates of chicken pepper soup. Soon, a huge thigh of chicken in a bowl of soup was placed steaming before me. I began to eat, careful about my table manners. Watching Linda secretly, I followed her lead.

'You know how wonderful you are, sweetie?'

I wondered what made me so wonderful. I was about to open my mouth to ask when somebody from behind said, in a most exhilarated tone, 'Hi Linda!'

Linda responded immediately. 'Hello, Alex. Nice to see you.'

I turned to look at the mature, plump and bearded man. A bunch of keys dangled importantly from his left hand. He went straight for Linda's cheek and the intimidating sound of a peck came from the contact. I winced.

'So how are you?' Alex asked, not minding that I was there. He probably thought I was not with her.

'I'm f-i-n-e,' Linda drawled, excited.

I felt like standing up to excuse myself.

Alex continued. 'You promised you'd come. What happened?'

'We'll talk about that later.'

'All right, all right,' Alex said, his happy tone deflating as he nodded rapidly.

He glared at me and then left. I tried to remain calm.

'So, how much do I mean to you, sweetie?' Linda asked.

'I don't know.' I kept my voice flat, bland.

'What do you mean you don't know, sweetie? That's not

a good thing to say to your lover. Do you know how much I love you?'

'I'm sorry. I am merely telling the truth.'

'Is that what you tell Millicent?'

I was amused and was about to respond when suddenly a tall man appeared beside Linda. He said 'Hel-lo' and arced over her, his right arm across her shoulders. His face would have been in contact with hers, save for a little gap.

I felt something snap in my bowel and farted.

'Hi, Bruno,' Linda said.

'You're looking so sweet, girl.' The man had a pleasant voice.

'You're sweet too, Bruno.'

Then Linda, perhaps out of guilt, stretched her right hand towards me. 'Meet my classmate, Murtala. Murtala, meet Bruno.'

Still holding Linda's hand, Bruno turned to me and said, 'Hello, Murtala.'

'Hello, Mr Bruno,' I said, stretching to shake his hand. But Bruno had turned to Linda in a hurry, as though I was an annoying distraction. My hand recoiled to my thigh.

Bruno lowered his voice and whispered into Linda's ear. I watched anxiously. This was the greatest mistake of my life. Why had I come here with Linda? As people came one by one to touch Linda or wink at her, it was clear that she knew almost all the men there.

Two more bottles of beer were served. I was alarmed. I had not even finished my first and my head was beginning to dull. Each sip seemed to make something stir in my stomach. Linda had already drained one bottle and had started the second.

'I can't take another bottle, darling.'

'Oh I understand. Always like that with beginners.'

'You're spending a lot.'

She giggled, slowly rocking her head sideways. 'Don't bother about the bill, sweetie. Bruno has offered to pay for as much as we can take.'

'Oh!'

'Now excuse me,' Linda said and stood up. She catwalked to the other side of the large canopy, her straight legs gleaming beneath the tight miniskirt. Try as I might to remove my eyes from her, I could not. People raised their heads to watch her. I saw a man whistle. She stood by another, bending to speak to him. After a while, she returned.

As soon as Linda sat down, I said, 'I'd like to ease myself, darling.'

'Go that way, sweetie.' She pointed to our left.

I stood up and seemed to sway under the gentle breeze. I realised I had grown lighter. Then I stepped away from my seat gently. Linda looked at me, amused. 'Easy, sweetie, easy,' she said, giggling.

I walked away slowly, afraid of staggering. Some adults looked at me with surprise.

I walked away successfully from the canopy towards the place Linda had pointed out. The electric lamp was extremely bright. The glitter was steaming with worms and stank of urine. I peed into it. Then I stood still as I felt my eyes becoming misty. I wiped my face and opened my eyes wide. Beside the gutter there was an alleyway that linked up with the next street. I glanced back to make sure that Linda was not watching me and saw yet another man talking to her. I walked away fast, almost trotting, then staggering. I found myself in the next street. In my pocket, I felt my ten naira note. I stopped a commercial motorcycle and hopped on it.

17 | *Imatum has been Packing Her Things*

I noticed Imatum had packed her things into the new bag she had bought.

'Mama,' Imatum called. She hunched up on the chair closest to the door, staring at the floor.

'Yes, Imatum the courageous one.'

'I want to tell you something.' Her voice was unsteady.

'Go on.'

Imatum hesitated.

'What's it?' Mama asked looking at her.

'I'm pregnant.' She sat up. Her face was on the door, her eyes darting from side to side.

'You're what?' And Mama began to cough.

I threw a cold look at Imatum. It was a hot Sunday afternoon and all my siblings were out. Only Ajara was in the front of our room, cooking.

Mama flushed and glared at Imatum. 'Imatum the courageous one.' Mama's voice was low, sad.

'Yes, Mama.'

'What did I hear you say?'

'I'm pregnant.'

A frightening silence ensued. I looked from Mama to Imatum. The lousy noise of our ceiling fan filled the room.

'Whose baby are you carrying?'

'You don't know him.'
'I want to know him.'
'I won't tell you.'
'Then why disclose the pregnancy?'

Imatum was silent. Suddenly, Mama sprang up, but it was too late. Her hand only caught Imatum's blouse from behind. Imatum was already outside the room, a piece of blouse in Mama's fist.

Mama burst into hysterics, stamping her foot on the floor and tapping her chest. 'Imatum! Imatum! So you've been going out only to bring pregnancy to me? You'll never end well. I grew up chaste, from my father's house to your father's house. I gave birth to you, as a wife faithful to her husband. If this is my path and you have chosen to take a different path, may it never end well with you! You'll live to regret it. May my ancestors take vengeance for me! If I gave birth to you through my anus, then you will live to deliver that bastard in your womb in peace. But if you came to the world through my vagina, then you shall never deliver that child in peace!'

Hearing Mama's raised voice, my siblings had rushed in, with other children following them. I politely sent them out and closed the door.

We begged Mama to be quiet. She wiped the tears from her eyes and sat down. Pulling her face in the ugliest way I had ever seen, Mama cupped her cheek in her right palm. She narrowed her eyes, staring vacantly. We left her alone.

She did not talk again until Baba returned from work. As Baba entered the room, Mama began a fresh outbreak, repeating her earlier words. He walked gently, almost noiselessly, to a seat and sat down, not disturbed by her outpouring.

In one short interval between Mama's statements, Baba asked me, 'Murtala, why has your mother lost her senses again?' Even though I sensed malice in his question, I answered. 'Imatum told us that she's pregnant.'

Baba's countenance was impassive. Then he screwed up his face in a sneer, his eyes roving round the room.

Mama continued, 'Why wouldn't she be pregnant when they all live like children without a father? Why wouldn't…'

Baba coughed and interrupted her. 'Will you stop disturbing the peace of my house?'

Mama sprang up, pointing her index finger at his forehead. 'You call yourself a man, a father? Shame on you.' Mama clapped her hands in his face, her body bobbing angrily. 'I say shame on you! Look at your daughter; she is now pregnant, because you can't take care of her. Look around and see if there is any person like you in this compound. Useless man like you…'

'Like mother like daughter,' Baba said quietly, as if speaking to himself.

Mama's outburst became harsher. 'No, it's like father like daughter. When you go to Sabon Gari to spend your time with bottles and prostitutes, do you see me there? Is it not because of the cheap pleasure of Sabon Gari that you've lost the direction to your homeland? That's what you've taught your daughter. The children are watching you. They take after you. Can't you see why you're no longer a man among men?' She raved on.

Baba absorbed it all, but he did not speak. He only looked askance, his face pained.

Imatum disappeared from home.

I asked Ajara about Imatum's whereabouts. She said she did not know. I met Fatima, her friend. She looked me up and down and said, 'I no know where she dey o.'

Like Imatum, Fatima had dropped out of primary school.

'I expect you to know because you're her friend.'

'Wetin you mean? Abeg make you no put me for trouble o.' So I left her alone.

Mama threw queries up to Jesus, demanding why she was fated to be amidst such senseless people: an alienated husband who preferred his family perishing in the city to living in the village; her first daughter, a symbol of motherhood in the family, whose reckless transformation had earned the family a disgrace; and her first son, that is me, for not standing up altogether to the challenges that faced the family. 'What could I have done? What could I do?' she would sigh. She sat alone for hours, resenting the proximity of Emayabo and Oyigwu.

After Baba had beaten her, I had spent some time sitting with Mama at home. She talked of the emptiness of life in the city. She talked about the type of people she saw in the market. Because it was only the poor that ate *alubo*, they came like stragglers, weatherbeaten and ghostlike. They bought next to nothing, but implored her to give more. 'The men are often abashed but, Murtala, in their eyes you'll see how the religious crisis has deformed their lives. The women come with tired smiles. They voice their pain. I always pity them. Why do they all have to live in the city? Why do we have to live in the city?'

Mama often took out her old photos and would stare at them for a long time. She particularly liked the one in which she was sitting on a small stool, wearing *atu*, platform shoes and a costly *odugbo* round her neck. She spent a lot of time dwelling in the past.

Even though she had not fully recovered, Mama returned to the market.

'Mama, you need more strength.'

'I can't lie down at home while hunger kills my children.'

One afternoon, after we had gone four days without lunch, Baba came home to find Oyigwu, Emayabo, Anyaosu and me drinking watery pap without sugar. I had returned from school and found my siblings lying down, very hungry and weak. When they should have been in the compound playing, they were lying helplessly on the bed and on the ground. After dropping my school bag, I went straight to the bucket of raw pap. Only a little remained. I prepared it and added water so that it could be enough for us. We drank like hungry dogs long abandoned. As Baba walked in and saw us eating, he stood still, his eyes on Oyigwu. He did not even answer our greetings. 'My children, this is how life has chosen to treat us,' he said in a low, shaky voice. I looked up at him. His eyes were teary and he looked deeply gloomy.

When he pulled off his uniform, he did not go to bed as usual. Instead, he got dressed. Then he went to the TV set, unplugged it and brought it down from the old, standing locker. He picked up a rag and dusted it.

'Baba, where are you taking it?' Emayabo asked.

'I'm going to repair it,' he answered, his attention not really on her.

'Baba, but it's working well,' Anyaosu lent her own voice.

'Nothing works well in this house, Anyaosu.'

Baba went away with the TV set, returning later without it. He gave me money to buy beans and sweet potatoes.

When Mama returned, we told her he had sold the TV. She only sighed.

18 | *Martha Jumps Up Happily*

'You promised to tell us the name of Mel Gibson's latest film,' Martha said, jumping up happily.

Mary sat on a rocking chair behind the set of sky-blue chairs, reading a book that looked unusually thick. There was a plastic cup of ice cream beside her.

'Hey Murtala!' she exclaimed, dropping the book and climbing out of the chair. She walked briskly towards me and stretched out her small hand. I shook it. She posed with her right hand on her waist, tilted her head and looked up at me. 'So, what is Mel…'

'Murtala, let's go up.'

Martha protested. 'Ola, Murtala promised to tell us the name of Mel Gibson's new film.'

'Yes, it was a promise,' Mary corroborated, her lips in a pout.

Ola looked at me sympathetically. He thought I was not prepared. I was. 'Okay, Mary and Martha. A promise is a promise. His new film is called *The Bounty*. Have you watched it?'

'That is an old one,' Mary said, disappointed.

I felt sorry for myself. I did not know any more of Mel Gibson's films.

'What's the new one?' Martha insisted.

Ola promptly came to my rescue. 'He hasn't made any films after that. I will read you a story about him in *The Guardian*.'

'Okay, thanks,' Martha said.

I was relieved. I followed Ola upstairs, into his room. The room was as big as our outer room and half of our inner room combined. It had two large windows and each window curtain was drawn to the side, making the room bright and airy. Ola's wooden bed looked new and had a big mattress. At the head of the bed, against the wall, stood a shelf filled with books. At the foot of the bed, against the wall, stood a wooden wardrobe. A door half opened to a toilet, neatly tiled in white.

'Have a seat, Murtala, and relax. My room.'

'You sleep here with your brother?' I looked at the large bed with two pillows.

'No. It's my room; I sleep alone. Why?'

'Well, I thought you and your brother slept on the same bed. '

'He has his own room.'

I sat on one of the two plastic chairs in the room. There was also a small plastic table on which lay magazines: *Newsweek, Time, The Economist, SportsWorld* and *Newswatch*. There were newspapers too, folded, lying on the rug. I dropped my school bag on the floor and picked up *Newswatch*.

Ola was undressing.

'My dad insists I read those magazines.'

'Why?'

'To know the world. Besides, they help improve my English.'

I flipped through the magazines listlessly. Then I stood up and moved to the bookshelf. Most of the books were new. Some of them I knew: *Brighter Grammar*, *Chike and the River*, *New Mathematics*, *Social Studies for Schools and Colleges* and *The Drummer Boy*. There were two folded maps lying flat on top of the shelf: *Map of Africa* and *Map of the World*. I also saw a globe, the type our social studies teacher had brought to our class one day.

Ola dressed in casual wear.

'Let's go see my dad. It's getting late.'

I had come home with Ola to thank his father for paying my school fees. In my mind I was still contemplating the words that would express my profound gratitude. I did not know that any man could decide to pay the fees of a child who was not his.

Though Mama was happy about my fees being paid, she was suspicious. 'Murtala the rational one, are you sure this friend of yours did not steal the money?' I told her that Ola had never told me a lie, none that I knew of.

We walked through the dining room into the kitchen where Aunt Becky was humming. She turned to us. 'Hey Murtala! Going so soon?'

'He has to go,' Ola said.

'Would've loved to include him in the dinner. We'll miss you, Murtala.'

'Thanks.'

She was peeling potatoes.

We walked into the large compound. To my right was

a large garage containing three cars: a Honda CRV, a big Mercedes-Benz and a small Toyota. The large compound was cemented, like ours, but there were no scratches and patches. At the other side of the wall, there was a large mango tree. I sighted Ola's father. Closer to the tree stood iron benches with backrests arranged in a circle, at the centre of which was a table. Ola's father sat on one of the benches, leaning back with his legs resting on the table. He was engrossed in a book.

As we drew near him, Ola said, 'Hello Dad.'

'Hi, Ola.'

I was shocked. Ola was addressing his father with as much friendliness as he did me.

'Hello, Murtala,' Ola's father said.

I bowed my head and said, 'Good evening, Sir.'

'Sit down, boys.' He took his legs off the table and sat up. He put the book on the bench beside him. 'Nice to see you again, Murtala. How are your parents?'

'They're fine, Sir.'

Looking at Ola, he asked, 'Have you had something to drink?'

'Yes, Dad.'

'Fine.'

'Murtala has come to thank you for the school fees.'

'You shouldn't have come for that, boy.'

I tried to make my statement, the way I had rehearsed it. 'I want to thank…'

He interrupted me, waving a hand at me. 'No, no, no, Murtala. It's nothing by the way.' Looking at Ola, he asked, 'Is he staying for dinner?'

'Nope, Dad.'

Speechless, confused, my words receded into my mind. Ola's father was behaving as if I had no reason to come all this way to thank him.

He tapped his pocket lightly, dipped his hand inside it and brought out a twenty naira note. 'Here, for your transport. And greet your parents for me. Study hard, okay?'

I nodded and took the money from him. Ola was smiling. As we walked away, I wondered about the kind of people I was getting to know. I thought of the happiness overflowing in Ola's house. Did Ola's parents ever get angry with each other? Did the children ever quarrel with one another? Did they ever feel hungry? Were they normal people?

Baba was becoming abnormal. Increasingly, he found solace alone in the inner room. I thought of what might happen to Baba without the inner room, without that bed, without the sleep. Did he actually sleep? The silence from his bed was awful. I grew afraid of entering the room to talk to him. My siblings too. If we had something to tell him, we would only talk to him either when he had just returned from work or when he was about to leave. In most cases I only spoke to him if he instructed me to wake him up.

His voice became rare in the house. He answered our greetings with mere grunts. To Mama he spoke infrequently and she did not mind him. At one point I thought a kind word from her might rescue him. One day I told Mama this. She gave me a long, angry look and said, 'If your father bewitches himself, it's he alone that can find a cure.' In a way I thought this was true, for I did not see why he withdrew so dismally into himself.

But Baba still listened to his radio. He did not miss the news. He still voiced his thoughts, murmuring along with the newscasters, contorting his face. Most often, he cursed the president of our country or a government official or the president of another country. He exclaimed the word 'SAP' so loudly that you would think he was in a passionate conversation with somebody. Occasionally he went out with one of the dog-eared books he had bought from hawkers.

One day Mama asked me, 'Murtala the rational one, I'm convinced that your father's madness depends on that word, 'SAP'. What does it mean?'

Exasperated by her attitude towards Baba and the mockery in her voice when she talked about his madness, I told her to ask him herself.

'A simple thing I want you to teach me,' Mama pressed.

'Baba is in a better position to teach you. Why don't you ask him?'

'Not in that mad state he is in.'

'Mama, no one is mad here. We're only poor,' I retorted.

'The rational one, you should know the difference between poverty and madness by now.'

I excused myself and left when it was obvious she was about to begin her usual self-righteous talk, which would only make me angrier.

A week after Imatum disappeared, Baba called me one day after returning from work.

'Where is Imatum?'

'I don't know.'

'Where did your mother send her?'

'Mama didn't send her anywhere.'

'If she didn't send her anywhere, she should've gone to look for her.'

I considered Baba's reasoning warped, yet I responded, 'Mama says she can't go after a wayward girl.'

'Is that how to be a good mother, Murtala?' Baba looked into my eyes, expecting an answer.

I wanted to bark at him: *Is this how to be a good father, sitting here and asking me now about your stupid daughter who disappeared from your house days ago?* But I said, 'I don't know. Maybe, you should ask Mama.'

'Well, Imatum is stubborn. Like mother like daughter, as they say.'

I kept mute.

That night I dreamt that Baba, drunk and drenched with sweat, fell into a well. Mama, my siblings and I sat round the well weeping. I woke up weeping.

19 | *I Start Extramural Lessons*

In the middle of March, thanks to the unending charity from Ola's father, I joined the extramural lesson preparing my class for the forthcoming Junior West African Examination Council exams. The class was held from 2.30 to 5.30 p.m. In the one hour interval between normal classes and the extramural lesson, I did not normally go home as some students did. Instead, Ola and I often idled around in the school. Sometimes, we strolled to Sabon Gari to eat something. At other times, we simply relaxed in an empty classroom, chatting and doing our assignments. This was when I busied myself with the news magazines Ola brought to school.

One day Ola brought *The Economist*. The cover had a large map of Africa. Inside it was a picture of a boy, very dark-skinned. His face was screwed up as though assaulted by the sun's rays. He wore a torn undershirt and a tattered beret. He carried a machine gun at the ready and a string of bullets strapped across his chest was flowing down his hips. Below the map, below the picture of the warrior, four words in dignified, upright red letters sought attention: *Africa: The Hopeless Continent*.

I looked at the picture for a long time and read the words over and over again, before I asked Ola, 'Would you carry a gun like this?' It occurred to me that I had asked the question the way Ukpo would have.

Ola was lying supine on two adjoined desks. He took the magazine from me and looked at it as if he were seeing it for the first time. 'No, I would not.'

'I wouldn't either.'

'Dad says most of the boys who fight in guerrilla wars are forced to do it. There are many such boys in Liberia. Mum calls them child soldiers.'

'I've seen some on TV.'

'Liberia is torn by civil war.'

'What's the cause?'

'Samuel Doe, an ordinary sergeant in the army, plotted a coup against the leader and succeeded. But Doe's regime was too violent towards people who did not support him.'

'But don't African leaders usually act violently towards people who oppose them? Remember what our English teacher said about them.'

'Oh yes, they do. Idi Amin, Mobutu Sese Seko, Jean-Bédel Bokassa and Daniel arap Moi. But Doe was not lucky like some of them. Charles Taylor and Prince Yormie Johnson promptly formed rebel groups against hint.'

'I see. But the other day, my uncle told me that the use of violence to seize power in Africa was copied from the West.' I remembered vividly how passionately Uncle Tony and Omodiale had spoken against the whites that day.

'He's right, Murtala. It was decided, I think, in Berlin, I can't remember the year now. That was when the white people shared Africa and started violent rule.'

'I see why most African nations are ruled by people who can plot coups.'

'Yes, Murtala. If you can plot a coup, you will rule even if you are a fool.'

My mind went over what Uncle Tony and Omodiale had said about our country. They lamented that we had never really chosen a leader for ourselves. All our leaders were either imposed on us or they imposed themselves on us. This was why most of our leaders were half-educated people who used crude methods to rule.

'Seen the video showing how Doe was killed?'

'No.'

'A terrible video. It shows his body being cut into pieces,' Ola said, looking out through the window.

I looked at the picture on the magazine again. I wondered how a boy, perhaps younger than me, could hold a gun at the ready with such confidence. How did he get the gun? The bullets were many. Were guns and bullets so common in Liberia that any child who wished could have them?

'Do they produce guns and bullets in Liberia?'

'Certainly not, Murtala,' Ola said, smiling. 'They obtain their arms and ammunition from Europe and America.' He took the magazine from me. 'Imagine the white people calling Africa a hopeless continent. Dad says they send arms and ammunition, instead of technology, to Africa.'

'But we buy the ammunition from them. Suppose we don't buy it. I don't agree with your point,' I said.

'You're right, Murtala. But the point is that they could refuse to sell to the few wicked men. By selling, they contribute to making the continent hopeless.'

'I don't think so, Ola. Perhaps only a few manufacture these arms and they want money,' I insisted.

'Well, we can get to know more someday.' He looked at his wristwatch. 'We have an assignment to do.'

Startled, I craned to look at her. 'I wasn't expecting you here. Didn't you go home?'

Linda, even this afternoon, looked very beautiful, as if she had just taken her bath. 'You've been running away from me, haven't you, sweetie?'

I lied. 'Why should I run away from you, Linda?'

I sat up on the adjoined desks on which I had been lying and let my legs dangle. I looked at her face. She was not annoyed, or if she was, she did not show it. She gave me the most charming smile and, touching my shoulder, said, 'Good guys like you shouldn't lie.'

I felt ashamed, disarmed. 'Well, I'm not a good guy.'

'You are.'

I had been avoiding her by clinging to either Millicent or Ola. She had chosen not to intrude when Millicent and I were together. She looked upon Ola as a rival who was using riches to keep me away from her. During our second outing, Linda had told me in the cab that I should disengage myself from Ola. She would give me more than whatever Ola was giving me. I told her I was not Ola's friend because of what he gave me, but she did not believe me. I told her that Ola had simply proved himself to be a friend. He had told his parents I was having problems paying my school fees and they had helped. In an important tone, Linda said,

'How much are the school fees anyway? If you promise to leave Ola, I'll pay your school fees from now till you finish school.'

'Where would you get the money?'

She giggled. 'Money isn't my problem.'

I looked into her eyes. 'Is it true that you were doing business in Lagos before coming here?'

Linda became upset, but quickly regained her composure. 'Who told you? Well, I was in Lagos. I made money, but I needed knowledge. I dropped out of Form One even though my father, who is a diplomat, desperately wanted me to be in school. Now I've realised I have to go back to school. Sweetie, you see why I need your help?'

'What help? You need knowledge and you're here to get it.'

'Oh yes, but with your help. The first day I started school, I went to our form master and asked him to name the best student in the class. He said it was you. I couldn't see you because you weren't in school. I need someone who can help me with my schoolwork. I was out of school for a long time. Understand me, sweetie.'

'I'll help you in any way I can.'

'But I'd like you to leave Ola; I'll do whatever you want, sweetie.'

I was piqued. 'What do you mean? I can't leave my friend. He's my friend.'

'Ok. Am sorry, but…'

'But what?'

She did not bring up the matter anymore. It occurred to me that it was better to keep Linda at arm's length.

Now Linda had caught me alone. Ola had gone to Sabon Gari.

Linda turned and faced me fully, her hands resting on my shoulders. She brought her face close to mine. She drew closer and opened her lips to kiss me, but I turned my face away, pushing her gently and coming down from the desks. I moved to the window. She came after me.

'Why did you behave like that, that day?'

'The world was too much for me.'

'You're not Wordsworth.'

For once, Linda was smart. The day before, our English teacher had taught us Wordsworth's poem, *The World is Too Much with Us*.

'I'll make you my heroine for being so smart.'

Linda's giggle filled the empty class. 'You're so funny, sweetie.'

'You knew what I meant by saying the world was too much for me, didn't you?'

'You left me in the cold, all alone.'

'But those men: Alex, Bruno and…'

'Sweetie, are you that jealous?' She giggled again.

'Jealous of whom?'

'Of me.'

Linda moved closer to me. I shifted away.

'How?'

'I wanted us to end the outing in my house.'

'Your house?'

She moved closer to me again. I moved away.

'Yes, my house was on the next street.'

'You didn't tell me.'

I looked at the time. It was twenty to three.

'Quite ungentlemanly, the way you left.'

'Sorry about that.'

I looked out of the window. It was quite sunny. The school compound was quiet.

'Sweetie, I want you to kiss the *I'm sorry* into my mouth.'

She moved closer to me. I moved away yet again, grimacing.

'Okay, wait.'

She walked hurriedly to the door and closed it, bolting it. She did the same to the four windows, the room growing darker as she closed each window. I watched her silently. I was weak.

The room was not quite dark. There were slivers of light filtering through the closed windows. We could still see each other. Linda removed her scarf. I could see her curly hair. She hummed Marvin Gaye's *Sexual Healing*. She unbuttoned her white blouse, pulled it off and put it beside the scarf. She pulled her undershirt over her head. Her small, pert breasts bounced free from the cloth. I had expected that she would continue to undress while I looked on, but in an unexpected leap, she grabbed me in an embrace. I felt the warmth of her naked breasts. My stomach growled. I felt an agitation in the lower part of my abdomen.

Linda was trying to take my lips in her mouth. I pushed her head gently and said, 'Linda, I've not eaten since morning.'

Maybe it was the way I said it. She stood divested of her energy, looking almost sisterly.

'You haven't eaten?' Her voice was soft and caring. 'I'm sorry about that.'

I watched her as she hurriedly put her clothes back on. She came and seized my hand. 'Let's go eat, sweetie.'

When Linda and I stepped out of the school gate, a man walking past caught my attention. A wave of sorrow and anxiety gripped me. I moved towards him.

Surprised, Linda asked, 'What's that? Do you…'

'Please, wait.'

The man was in rags, his Afro dishevelled and matted. He carried a filthy sack on his left shoulder. Flies perched on his body and on the sack. Now and then he stooped, picked a stone, grumbled and threw it. It was obvious that his target was invisible. He noticed I was drawing closer to him, turned to me aggressively and, with an empty hand, made a gesture of throwing a stone at me. I took a step backward. My eyes misted. My body was tense.

'Sweetie, what's the matter? What have you got to do with that madman?'

I turned and realised how far I had moved away from her, towards the madman.

'He's Helen's father,' I said sadly.

'Who's Helen?'

'Well, forget… never mind… let's get back to the class.'

'But you want to eat.'

I stood stiffly, looking at Helen's father as he walked away, throwing stones.

That day, I returned home in the evening and found Baba

Eddy, Baba Tindele, Baba Fatima and Omodiale talking passionately under the tree near Baba Fatima's door in our compound. It was a long time since I had last seen them so excited. Their enthusiasm was infectious and instead of going directly into our room, I joined them under the tree. A couple of youths were there, listening with rapt attention.

Omodiale, a small camera hanging from his neck, was making a point, gesticulating. 'Y'know, the man thinks he's doing a great thing for our country, like repositioning it to meet international challenges, y'know, but he's killing the country. Y'know, he's killing us.'

Baba Fatima said, 'But na fool he be. I tell you, dat military president na complete fool. I tell you…'

Baba Eddy interrupted. 'Na lie o! He no be fool. De real fools na dose people wey dey make plenty noise for newspaper and dey no fit take action. We dey fear soldier too much. And all dose book people for Yorubaland, I know no wetin dey worry deir heads sef.' Baba Eddy's large tummy danced up and down as he spoke. His voice was loud.

'Nonsense. Wife of head of state dey push cocaine? Ehm? Which kin' money e dey look for, ehm?' It was the thin Baba Tindele whose utterances, on almost anything, cut him out as an impatient cynic.

'You no go keep your mouth shut? Dem fit send you letter bomb now now.' Baba Eddy had his finger across his lips.

'Ah may his soul rest in peace, my brother Dele Giwa,' Omodiale said.

Baba Fatima, who was sitting on his wooden chair, said, 'Look, de problem with dat soldier be say he wan turn Nigeria to America overnight. Na CIA dey control am.'

'Baba Fatima,' Omodiale bounced towards him, 'these days you don't talk of CIA any more, you talk of the IMF and the World Bank. Y'know, the Bretton Woods evils. This duo has a clever way of dealing with you. Like mice, they bite you and blow air on the wound at the same time. Y'know they lured him into clamping SAP on us!'

Baba Eddy said, 'Sroctoral Adjusmen nonsense! No be dem suppose adjus deir lives? All of dem wey get five, ten, twenty car make dem donate de car to de country. Make dem get only one car each. Na me dem say make I no born pikin, make I dey chop small food, make I go village go farm. In short dis SAP na *yeye* ting. I no know say people wey go school get bad brain to make some ting like dat.'

'Look here, gentlemen,' Baba Tindele began, his face already in a scowl. 'My own problem na price of food wey de go high anyhow. You know how much *mudu* of rice cost now? Even ordinary *garri*? You know how much a gallon of kerosene cost? My salary no fit buy food for my family again.'

'Now make you ask yourself,' Baba Fatima said, 'how many people fit afford to buy kerosene? Imagine dose people wey dey village. Imagine as raining season dey come; your wives no go use charcoal and wood again. Look, dose people don plan to wipe poor people comot from dis earth. I swear!'

Omodiale promptly took over. 'But the fool has said there're no poor people in *Naija*. Y'know, he is suffering from the national disease called *Dikkonism*!'

'Wetin be dat?' Baba Eddy and Baba Fatima asked at the same time, really confused.

'Don't you know *Dikkonism*? Well, for security reasons, I won't explain.'

Baba Eddy, still confused, asked, 'Dat too na English word?'

The others laughed.

Baba Eddy continued. 'De oder day, he say our country people too rich. He say he dey see family wey dey get two, three cars. But he no get eyes to see say family like us dey. No single bicycle sef. '

'Oh yes,' Omodiale corroborated. 'Supposing he comes here now, he'll see that in this compound, as many as we are, nobody has a car. Y'know, no single car owner in this fateful house. Yes, as you say, Baba Eddy, the fool does not have the eyes to see us.'

'On top of dat dey wan kill us with religion riot,' Baba Eddy said.

'But wetin bring dat Bonnke here sef? Na him cause am,' Baba Fatima said.

'Na lie!' Baba Eddy blurted out belligerently. 'I no agree with you. Na so you Muslims dey talk dat nonsense. Wetin…'

An angry Baba Tindele cut in, shouting, 'Why you dey abuse Muslims like dat? Mind your language, my friend. You know say we be Muslims here.'

'And so what? I no go fit talk de true because you dey here? Wetin concern Muslims with man wey come to preach in church. *Abi* he tell you say he go enter mosque preach?'

'Baba Eddy,' Baba Fatima's voice was levelled, 'if you get sense…'

Baba Eddy flared up. 'Me I no get sense? I no get sense

because I talk de true. Na you no get sense. Na all of you no…'

'Look, Mr Man, if you insult me I go deal with you!'

I saw Omodiale bounce backwards, turn and slip into his room.

'You be fool!'

'Na you be fool!'

Baba Eddy and Baba Tindele stood glaring at each other like two angry cocks.

I left them and entered our room.

Baba was listening to the evening news, gazing intently at the wall. I greeted him. He grunted a reply.

20 | *A Hulking Man with Blazing Eyes*

It is a hulking man with large, blazing eyes, clad in a white cloak. Long fangs stick out of a wide, red mouth. Thick smoke exudes from the opening. His arms are spread and his fingernails look like swords. His legs, half exposed, pinkish in colour, are like those of an elephant. His steps shake the earth. As I retreat in terror, another ogre suddenly appears beside him, of the same height and with the same colour, the same fangs and cloak. But his bobbing head is turbaned.

The monsters are approaching, hungry for me, eager to grab me with their sword-like fingernails. I take to my heels, running as fast I can. *Grandmama, where are you? Hold me with your arms of the Wind. Let me elude this violence.* I keep running. They are after me in hot pursuit. I race into Egbe Road. I race into Onitsha Road, into Aba Road, into Benin Road, into Calabar Road. They are after me. I burst into Yarkura Market, now a desolate, haunted arena. I feel the heat of fire behind me and turn. Their tongues reach out with flames. *If only I could fly. If only the Wind would rescue me… If only Ukpo could… If only Helen…* I am across Murtala Mohammed Way, across Kantin Kwari, up to the emir's palace, descending to Gwale. Their flames are hot on my back. I hit the path to Sharada, detour to Zoo

Road, head for Hotoro and Tarauni. Still they are after me. Towards Maiduguri I am headed. I feel my feet rise, rise and rise… *Oh Wind, rescue me.* I rise, my arms outstretched. A loud, unearthly explosion brings me crashing to the ground. I see the monsters explode, turning into blood. The blood gathers, streams, expands. It is rising. My feet are in it, my knees, my thighs… The stream rises, swathing me. An invisible hand grips my arm and flings me up. I roll into the air and hang suspended above the rising stream. Then in an instant the blood dries up. I begin to see destruction. A huge cathedral is crumbling under the thick smoke of flames. A mighty mosque is burning in the centre of the city. A huge flame rages through the entire city, razing houses, barracks, estates, offices, banks, warehouses, industrial buildings, supermarkets, shops, stalls, schools, parks, vehicles, airports, bus stations and trees. All, all.

I see a multitude of people, half naked, their bodies covered with ash, trekking eastward in terrible despair. I see our military president, fully dressed in khaki, suspended in the air, reading aloud a national mourning. I see pastors, reverends, bishops, overseers; and *mallams*, imams, muezzins, sheikhs, their gleaming robes untouched, suspended in the air, in solemn prayer for the destroyed.

Suddenly, I find myself lifted to a higher terrain. I see a man, his beady eyes in a belligerent stare, his head turbaned. I see two skyscrapers crumbling, a mighty nation watching, passive. I see a man with a pained face making a thunderous speech to the nation, his fists raised in ire. I see another plummeting helplessly from a tower. I see numerous fighter jets, beastly in shape, dropping bombs and food simultaneously. I see monstrous jets, *Learsi* boldly printed on them, hugging the sky in a dance of death. I see soldiers, wild with guns on the west of a river, on hills, in deserts, giddy with the lust for death.

I see massacred bodies spread across lush, green ground and an ecstatic banner, draped across the corpses, reads *Cinhte Gnisnaelc*. A number of monsters, some wearing mufti, others khaki, are seated at a table, eating human flesh served from a cauldron. From their lips resounds a dazzling incantation: '*Ytinu Nacirfa Fo Noitazinagro*'. I see a multitude of hyenas, hungry and angry. Above them fly the flags: *Allobzeh, Adeaq-la* and *Nabilat*.

Then in a split second all the places and people roll into one. Turn into a huge ogre. And the ogre is shifting, shifting, and shifting. The ogre is becoming a rhythm. The rhythm is becoming a dance, dancing westward to the highest flame. It is too much for me and I collapse. The pain is unbearable. The first two ogres spring up again from nowhere. They merge into a hulking Owuna masquerade, roaring towards me menacingly. I want to scramble up and run, but I cannot. My limbs are dead. I scream.

I awoke to find myself on the two adjoining benches, lying on my back. I sat up abruptly, looked around, turned round and felt my forehead with my hand. Ola and Millicent were standing near me, staring at me, nonplussed. I was sweating profusely. I considered myself again, embarrassed and ashamed. Silently, I looked out through the window. The sun was behind a dark cloud. The sky was overcast, a gathering wind sweeping the ground.

'A terrible scream, Murtala. What did you see in your dream?' asked Millicent, in a tender voice, more tender than anything I had ever heard.

I smiled wanly and looked round the classroom, glad to see that they were the only ones. *Why must you invade my noonday nap, Owuna? What have I done to deserve this disgrace from you? What will Ola and Millicent think of me now? And where are you, Ukpo, Helen?*

Tears stung my eyes, but I tried to be brave. I realised there was nothing left for me other than to be brave. This was an aspect of my life I could not control, not even explain. I did not say anything, although Ola and Millicent were expecting a reply.

His hands across his chest, Ola said with a look of deep pity, 'Let's go out and stroll. We've got some minutes before our lesson.'

I was glad that they did not press me about what I had seen in the dream. How could I explain the things I had dreamt of?

Woodenly I sat throughout the lesson hours. I should have left, but did not want my friends to worry about me.

After the lesson, Ola said goodbye and left. Millicent would not let me go. Her concern was there in her teary eyes.

She spoke to me in a low voice. 'Are you all right, Murtala?'

I nodded.

'Do you want me to get something for you?'

I shook my head.

She felt my forehead with her palm. 'Do you feel any pain?'

I shook my head again.

Instead of boarding a bus, she followed me up to Airport Road. We stood under a mango tree beside the now busy road. It was getting dark. The clouds had not given up.

'I'll walk home with you, Murtala.' Her voice was soothing.

'No, thanks. I'm fine.'

'But you're not all right.'

'Believe me, I am.'

She moved closer to me, facing me. Moved by the tears glistening her eyes, I looked at her steadily. In the falling dusk, her face was a shining moon.

'I love you,' she said quietly.

Tears dropped from my eyes. The image of Helen was still too strong. *No, I can't love you, Millicent.* I backed away.

Millicent moved closer to me. She brought out her handkerchief, fragrant with powder, and dabbed my cheeks. At the same time, two lines of tears ran down her cheeks.

'You must go home now,' I told her.

'If only we lived in the same house.'

I noticed two men, sitting on a wooden bench, looking at us slyly. They were talking in low voices.

Millicent and I walked to the road, her hand in mine. We stood silently on the kerb for a short while before she got a cab. She waved me goodbye.

21 | *Who Writes these Things?*

'Who wrote these things?' Ola raised one of my exercise books for me to see.

I took it from him.

On the inside back cover there were expressions scrawled in slanting shapes. One of them was; 'Such is life'. Others were: 'Life is beyond reason', 'Life moves backward', 'Even God forgets people', 'Life is a mysterious', 'What is the meaning of life?' and 'Violence upon violence same violence'.

I recognised Baba's handwriting.

'It must be one of my sisters,' I lied.

'The thinking is bad, Murtala.'

'And the grammar is poor,' I said trivially.

I remembered the times that I had gone to bed and left my books on the table.

Mama looked around the room and asked me, 'The rational one, do you know your father is not around?'

It was late in the evening and raindrops were tapping a familiar rhythm on our roof.

'He's been coming home quite late these days.'

'Is he tired of the inner room, his paradise?'

'Mama, I think Baba has a problem.'

'What problem? Your father has always been like that. He bewitches himself.'

Mama stood up, stretched her hand and took her Bible from where the TV set used to be.

'Mama, I have a strong feeling that something is wrong with Baba.'

'Many things are wrong with your father. He's sick. As long as we continue to live in Kano, as long as he slaves for the police, he'll be sick.'

'You always say this. It's not the way to help Baba…'

Mama flared at me. 'What do you want me to do? Tell me, Murtala the rational one.' Lowering her voice abruptly, she said, 'Go ahead, tell me. You're a college boy and should have more sense than I do. Tell me exactly how to handle your father.'

I was silent, touched by the desperation in Mama's voice.

'Tell me,' her voice became shaky, 'that this and this and this are the ways I should treat your father. I'm tired of singing the village song. I even moved my children home, but what happened? Because your father was not happy with my moving home, ill luck befell me and I'm here again. What else did I not do? Where did I go wrong?' Mama was on the verge of tears.

Ajara and Anyaosu stared at us.

'I understand you, Mama. I just have a strong feeling something is wrong with Baba.'

'Ask him; he listens to you.'

After some silence, I asked, 'And what about Imatum?'

Mama bowed her head and did not answer immediately. Then she raised her head: 'Murtala the rational one, I'll let my pride sustain me as far as Imatum's case is concerned. If she returns, I'll welcome her. After all, I didn't chase her out of this place. But I'll never go after her. What kind of mother would I be? What message would I be giving my other daughters?' Mama looked at Ajara and Anyaosu. 'That you can bring evil home and I'll accept it with both hands? I think of her every day and by thinking of her, I think of life. Perhaps the thing that throws your father into the path of the police has thrown her into the path of waywardness. Murtala the rational one, who knows, maybe tomorrow you'll decide to take your own path. Do I kill myself? No. I live.'

'Mama, I won't disappoint you.'

The rain was getting heavy. I was beginning to get cold. Pulling her wrapper up, Mama covered her body with it. I pulled my bedcover from the bed and wrapped myself in it. Emayabo and Oyigwu were sleeping soundly on their mat under their own cover.

'Ajara and Anyaosu, you'd better cover yourselves,' I told them.

Anyaosu stood up and entered the inner room. Ajara told her to bring a wrapper for her.

Mama continued. 'Mhm, you'll not disappoint me, you say? Murtala, our tongues are always ahead of our acts.'

'Baba says actions speak louder than words.'

'That's when the two of them speak at the same time. In most cases, action follows tongue. But action often disgraces tongue.'

'What do you mean, Mama?'

'Your sister did promise me that she wouldn't get pregnant

outside matrimony. Murtala, the very first thing a woman feels when she knows that her daughter has an unwanted pregnancy is humiliation. It is. When my friends, my tribal people, my church people, come to me and say, "Oh we heard what happened to your daughter, it's a pity; you know children these days", they're actually reminding me that I'm a humiliated mother. Some will ask, "Are you sure that's not how her mother came to her father's house?"'

Mama told us many things that night.

I always kept the door open for him. Baba returned when we had gone to bed.

I came out of our room and sat under the tree. It was late morning Saturday. I needed some fresh air, relief from the heavy odour in our room.

Daniel, Emayabo's friend, ran out of his family's room, hotly pursued by his mother. 'Uncle Murtala! Uncle Murtala! Uncle Murtala!' he was crying, running towards me. She caught and spanked him before I could intervene.

'Stupid boy! God go punish you and your papa!' She was a tall, fat, unsmiling termagant. She stomped back into their room.

'Sorry Daniel, I couldn't help you,' I told him.

Daniel, crying louder, stamped off to the gate and leant on it. Rekiya came out of their room, her right palm wet with soup from eating. She walked straight to Daniel. 'Sorry, you hear, no cry again. No mind dat your wicked mama.' She patted his head with her left palm. Daniel stopped crying, staring at her. Two thin lines of tears ran down his cheeks. She wiped away his tears. 'Come, come to our room. Make we chop.' Daniel did not move. She held his hand and pulled him. He followed her, looking at me shyly. I smiled at him.

'M-Boy!'

I looked back and saw Omodiale's glowing face.

'Good morning.' Although I greeted him, I felt like leaving.

'Come with me to my room; we've got to chat a bit, y'know.'

He had already put his hand on my right shoulder. It was too late to decline.

'Have you heard from Tony?'

'No.'

'A great guy, Tony. I wish you were like him.'

What did he mean? I followed him into his room, fighting the urge to like and hate him at the same time.

There was cool music emanating from a huge tape player on one side of the room. The speakers were on the other side of the room, beside a big TV set. They were the only important things he had in his outer room. No chairs, no table. But the entire floor of the room was covered with a lush, blue rug that still looked new. He had painted his room blue, maybe to match the rug. He beckoned me to sit near a heap of magazines. I saw *Hints, Love* and *Newswatch*.

I sat down, glancing towards the door to the inner room. Maybe Fatima was lying in there. I wondered how Omodiale felt committing immoral acts with Fatima, whose father was his next-door neighbour. I once asked Uncle Tony about it and he told me to mind my own business.

The music suddenly possessed Omodiale. He sang along, whistled, snapped his fingers and bobbed his hips. Amused, I laughed.

He looked at me, bobbing his body even more. 'M-Boy, do you know this is the song in vogue? Y'know, it's the latest hit. It's called *My Baby Girl*.'

I stared at him.

The dance was getting intense. It seemed if it did not end we would not begin the chat. But he had not called me just to watch him dance. 'Y'know, M-Boy, you don't look like someone who respects dance. Y'know, you look so involved in books that you're dead to the world. I understand you want to be a medical doctor.' He danced as he spoke. The rhythms and flexibility of his plump body were a marvellous sight.

I watched him quietly.

He whistled and danced with relish. 'Y'know, M-Boy, music is the only free thing the poor man has to live on in this country.'

To my relief the music ended. Before he sat down, he switched on the ceiling fan. He was sweating all over.

'Now to serious matters,' he said, sitting opposite me, looking straight into my eyes.

I averted my eyes.

'Y'know I've been trying to tell you this for some time now but I didn't find the courage. As young as you are, you carry a scowl that scares even adults like me. M-Boy, why have you decided to make life so dry?'

I wanted to scream at him to shut up. What was his business with my countenance? I wanted to tell him that it was my choice to scowl instead of smile. But I did not have the guts to talk.

When he did not get a reply from me, he looked at my expression and understood. He said, 'Look M-Boy, try to be friendly. Now that Imatum is not here, we can be good friends.'

'Who is talking of Imatum?' My voice was strong and full of anger.

'Take it e-a-s-y, M-Boy. Don't spoil this chat. It's very important to you, y'know. Yeah. I suppose you love your dad?'

What was it about Baba? I said yes.

'Okay, listen to me. Burn that scowl on your face. Oh you're so sullen! Life is dangerous to people who are sullen, y'know. Yeah. It's vivacious people like me who laugh that disarm life. I soak my *garri* and eat and laugh. Over there, look,' he pointed to some large brown envelopes. 'My university degree coolly lies there: seven years after graduation, no job. I look at it and laugh, y'know. Each time the fool who calls himself our military president multiplies his SAP-reforms to make life unbearable for me, I just laugh, y'know. I laugh the laugh life doesn't want and I survive. But,' his voice came low, his right hand rising instinctively to his chin, 'M-Boy, permit me to say this: something is really, r-e-a-l-l-y wrong with your dad, y'know.' He lowered his voice even more: 'Each time I go to the graveyard to take my herb, I see him sitting under a tree like a ghost. I mean it, M-Boy.'

I grew cold, staring at him.

At 5 p.m., I followed Omodiale to the graveyard, walking behind him. My eyes were on his rhythmic steps, but my mind was crammed with thoughts. He turned back repeatedly to look at me. He tried to make me talk, but I refused.

We passed the well where I used to fetch water. We walked through the green undergrowth, most of it thick and thorny. We walked across the graveyard to the large piece of land on which many Hausa men had their irrigated farms. Large *dogonyaro* and mango trees bordered the graveyard and the land.

'Come, M-Boy, look over there.' Omodiale pointed to one of the *dogonyaro* trees.

Under the tree sat the unmistakable figure of Baba, his back to us.

'Now I leave you with the revelation. I've got to soul up myself with my herb before this rain pours cats and dogs on me, y'know.' He walked away.

I stood still, confused at first. Should I go to Baba? How would he react?

I trod slowly, my legs reluctantly obeying. My heart pounded heavily as I approached Baba. He sat on a huge stone. I could see mostly young men in groups, some sitting, some standing under the trees, smoking and holding their spliffs in their half-closed palms. Some of them looked at me strangely as I passed. They started hurrying away from the rain. The clouds had fully thickened and it had begun to drizzle.

'You shouldn't have come.'

I halted.

He turned to face me. His eyeballs were sunken.

'Let's go home,' he said as he stood up.

I walked behind him silently. The rain had begun to fall. In the rain we walked unhurriedly and reached home, thoroughly soaked.

22 | *Mama Returns, Agitated*

Mama returned from the market, agitated. She ignored Oyigwu and Emayabo who, as usual, greeted her with excitement in expectation of what she might have bought for them. She shouted my name. 'Murtala!'

'Yes, Mama.'

'Call all your younger ones into the room and lock the door!'

'What's the problem, Mama?'

'If you're indeed rational, obey my instruction!'

I obeyed.

Since I had come home with Baba, he had gone to bed in the inner room. He would not talk to me and so I could not ask him anything. Again and again, I went into the inner room to steal a look at him while pretending to do something else. He lay supine, one knee raised, the other leg flat on the bed. His left hand pillowed his head, the right raised against the wall. With his finger, he drew an imaginary figure on the wall. I was angry with myself for not being able to gather the courage to ask him the questions raging in my mind.

Anyaosu was already in the room and I found Ajara in Baba Eddy's room. I went outside the compound, to the house next to ours, to get Yakubu. I found him eating in

Denis's room. I was so angry that I smacked him on the head when we were out of the house. 'Why must you follow your friends to their houses to eat all the time?'

Yakubu murmured something and sprinted off, ahead of me. Inside the room I found my siblings standing, looking at Mama whose appearance, once again, had become that of an embattled mother hen. She turned to me, her eyes misty: 'I doubt your father is home.' There was trepidation in her voice.

My heart sank. What was it about Baba again? 'He's in the inner room.'

She showed surprise. Then lowering her voice, she said, 'Call him, Murtala the rational one.'

I went into the inner room. Standing by the wooden bed, I called, 'Baba.'

'Hhm,' he responded, turning to look at me.

'Mama is calling you.'

'For what?' His voice sounded strange.

I heard Mama, now sniffling, imploring. 'Come out, Father-of-my-children. Come out, let's talk.' She broke into a sob.

I was confused. My younger ones came, crowding near the door to the inner room, behind Mama, behind me. Emayabo began to weep along with Mama. In their weeping, the unspoken petition was for Baba to get off the bed and come out of the inner room.

He did.

We moved back into the outer room. Mama and Emayabo were wiping tears from their cheeks.

Mama was trembling and could not sit down. Baba sat

down, looking as tired as if he had been labouring all day. Oyigwu placed his small hands on Baba's thighs and looked up into his eyes. Emayabo stood away from him, staring with her teary, unblinking eyes. Yakubu hunched up on a chair, his hand cradling his cheek, lost in his own thoughts. Ajara and Anyaosu, holding each other's hand, sat on the bed.

Facing Baba, still sobbing, Mama said, 'You lost your job and you didn't let us know. Why, Father-of-my-children?'

Mama's words did not surprise me. This was something I had been fearfully waiting to hear. I had refused to think of it, even though I knew a policeman was not allowed to grow a beard. I had doubted that Mama knew, that my brother and sisters knew. The beard was an unmistakable sign of disconnection. But I was frightened. I could not tell Mama what I thought was wrong with Baba. I was sad, though, that Mama had not noticed it. I had felt bitter about Mama's backhanded dismissal each time I wanted us to discuss Baba. That said, it was clear to me that she too had her problems.

Baba sat calmly, as if nothing had happened, as if we were making a riot of emotions about nothing. He was patting Oyigwu's head the way a man would pat the head of his dog. We all waited. Anxiously. After some time Baba spoke up. His voice was amazingly flat. 'Sit down and listen to me, woman.'

Mama sat down promptly, her hands across her chest, staring at Baba.

'What do you want to know?' His voice was cool.

'Father-of-my-children, don't ask me a childish question.

We want to know why you stopped working; why you chose not to share the problem with us.'

'I've been dismissed from the police force. An armed robber under my custody disappeared. I won't explain what happened other than to tell you that my DPO was bent on seeing me removed.'

'But why didn't you tell us, why?'

'Because it would widen my wound. Now that you know, I expect you to open your big mouth wide and laugh at me. Laugh and laugh and laugh until you're tired. Your prayer has been answered.' Baba stood up and headed back to the inner room.

Mama sat still, brooding.

We watched her quietly. Oyigwu moved closer and leant on her. Ajara and Anyaosu were whispering to each other. Yakubu remained in his position, looking up, his eyes riveted on a leak in the ceiling. Emayabo with wet, expressive eyes stared at me. *I can't help, dear sister. No, I can't. Ask God – not me – why we're so doomed. Like you, I don't know where life will lead us. I don't.*

Mama looked at me, looked at my younger ones and said, after sighing, 'What else, my children? Now we must know the road that leads to our village.'

That mournful air was still heavy in our room when I returned from school the next day. Oyigwu and Emayabo were outside playing, but withdrew from their friends and followed me into the room when they saw me enter.

Mama had not returned from the market. She had gone to

pack her things, to sell her remaining goods and to relinquish her stall to another woman. She had chosen to whom to give the stall: Owagoyi, the newly married young lady from our village. Mama would also inform our church members, tribal people and her friends that our time in Kano was up.

'But has Baba spoken to you? Is it his wish that we return to the village?' Although I knew this kind of question infuriated Mama, I still asked it.

'Murtala the rational one, your father has become strange. Too strange for me to understand him. I hope that the worst does not happen. How are we going to handle it? We must return home. Do you hear me?'

'We need to know what's on his mind, Mama.'

'Does he still have a mind, Murtala, does he? When I talk to him, he stares at me like a *malu*. There's nothing else we can do than head home. If he goes with us, fine. If he doesn't, your uncles will come and get him before something else happens to him. Do you hear me?'

I nodded my consent. However, I thought of my school. Was this the end of my schooling? Could I find a good school in the village to attend? Would Mama be able to pay my school fees? Would I eventually study to become a medical doctor? I was confused. I could not say no to Mama. As Baba continued to drift away, she was the only parent we had. An uncanny fear gripped me at the thought of us living without parents.

I did not see Baba in the inner room. I asked Anyaosu, 'Where has Baba gone?'

'I don't know. He went to the market twice in the morning and bought foodstuffs. Then he went out.'

She showed me the bag of rice he had bought, the half-bag of beans, the yams, the half-bag of *garri*, the packet of Ajino Moto and the smoked fish.

Mama returned home later, exhausted. She brought home some large basins she used in the market. When she entered the inner room, she called me.

'Where's your father?'

'I haven't seen him since I returned from school.'

She noticed the foodstuffs. 'Did he buy these foodstuffs?'

'So Anyaosu said.'

'Preparing for our going home. We need the foodstuffs to survive on. We're lucky we're going when it's almost harvest time.'

Although Mama surprised us by being sad over Baba's sacking, whose obvious consequence was our leaving Kano, I could discern the undertone of joy in her voice each time she mentioned home.

Mama took her usual seat in the outer room. She was eating when we heard knocking on our door.

'Yes, come in.'

The door opened wider and a slim woman of average height walked in. She was the leader of the women's fellowship in our church. She spoke our language.

'Ah welcome, Mama Ojiri. You really are a good farmer coming at this time.' Mama stood up for her.

'My sister, we're all farmers in our part of the world. If not for our lazy men who pull us to the city, you can imagine what I would have become with my farms. Truth is that my farms would intimidate you.'

They laughed. She sat down and responded to our greetings by calling our names. 'Oyigwu, my husband,' she said, lifting him to her lap.

Mama joked, 'You can see Oyis is becoming a man. You either grab him now or lose a good husband.'

'I'll grab him,' she said, cuddling Oyigwu who was grinning broadly. She then turned to me and asked, 'Where's your father?'

'He's gone out.'

'May Almighty God show us a better way in life.'

'Amen.'

Mama Ojiri touched Oyigwu's cheeks and navel playfully. 'Will you be a good husband to me?'

Oyigwu nodded.

She untied the edge of her wrapper and removed a coin. 'Here, my good husband.'

Oyigwu seized it from her hand and closed his hand on it, holding the fist to his chest. He grinned. She let him go.

She looked at us and told Mama, 'My sister, you're blessed with children.'

'Thank you, they're my wealth.'

'May God keep them for you; may they become useful to you.'

'Amen, my sister.'

After some silence, she began in a low voice. 'I bring the message of the women's fellowship to you. We're going to miss you. We sincerely sympathise with you over what has happened to your husband. We urge you to pray; we'll pray with you. All things good will come your way.'

'Thank you, my sister,' Mama responded. 'Tell the fellowship that I'm glad they sympathise with me. I deeply appreciate your prompt response. Yes, I'll continue to pray and I need your prayers too. Thank you.'

Mama Ojiri continued. 'In view of your request and considering the short time, we have decided to do your send-off party three days from now. We hope that'll be fine by you.'

'Yes, thank you. I'm grateful for your understanding.'

After speaking to each other for a while, Mama Ojiri left.

'Mama, are we going to the village again?' It was Ajara.

'Ajara the beautiful one, I hope you understand what has happened to your father?'

'He's no more a policeman.'

'But he can work in another place,' said Yakubu.

'Yakubu the powerful one, do you have a job for your father?'

'I don't know. Instead of him sleeping always, he can go look for work in Sabon Gari.' Yakubu pursed his lips.

'Or he can become a soldier. Soldiers are better than policemen,' said Anyaosu, lying on my bed.

'But Mama,' Ajara said. 'The village is not good for us; we'll fall sick again.'

'No, you'll not fall sick,' Mama said calmly. 'This time we're prepared for the village. There's a better life in the village, as I've always told you.'

'What about Imatum, Mama?'

'Ah! Imatum the courageous one is an independent

woman now. Whenever she wants, she'll meet us at home. Don't worry about her, Anyaosu the quiet one.'

I listened to my siblings tasking Mama while I watched the time. They did not know the night was deepening. Usually by this time they would have gone to bed.

When it was midnight and Baba had not returned, Mama and I became apprehensive.

'Where could this man have gone?' Mama muttered over and over.

I remained quiet, imagining horrible things. Perhaps Baba was lying somewhere, dead! Perhaps a certain Alhaji had kidnapped Baba for ritual purposes. Did we not hear stories of men desperate to become rich who used human blood for rituals? But Baba was too old to be kidnapped and killed. I consoled myself with the thought that they only kidnapped children and women.

I stood up and went into the inner room. I felt Baba's torch under the pillow. I put it inside my shorts' pocket and sat down briefly with Mama in the outer room. Then I walked out, giving Mama the impression that I was going to pee.

Our gate was already locked. There was no electric power. If I opened it there would be noise, so I climbed over our dwarf fence and jumped down outside. The mosque opposite our gate was open. I wondered if they ever closed it.

Turning right and right again, I plunged into the eerie darkness of the cemetery. I walked fast with the help of the faint torchlight, willing myself not to look back. I remembered the story of Lot's wife in the Bible. *And she turned back and became a pillar of salt. If I turned back, what would I become? Maybe a pillar of pepper.*

I heard the chirping of crickets, some uncanny whistling and certain movements of nocturnal animals as I walked on. The wind was gentle, friendly. *O Wind, come to my aid.* The image of Grandmama flickered in my mind. I felt as if I had melted into the darkness and the world was at a standstill. I wished I could see some of the men smoking. At a certain point I stopped, raised my head and discovered that I was going the wrong way. I detoured and, convinced that I was now on the right path, walked on, my gaze on the ground, following the faint light before me. I was afraid to raise my head.

I reached the tree and saw the stone. Sadly, Baba was not sitting on it. I stood still and my stomach heaved. *Baba, where are you?*

I turned and began to walk away.

Then I heard the weird cry of a night bird splitting the silence. It was so close that I sprinted in terror. The torch fell from my hand. I stopped and picked it up. Then I walked faster, trotting, almost blindly. I hit my left foot hard on a cemented grave. It hurt so much that I limped. I tried to compose myself, to walk normally. When I was close to the first building, which was a school block, I looked back. Convinced that I saw a monster coming after me, I sprinted. I did not stop and did not look back until I reached the last turn to our gate.

It was open. Mama, Baba Fatima, Omodiale and Baba Eddy were standing in front of it. Mama was weeping and the three men looked confused.

'Where you dey come from, Murtala?' It was Baba Fatima, his hands in his trouser pockets.

'You wan give your mama heartbreak?' Baba Eddy had his arms across his chest.

I stared at them.

'M-Boy, why don't you give us an explanation?' For the first time Omodiale's voice sounded exasperated.

I walked straight past them into our room. When Mama came inside, I was already beneath my bed cover.

After addressing me twice and getting no response, Mama started muttering to herself.

A few days later Fatima, Imatum's friend, informed us through Ajara that Imatum had given birth to a baby girl. Though the baby was healthy, Imatum was not. She had suffered a vesicovaginal fistula during the birth. Her vagina was ruptured so badly that she shat and urinated without control through it. I felt sad. 'I'll go see her in the hospital,' I told Mama.

'Don't! You dare not.'

'Why, Mama?'

'When a child asks for meat out of greed, give her a huge bone. Imatum is chewing her bone. She'll chew it alone. If you are from my womb, you dare not see her!'

I pressed. 'But Imatum is ours. What if...'

'She dies?' Mama shouted. 'Your sister has sought death and if she finds it, good for her. Don't talk about this any further.'

I stared at Mama strangely. Then she took her Bible and began to read.

*   *   *

I should've exploded against the world, wrenched her sanity, displayed all I knew about the dance of death. I should've taken a belt-fed machine gun, discharged a riot of bullets, first, into the evil-fattened belly of SP Ibekwe, into the skulls of the rank and file on duty; and then burst onto the streets, shooting at any human in a commando-style mania. But my fingers, in spite of the readiness of the trigger, froze in cowardice. Utter cowardice. And I reflected later: why wasn't I brave just for once? Why didn't I, for once, rise to manhood that sought expression through lurid violence? Why was I like this – so cowardly – in a world whose philosophy was expressed in eloquent violence, whose vision envisaged the end of flesh?

I should've exploded against the world. Like Sergeant Tukura when he got the shock that his twin daughters, the only loved ones for whom he lived, had been slain by religious killers. A small but brave man, he danced to the tune of violence instantly. With the gun given to him as a member of a patrol team, he cut down the life of ASP John whose order was that Sergeant Tukura could not be released to go see the remains of his daughters; he was a son of the Federal Government, performing a crucial duty; he had to keep peace in a delirious religious riot. Wide-eyed, Sergeant Tukura was calm. But in the next minute, he rattled the idiot with bullets. Kill him! Fire him! Kill him! one of Sergeant Tukura's superiors was said to have been yelling. They crowded on him, but before they killed him, Sergeant Tukura cleanly took the lives of five able-bodied policemen.

I should've exploded against the world, or, at least, against SP Ibekwe. I did not. I could not. I only stared, head bowed, in front of SP Ibekwe's table. He was a large man with hooded eyes. He was my new Divisional Police Officer who came with the strange talent for putting the police on the right path. What he considered the right path was an extension of the sickened imagination of a self-conceited neurotic. Not entirely so, perhaps. It was said of SP Ibekwe that idealism was the seed sown in his pre-cadet life, but a violent realism replaced the seed in his post-cadet career. Therein lay the disorder: abruptly turning from a stoic idealist into an incensed realist. SP Ibekwe had just been confirmed a full superintendent of police in Kaduna and teas at a party celebrating it when he got his own terrible news: his parents and two siblings had been slaughtered in nearby Kano. No premonitions, no nightmares. He got the news at 4 a.m.: they were slain at midnight while he was quaffing whisky with friends.

And it came to pass, as the story said, that SP Ibekwe, drenched in whisky-flavoured sweat, belched, took a calm look at the world suddenly turned strange, and exploded into a vow, giving up the probity of his profession, the benevolence of his conscience, and declaring war against the religious killers and all peoples associated with them. It was but a cold war. How could he, a respected police chief, take up arms against the religious killers because they had killed his parents among thousands in a religious crisis? There were many quiet ways of striking back against the Hausas, the northerners. A man of remembrance, he connected with the civil war during which his ethnic people were massively slain in the North.

In this same north he was born, raised, educated and given books, thanks to his iconoclastic economics teacher, that drilled his mind along the path of useless idealism. Now, SP Ibekwe clearly saw a disorder in his world, a terrible disorder in the form of the violence caused by alien religions and colonial tribalism, casting a pall on the vision he had laid out for himself as a young man. He became dangerous, with an excuse, with a conscience. A DPO with such a diseased conscience, putting the police on the right path became the silenced barrel for his cold war. His noiseless bullets were lethal and came with the speed of light.

He got me.

Staring at me menacingly, belching, he asked the state I hailed from.

Plateau State.

In the North.

No Sah, it's in North Central.

North is north, nothing like central nonsense. Plateau, Ha-wu-sa. The anger was mounting.

As you like it, Sah.

You mean to say, to tell the Federal Republic of Nigeria, that in your twenty-something years of service, you don't know how to handle a common Sabon Gari thief? Tell me, where is your experience?

Well, Oga, I tried to…

You were expected to handle situations, not to try. You were to…

Sah, I beg you to pi…

Shut up!

Yessah!

I see why you're a bloody corporal after all these years in service. Inefficiency. Impropriety. You're a misfit in the police force!

Not so, Sah. You see Oga, promotion…

I say shut up your stinking mouth! How dare you talk of promotion when a common thief under your care slipped away? How dare you talk of promotion when you aided and abetted criminals!

Hei! Oga, you don finish me. I didn't aid and abet…

I give you twenty-four hours to bring that criminal or you're fired!

I closed the exercise book. I could not finish reading it.

23 | *I Cannot Sleep*

I did not sleep the second night after Baba disappeared. Mama kept a passionate vigil. Much as she tried to keep her sniffling low, it disturbed me. Besides, I heard the mice racing around, uttering sharp whimpers. I heard them under my bed, struggling, pulling and fighting. From the inner room, I heard them scampering over plates and pots. I heard their scratching sounds. I did not move. The room was dark. I felt Yakubu's breath on my arm. I pushed him away.

I thought of Baba's whereabouts – where would he be now? At the cemetery? In Sabon Gari? Out of Kano? Had he got another job in another city without telling us?

I sensed that Emayabo and Oyigwu were disturbed in their sleep as they kept turning noisily on their mats. I wanted to go and hold them in my arms, to soothe their disturbed souls.

I heard some of what Mama was saying: 'My God… my husband… my children…' I concluded that if God ever listened to her, all would be well the next day. *But God, won't you ever listen to Mama? Won't you? God, won't you just pity Mama now that she is spending the whole night crying to you? Did you not say we only needed to ask, seek and knock?*

Mama has asked, sought, knocked. Now she's crying. Please, listen to her.

It struck me that Mama was wasting her time. I would certainly not spend so much time begging God to help me. If I ever met God, if I ever convinced myself that he would actually listen to me, I would ask him just one question: why did things never go right for my family?

Mama woke all of us at dawn.

She looked like a woman just bereaved. Like the day Ukpo died. We began with devotion, singing some gospel songs: *My Redeemer Liveth, Abraham's Blessing, Jesus, We're Here*, and *In the Name of Jesus, Every Knee shall Bow*. We sang quietly, our lips heavy. Emayabo and Oyigwu were singing and dozing. I could not remember when we had last woken up so early to sing and pray. When Mama had tried to initiate us into this Christian tradition in the past, we revolted. And Baba had supported us. I knew that if Imatum were here, she would not have joined in.

Each of us was asked to pray, beginning with Oyigwu. At first Oyigwu looked confused, then he brightened up with a sudden grin. We all closed our eyes and he said, 'Oh God, oh Jeshush klaish, oh God, our Baba losh. Amen!'

All except Mama and I said 'Amen.' I opened my eyes to Oyigwu's staring eyes. He smiled at me smugly.

'Oyigwu, our father is not lost,' I said.

He challenged me. 'Where ish Baba? He losh!'

'Emayabo the wise one, it's your turn.'

Emayabo stifled a yawn. With her thin voice, she picked her words slowly. 'Almighty God, Baba has not been sleeping at home. Mama is not happy. Murtala is not happy.

Ajara is not happy. Anyaosu is not happy. Yakubu is not happy. Me too. Please God, bring our Baba back. In the name of our Lord, Jesus Christ.'

'Amen,' we all chorused.

'Yakubu the powerful one, it's your turn.'

Yakubu sprang up and posed as if he was going to say a great thing. He shouted, 'In the name of Jesus...'

I interrupted him. 'Yakubu, lower your voice.'

'Okay, I hear.' He glared at me. Then he continued. 'Our Father in Heaven, listen to me or I will cry now. Have you not been seeing Mama crying? God, where is Baba? If you bring him back, make him not to sleep again, so that he can go out to look for job and buy me a good pair of jeans. Then we will have good food and I will not eat in Denis's house again. In Jesus' name I pray.'

'Amen.'

'Yakubu, that's not a good prayer,' I said.

'Mama said I should pray and I did. That's my prayer.' He turned his face away sulkily.

'It's your turn, Anyaosu the quiet one.'

She was sitting near Ajara, holding her hand.

'Let's pray,' she began. 'Our Father who's in heaven, our father who's on earth is not well. We've not seen him. Bring him back to us so that when our foodstuffs finish we'll not die of hunger. Give him another job. He's no longer a policeman. In Jesus' name we pray.'

'Amen.'

'It's your turn, Ajara the beautiful one.'

Ajara squeezed Anyaosu's hand, shifted on her seat and beamed. Even with her unwashed face, she appeared very beautiful. She covered her hair with a scarf properly before praying. Then she began. 'Our God, we know that you know where Baba is. He's not well and has not been sleeping at home. We beg you to bring him home this morning. Baba has no job now. Give him another job. But if he doesn't get a job and we go to the village as Mama insists, then let us not fall ill again. In the name of Almighty Jesus I pray.'

'Amen.'

'Murtala, it's your turn.'

I did not want to pray. I wished I could tell Mama that we were wasting our time. However, because I was afraid of her bad temper, I prayed. Mama prayed too, although I thought having prayed all night she would not need to pray again.

After the prayers, we began our usual chores.

I did not prepare for school. Since Baba's disappearance, I had reasoned that it was unwise to return. Ajara, Anyaosu and Yakubu were preparing for school, however.

Mama and I grew more confused about Baba's whereabouts. Oyigwu's short prayer had triggered in me the thought that I had been all the while avoiding. What if our father was really lost? He might have strayed somewhere in his ghostly stridings and be unable to return. It was not uncommon to hear on the radio that someone had disappeared. Either their families were unable to find them or the other way around.

Once, before Baba had sold the TV, a little boy was shown, a sad look on his face. He was wearing a T-shirt and jeans. It was explained in Hausa that he had been found in the street roaming all alone, not knowing the directions back to his house. He could talk, but his answers to leading questions gave no clues. They asked him the name of his father and he said: 'Daddy.' That of his mother: 'Mummy'. That of his sister: 'Baby'. And that of his brother: 'Junior'. It was announced that whoever his parents were or whoever recognised him should go to claim him. Emayabo, who was also watching, burst into laughter and said, 'That boy is a fool.'

Baba, just returned from a heady outing, had asked Emayabo, 'Are you better than he? Do you know my name?' She looked at him, tilted her head to the right and said, 'Your name is Odula Osusha Ede.' She earned a coin from an impressed Baba.

Mama and I conferred on how to look for Baba. 'We should go to the police station first,' Mama suggested.

'Baba is no longer a policeman.'

'That's the right place to go when someone is lost.'

I asked, 'Is Baba lost?'

'Three days and you think…? Murtala the rational one. I'm old enough to know something is terribly wrong.'

'What are we going to say at the police station?'

'We'll tell them we've not seen him for days.'

'They'll convince us he'll return home.'

'Are you sure?'

'Or they'll promise to look for him, but will not.'

'I see what you mean, the rational one. In any case, we must go and report to them in case…'

'Baba doesn't return. I agree, Mama.'

Later in the afternoon, we silently trekked to the police station. I kept looking at the sky, seeking the sun. It struggled with dark clouds and some of its rays stubbornly penetrated them.

People, most of them in mufti, crowded around the front of the police station. They were standing in groups, talking to a policeman in low voices. I saw a woman with a swollen eye, crying and talking all at once. The policeman listening was telling her to either talk or cry. I also saw a car, the bonnet smashed, parked behind one of the dilapidated police trucks. There was, beside it, a mangled motorcycle, the front part of it bloody.

We moved into the police station.

'Ehm Madam, wetin be your problem?'

'I be Odula Ede's wife…'

'Who be Odula Ede?'

Mama did not answer. She seemed confused.

A policeman who had been listening to another man turned to Mama, interrupting. 'Ah Odula! You be his wife?'

'Yessah,' Mama curtsied.

'Sorry ehn, Madam.'

'Tank you.'

'Na him son be dis. Even from de ears you go know,' he was pointing at me.

'Yessah,' Mama replied.

I did not talk.

'So wetin happen?' The policeman abandoned the man talking to him. The other policeman withdrew, glaring at the intruder.

'Since three days, we no see am. He no sleep for house.'

The policeman did not reply immediately. He looked out through the window thoughtfully, then he turned to

Mama, interlocking his fingers as he placed his elbows on the counter. 'Madam, you no need to fear say your husband lost. No be adult him be? No be trained policeman him be? Just go home and relax. He go come.'

'But…'

'But wetin? I don tell you be dat. How you go dey waka about dey complain say you no see your husband because he comot from house? Must he sleep for home? Me I dey sleep for outside most of de time. You no know say na policeman you marry?'

Mama listened to him with bowed head. Indignation was stirring in me. Why had we brought ourselves here to face the antics of another cranky policeman? Did he not know that Baba had been dismissed?

We walked out of the police station as silently as we had walked in. The clouds had merged. We had not gone far when it began to drizzle. I saw the rain in a windy fury in front of us.

'Mama, it's raining heavily ahead of us.'

She did not reply. I walked in silence beside her.

As we walked on, we got drenched. The atmosphere darkened and oncoming cars had their full headlights on. I did not see anybody trekking in the rain apart from Mama and me. I saw her washed fists holding her wrappers tight, preventing the wind from exposing her body. Now and then the whooshing of the rain deafened me, the slanting raindrops blinded me. I kept wiping my face with my palm. I tried to keep my eyes on Mama. She walked on slowly, steadily, fighting the wind, her head bowed. She did not turn once to look at me.

When we reached home, I heaved a sigh of relief. The rain had not abated. In front of our house I saw goats, sheep and hens with their chicks against the walls of our house, drenched, their heads drooping. I stood watching the fowls and animals in their silent resignation to nature when Mama's voice tore through the rain: 'Murtala!'

I started and then stepped into the compound. She was already inside.

'Hhm, something smells in our room,' Emayabo told me, looking concerned.

'What else other than your urine? Why can't you stop wetting?'

'It's not urine. I told Mama yesterday. Our room smells.'

I opened our window and the fresh morning air came in.

Anyaosu added, 'Brother Murtala, it's the odour of a rotting mouse.'

I consciously sniffed the heavy air in the room. The odour was there, mingled with the smell of urine.

'Ajara used the rat poison,' Anyaosu said.

'Oh my God. Didn't I say nobody should use it again?'

Knocking at the door caught our attention. Baba Fatima entered our room, his lined face looking genuinely sad. Mama came out of the inner room, welcomed him and thanked him for his help the day I had gone to the cemetery to look for Baba.

'Where you go dat night, Murtala?'

I did not answer him, not being in the mood to talk.

He was standing and so Mama asked him to sit

down. He perched his buttocks on the chair nearest the door.

'So your husband never come?'

'No,' Mama answered, looking sideways.

'Oh sorry about dis, my dear.'

A silence followed Mama's response.

'You don tell your people, your church members and some people wey go fit help you look for am?'

Mama nodded with a barely audible 'Yes'.

Baba Fatima left.

On my way to the bathroom, I saw Baba Fatima sitting on his armless chair, telling Baba Peter, 'Ah you don hear? Policeman don disappear o. His family never see am since four days now. Abeg go greet de madam.'

'Na which kin' joke be dat?'

'Me I look like a joker to you? Dey no see de man o.'

I felt the urge to shut Baba Fatima up, but I could not confront him because of his age.

Omodiale bounced into our room. He had a pained expression, his right palm in his left palm. He refused to sit, stood by the door and looked out now and then. He assumed a sober pose, as though he was partly responsible for our grief. Really, despite some of his bogus mannerisms, Omodiale was the most humane of all the men in our compound. Though he could be intrusive – and irritatingly so – he had a quick and genuine manner when responding to other people's pain, be they adults or children.

He looked away shyly as he spoke to Mama. 'I'm sorry about everything, Madam. Y'know, I watched your husband and I knew that all was not well with him. I even told

M-Boy, didn't I?' He looked at me. I nodded, praying that he would finish quickly and take his histrionics out of our room.

'I'm sure a policeman can't get lost just like that. But y'know that beard of his...' He had his hand on his chin, staring at me.

In his eyes, I saw the rest of the sentence. Perhaps he expected me to say it. I could not. *How can I tell anyone that my father has been dismissed from the police? How? Now I know that some things cannot be said. Now I believe in Mama's admonition: 'Let some words rot in your mouth. They're not worth letting into the air.' But how can I keep this from Ola? How can I keep it from Millicent?*

Omodiale took another course. 'Madam, y'know I think you should consider doing an announcement on the radio and the TV.'

Mama nodded her consent. Always.

Omodiale left when it was obvious that any further comment from him would undermine the very reason for his visit.

Baba Eddy entered our room, exclaiming 'Holy Mary!' and making a hurried sign of the cross. A security man with Union Bank, he was still in his uniform. 'Mama Murtala, sorry o. But where Baba Murtala come go sef? You sure say he no leave any message, say a note or anyting to show where him dey?'

Mama shook her head.

'Ha! Dis na pity. Where we go go look for am now? How I go fit help you look for am? And dis my work wey no dey give me time.' His big stomach heaved as he asked his questions.

He pulled out a handkerchief from his pocket to cover his nose and left, his questions unanswered.

A deadpan expression was what we got from Baba Tindele. After the initial enquiry, to which Mama shook her head, Baba Tindele stood in one place, with his head bowed, rejecting the seat offered. He seemed to be feeling some pain for us. When he was sure he had reached the end of his stay, he told Mama, 'Madam, sorry ehn?' and left.

The wives and children of the men came into our room all looking sympathetic. Some curtsied to Mama before expressing their feelings. Some of the women were eager to converse with her, to get her to really unfold her woe so that they could fully empathise. Mama was simply impenetrable, only nodding yes and shaking her head no. Most of them felt uncomfortable in our room.

Of course there were others who did not come to our room at all. Like Baba Rafatu. There were the two young men living in the room immediately after Baba Tindele's. Baba Peter too. And the two Hausa men. They spoke to Mama outside in the compound. Some did not bother at all.

Some of the children had come to understand what it meant for a man to disappear. Oyigwu kept explaining to his friends that Baba was lost. At a certain point, Ajara smacked him on the head when she caught him right in the midst of his friends, regaling them with the story of Baba's disappearance. He came to me, crying, and I consoled him. Not long after that, we got a report that Yakubu had struck a boy so hard on the nose that he bled from the nostrils. The boy's offence was that he had told Denis that our room stank.

We had spent the whole day looking for the rotting mouse, but could not find it.

'It must be in the inner room,' Ajara said.

'No. The outer room,' Anyaosu countered.

'It can't be in the outer room, we've searched everywhere,' Ajara insisted.

'We've not ransacked the inner room. Let's do that,' I told them.

Glad that there was electricity, we began to do that. Mama sat in the outer room, brooding, while we all moved things in the inner room. We dismantled Baba's wooden bed, searched the bags, unused pots, police boots, cartons and other objects stashed under it. I moved under the metal bed on which Ajara and Anyaosu slept and started pulling out sundry household wares there.

'Here it is!' Yakubu shouted. He held an old, dusty police boot out towards me.

'Keep it on the floor.'

The swollen body filled the boot, with its tail hanging out, broken. The stink intensified. My siblings crowded around the boot.

'It's bigger than the previous one,' said Anyaosu.

'We have big, big mice in our room. Big meat!' It was Yakubu.

Ajara laughed. I could not help laughing too.

'Ajara, where is the rat poison?'

'In the outer room.'

'Give it to me.'

* * *

I started out of the deep sleep that had long defined my life and sprang into action. My fate lay hotly in my hands: to find the criminal or be dismissed within twenty-four hours. Sergeant Abu came to my aid, proving himself a soulmate. Together, disguised as street men, we trekked the length and breadth of Sabon Gari, asking: Did you see Odia, the handsome boy from Benin, famous for his glib tongue? We did not call him a robber; in fact, we said he was our friend and we had some urgent business for him. But alas! Sergeant Abu and I were well known in Sabon Gari. They said, Ah Oga, which time you don be Odia's friend? Abi, you dey look for am to catch? We hear say he dey for una hand.

From bar to bar, nightclub to nightclub, prostitute to prostitute, we took our search, with disguised moods, sly eyes and superlative tongues. Minutes were melting, hours were hurrying and my anxiety mounted.

In the night I saw Odia in my dreams, smiling, chuckling, singing and dancing the makosa. Once, in a dream, he even bought me beer.

You see, Oga, you be nice policeman, I go buy you drink – I know say na beer you dey drink. Sidon, stay cool and pour de ting inside your belle, nonstop. I don declare one carton for you. You dey smoke cigarette? Or na ganja? I know plenty policemen wey dey smoke ganja. Take ganja, e good for you, especially with dekind tension wey your work dey give you. E go scatter highbloodtension comot from, your way. Smoke am.

Tank you, Odia. You be nice guy.

No, no, no, na you nice pass, Oga. I know say na great kindness you do me when you say, Go meet your sister outside, even say my sister dey dash you money. I swear to God, na you nice pass.

And I drank my beer, rocking my head to the booming makosa, in the smoke-filled bar. I felt gay, so gay that I sprang up and did some makosa dance steps. To which Odia, sitting opposite me, chain-smoking, said, Ah officer, you sabi do am o.

And I emptied bottle after bottle, moving into light, approaching heaven, getting close to God, really closer and closer. And I found myself sitting opposite God, awakening the great Sage for a talk:

You see, God, if there were no beer; I mean if the world were devoid of liquor, something would have been wrong with its creation. I start by thanking you for creating beer.

Who told you I created liquor, Odula?

But who else would have created it? Satan, your archrival, the Bible says, is a destroyer. You're the only creator, God.

Human beings, in my own image, also create.

I see, God. But you've not given me that talent to create. Why?

It's there, except that you're not using it.

Well, God, that's not why I've come for a talk.

So, what brings you my way, Odula?

A great evil is going to happen to me, God.

What?

In precisely seven hours, I will be fired from the police force. I have seven dependants: a wife and six children.

The dismissal will not be an action in isolation, will it?

What do you mean, God?

I mean did anybody simply wake up and say, Look man, you're fired?

I did not answer for a long time, only belching.

Well, Mr God, you're Almighty, you're All-powerful, and all you need do is help me, not ask questions.

You're wrong, Odula. To reach the end, we must know the beginning.

You don't want to help me, God.

Truth is that I can't help you.

How can you, God, say you can't help me? I shouted in anger, waking up. I found myself on my bed, Ijaguiua's arm, unusually adventurous, across my chest.

How foolish of me not to have grabbed Odia in that dream to drag him into reality. How foolish of me to have accepted a drink from him, when it was with such kindness that his sister had turned me into an idiot.

She tried seduction first; but it occurred to her that I could have my peace even with thousands of naked, breast-pointing women around me. Her gifts were crisp banknotes, laid inside new brown envelopes, making me, already used to squeezed banknotes, feel very important. The amounts were impressive: one hundred, three hundred, six hundred, calculatingly geometrical. Officer, dis na for you to drink, she would hand the envelope to me. I knew it would not only take care of my thirst for beer but also my children's school fees, my children's hungry stomachs. I could also save to buy some clothes for my loved ones; for long, I had not given them new clothes. Odia's sister – I did not even know her name – kept coming with the envelopes. She must have cast a spell on me. For although every policeman was used to taking gifts, the frequency with which Odia's sister gave me gifts should have alerted me.

Na for your drink, officer. You know say my broda no do

anyting; na friends put am for trouble. Officer, you fit help us shey?

Okay, I go try my best. You know say our new DPO na very strict person. I go talk to de divisional crime officer wey dey handle criminal cases.

She kept disturbing me and I kept promising her. The gifts multiplied.

That fateful day, she came when I was on night duty. After giving me the usual gift, she said, Abeg make you allow my broda come meet me outside make I tell am something small.

No problem, you be nice woman.

The sergeant on duty, when I told him, glared at me and said, At your own risk. We were used to letting people out of the cell to meet their rich relations who would tip us and make sure the suspects returned to the cell.

Odia came out of the cell, beaming. Oga, God bless you, as you let me see my sister. As I dey here, I dey see say na you nice pass everybody.

Normally I should be close to him, alert to any unusual move. But as he moved out, shouts erupted in the cell. The inmates were shouting that they too wanted to come out and have some air. They were screaming about partiality. Confused, I moved towards the cell, the sergeant coming after me.

Odula, you see wetin you don cause?

I ignored him and shouted at the criminals: Oya, make una shut up!

Then something struck my mind. Abeg, Sergeant, make I go watch Odia.

I rushed out. Odia and his sister had become thin air. Ede, my father! I went round the police building, shocked, trembling. A few Hausa men were selling cigarettes, kola nuts, sweets and other items. I shouted at them to tell me where Odia and his sister had passed. Embarrassed, they stared at me. I moved round the stalls, my eyes keen on the hideouts. Outside the gate of the market, commercial motorcycles, cabs and buses were moving in two directions. I stood, totally confused.

Three hours left! My comings and goings had proved futile. I resigned myself to my fate. Let me be brave once again, as I had been when my father kicked me out of school. The end of my being a policeman would not be the end of my life. I would make another vow and seek another vision.

Look, Sergeant Abu, let's forget about this. I've done my best. I'm ready to be dismissed.

Foolish talk! Sergeant Abu spat out.

I mean it.

Don't. Until my babalawo confirms that it's the dead end for you. Let's go see him.

You mean I should take my case to a soothsayer, a diviner, a shaman?

Yes. Hope you know, it's not only Jesus who can turn water into wine. Don't underrate my babalawo.

I threw my head backward, laughing, despite my heartache. Forget it, Sergeant Abu, even God told me he couldn't help me when I spoke with him.

Where did you speak with God?

In my dream.

Sergeant Abu collapsed in a fit of laughter. Now I see your head is about knocking off. We must go to the babalawo now. Oya! Hop on the Vespa.

I did. I looked at the wristwatch I had bought in order to keep track of the fateful twenty-four hours. I pitied myself.

The babalawo, a scrawny, bearded and dirty man, riveted his beady eyes on me. He shook his head slowly. He threw the cowries on the ground again. Then he burst into an impassioned incantation in Yoruba. Ogun. Sango. Obatala.

Only one hour left!

Em Shergeant, your friend's case dey too bad. Wallai tallai. E don pafuka! But we go fit get hope. Shebi, dem say so far life dey, hope dey. Yes, ke. I go give am someting wey e go carry for body when e go go see your DPO. Shey you dey hear me. When de DPO see am, e go love am instead of hate am.

What cheap nonsense!

And so he gave me a talisman, some herbs and powder. Unbelief was written all over my face. Sergeant Abu was totally sure that my problem was over. Don't you see that sometimes I commit offences and go free! I depend on my babalawo.

Thirty minutes left!

I barged into the DCO's office and dropped on my knees. I spoke Hausa to him: Please Oga, beg the DPO for me. I have six children. If I'm dismissed, how will I feed them? Where do I go!

Look, Odula, I have spoken to the DPO many times about you. He's adamant. That's the position he takes if the culprit is from the North.

But I'm not from the North.

Are you denying that you're a northerner because you have a problem? Plateau State is in the North.

No sah, sorry sah, it's in North Central.

North Central is north, not south or west.

Sorry, sah.

Well, sorry about it, Odula. We're not happy. And we're plotting the transfer of the DPO.

So, there's nothing I can do?

I don't know, Odula. He has asked me to prepare your file. It'll move to the office of the commissioner of police today.

Then I burst into hysterical laughter. The DCO was alarmed.

Are you laughing or crying?

I staggered about, laughing. I bent down, laughing. I sprang up, laughing.

He called one of his boys. Please get Sergeant Abu for me quickly.

I kept laughing, just laughing. Sergeant Abu came. I was still laughing.

Please, take your friend home. I am afraid…

I stopped laughing suddenly. Don't be afraid. I'm perfectly sane. For a long time in my life, I haven't laughed – in fact, since I became a policeman. Now I have to laugh all the laughter bottled up in me.

That's weird, Odula.

I agree with you, sah. And let me add that I haven't seen anything in this world that isn't weird. Until I seek a new vision.

I closed the exercise book and listened to the movement of mice in our room, unable to sleep.

24 | *We Visit Our Pastor*

Mama and I visited our pastor in his office. The single room with a large window was sparsely furnished. On the wall above the seat of the pastor, a large portrait of Jesus hung, a halo over his head. I saw posters of the twelve disciples, of the Virgin Mary, of the baby in the manger and of the crucifix. A huge Bible lay on the rectangular table, open. It looked as if it had been open for ages.

The pastor was a tall, thin man. His Adam's apple raced up and down as he spoke and his eyes blinked. He spoke our language. 'Madam, you look sad. Your eyes are swollen.'

'Yes, Pastor. My husband left home a week ago and we've not seen him.'

'Jesus Christ! What do you mean, Madam?'

'We can't find our father,' Mama said.

'You mean your husband is lost?'

'Yes, Pastor.'

I watched his eyes closely. I had never before seen eyes that blinked with such frequency.

In a low voice, turning his face away from Mama, he mumbled to himself, 'A policeman lost? A policeman lost?' Then he spoke louder. 'Did anything happen before he left home? Did you quarrel? Was he handling a complicated case? Did he have any problem? I've not seen him for quite some time.'

Mama bowed her head, tilting to the left. 'He lost his job.'

'Oh I see. But that's not enough for a man to leave his house. What do you think, Madam?'

'He had been very sad over it.'

'Sure, he'd be sad. And he didn't mention anything to you about leaving home?'

'No, Pastor. We're thinking something may have happened to him.'

'It's the work of the devil, Madam. The Lord shall see you through. Take heart.'

'Thank you, Pastor.' Mama looked meek, her voice very soft. Her eyes were swollen. She did not look at all like the Mama who would pucker her brows, hurl insults at us and watch us sulk in bitterness.

'The devil!' the pastor suddenly shouted. 'Hhm the devil. We'll deal with him. I'll talk with Joe and we'll hold a three-day prayer vigil with fasting. ' He glared momentarily at me as if I were the devil. 'Send your boy here tomorrow to know the date of the vigil. You ought to attend.'

Mama nodded.

'Take heart, Madam. The Lord does not forsake his own. You've been dutifully attending church, paying your tithe and participating in women's fellowship. Your husband will return home. The devil is a liar.'

'*Chaakokoo!* How are we going to tackle this matter? It's so strange to me.' It was Adimetu, one of the market women close to Mama, speaking our language.

'That's how I see it too, my sister.'

'Our ethnic people must help you look for him.'

Mama was silent.

'It's a painful thing. How do you cope with the children? The Lord will help you.'

'Thank you.'

The next day, a group of three market women came. Two were fat and the third was young, slim and tall.

'*Ewooo!* Mama Murtala, wetin we dey hear?' the oldest of the women said, sitting opposite Mama and looking at her with much concern. She was Igbo.

'Hhm,' Mama uttered.

'Na true?' the other fat woman asked, her eyes intent on Mama.

'Yes.'

The oldest woman said, 'How we go esplain dis, Mama Murtala? Your husband na gentle man. He no look like man wey dey follow anoda woman outside. I for say na woman take him brain.'

'Hhm.'

'Mama Murtala, sorry o. Na God go help you,' the young woman said. Her lips moved with grace. Her voice was soft.

I listened to them carefully. I was always by Mama's side, trying to make sense, to trap the insinuations and measure the weight of the feelings of the people that came. Some of them answered my greeting calmly, asking Mama, 'Is he the Murtala?' and she nodded her answer.

Hadiza also came. Her body looked the same, charred,

burnt and reddened. She wept as she listened to Mama. Her conclusion was a sad one: 'Given the way people kill people anyhow in this city, we can't delude ourselves with any hope.'

Ola came to my house. 'I'm worried that you have not been in school for some days. The exams are coming.'

I did not want us to talk about my absence from school at the moment. 'I can see you've got a new uniform. Congrats.'

'Thanks. Is your mum at the market?'

'No, she's gone to see a friend. She's not been going to the market these days.'

'And your dad?'

'It's because of him that I've not been regularly in school.'

Ola was wide-eyed. 'What happened?'

'We've not seen him for a week now. We don't know his whereabouts.'

'That's serious.'

'Ola, we're all confused.'

'A week! Didn't he leave any message?'

I narrated to Ola his sacking from the police force and his strange behaviour, how I found him at the cemetery and his subsequent disappearance without a word. Ola gaped at me as he listened. I stood up and switched on the ceiling fan.

'Maybe you should announce it on the radio.'

'I'll discuss that with my mother.'

Ola was about to leave when Mama came in. She looked worn out from a long trek. Her eyes were no longer swollen but shrunken. She had lost much weight.

'Mama, this is my friend, Ola.'

'Good afternoon, Mother,' Ola greeted Mama in Hausa.

'Welcome, my son. How are you?'

'I'm fine, Mother.'

'I know of your kindness to my son. Almighty God will reward you.'

'Thank you, Mother. Murtala has been a good friend. My parents like him.'

'They must be very kind. How are they?'

'They're fine.'

'Please, greet them for me.' Mama turned to me and said, 'Maybe we should go and thank them someday, Murtala.'

'Thank you, Mother. Murtala has just told me of what happened,' Ola said.

'About his father?'

'Yes.'

'We're confused, my son. Help us pray.'

'I will.'

I walked with Ola to the main road. Before he boarded a cab, I faced him and looked imploringly into his eyes. 'Please, don't tell any of our mates about my father's disappearance.'

He understood. 'I promise.'

I decided to go to school. On my way, I went to the rock near the cemetery hoping to find Baba sitting on it. A night rain had brought cold to the early morning. I saw a few people moving around, smoking, but not Baba. I only heard the wind soughing in the leaves as I stared at the stone intently.

Like the stream near our village, you've witnessed my father's decisions. I implore you, tell me my father's whereabouts.

The odour of ganja wafted towards me. It was so strong that I covered my nose with my hand.

I left the rock, feeling sad. At a slow pace, I walked out of the bush between the cemetery and the double-lane Airport Road. A few cars were speeding to and from the airport. I crossed the road and took the street to my left. I saw a huge storey building on my right, burnt. There was a small mosque beside it, also burnt and two burnt kiosks beside the mosque. I walked down the street and saw, on my left, a small heap of debris, beaten by rain. The sun had spread out its splendid rays.

I was shocked to see Linda standing on the roadside, looking towards me. She was in her uniform. I knew this was not her route.

As I approached her, I wondered aloud, 'What are you doing here, Linda?'

'What happened to you, sweetie? I have been coming here every morning for three days, waiting to see you.'

She held my hand and pulled me towards a roadside shop. I did not resist her. I tripped and almost fell.

'O sorry, sweetie.'

Her bag was on a bench in front of the shop. She chuckled and gestured me to sit down. Instead of sitting, I told her, 'We'll be late, let's go.'

She picked up her bag and we walked on.

'Have you been ill?' Linda looked at my face each time she spoke.

'I'm well.'

'You've grown lean.'

'I'm becoming a man.'

She giggled. 'I hope you'll behave like a real man around me.'

I was amused. 'I don't understand what you mean.'

We walked on silently for some time.

'Sweetie, the JSSCE is drawing nearer. What plan do you have for me?'

'I don't understand.' I looked at her.

'That's how you answer when you're up to some mischief.'

'Well, I'm not up to some mischief.'

'But you know I can't write the exams without your help.'

'That's malpractice. I can't help you.'

'But I need your help. I know you can. Besides, I've explained things to you.' She looked at me. Our eyes met, she giggled and I grinned.

I asked, 'How can I help you when I'm also writing the exams?'

'I've talked to Mr Ejiro about it. He'll help.'

I stopped and turned to Linda. She bobbed her head to the left and to the right, opened her lips in a low laugh and wagged her tongue sensually.

'Are you referring to Mr Ejiro, our Exams Officer?'

'Who else?'

I burst into laughter and began to walk again. Mr Ejiro was the strictest teacher in our school.

Linda was walking close to me, her hip touching me.

'So what do you want me to do?'

'Two options, sweetie. Either I sit close to you to copy your work or he'll give you two answer sheets, one for me.'

I became mute.

We walked on slowly, my eyes scanning the horizon. The day was bright, the sky blue. The sun seemed to be making a grand appearance, but I knew the clouds would come later.

I felt Linda's long fingers round my arm. I did not respond. Then she tugged at my arm, but I did not say a word, nor did I look at her face. We were close to the school. She held my arm. My eyes were on the ground as I walked.

'S-w-e-e-t-ie,' she drawled, 'please tell me something.'

My anger was growing. Abruptly, she let go of my arm. I raised my eyes from the ground and saw Millicent.

I reached home late in the evening. My younger ones had just eaten their supper. Oyigwu sat on a chair, dozing. Emayabo was playing with an old toy. Yakubu was absent. Ajara too. Mama was in the inner room, looking frail, lying on the bed. As soon as I stepped into the inner room to undress, she spoke to me.

'What took you so long, the rational one?'

'I was with a friend.'

'Do you want to give me more worries?'

'I'm sorry, Mama. I didn't mean that.'

'Isn't it better for you to stop going to school so that we face the problem at hand?'

Stung, I said, 'Mama, even the Bible says the dead should bury their dead.'

'Yes, but we're not sure if your father whom you love very much has joined the dead.'

'I've heard you, Mama. Our exams begin next month. It's

called JSSCE, meaning that we'll be given a certificate for the first three years of secondary school. So please, let me take the exams and then we'll go to the village.'

I was standing by the bed, not able to pull off my uniform yet.

'The foodstuffs your father bought are running out. There'll be no food to live on.'

I implored, 'I know, Mama. God will help us. If I don't take the exams, it'll be a terrible setback for me.'

'Murtala, I understand your point.'

I hoped she did.

'Church members have given us five hundred naira. The pastor says if we're ready to go home they'll release the church bus for us.'

'Thank God.'

'On Sunday, we'll tell the pastor to thank the church on our behalf.'

'That's good, Mama.'

Relieved that Mama had not stopped me from taking the exams, I undressed and came to the outer room in my shorts.

It had begun to rain outside.

Later in the night, as I was unpacking my school bag to begin studying, I saw a small brown envelope inside my economics notebook. It was settled. I held it up and turned it over. There was no writing on it. I tore the edge carefully. I pulled out new twenty naira notes, and with them a slim white sheet of paper, almost the size of the notes. I raised the lamplight and read what was written on it. A single line: *Assistance to the family, please give to your mother.* The money totalled one hundred naira. I was sure it was Linda's design. Was this her plan to outdo Ola?

I could not read further and put away my books. Quietly, I climbed onto the bed and lay beside Yakubu.

Sleep eluded me. Where was my life heading? The fear of Mama suddenly taking a decision that would prevent me from writing the JSSCE gripped me. I knew she could suddenly make a decision any day, any minute. If only Baba had not disappeared. Where could he be now? What was he doing now? Did he have a place to lie down and sleep?

If only you were here, Ukpo. Now I need you to be by my side, to give me your knowing grin and to lend your voice to what I feel. If you were here, we would have together sought answers to the mystery of Baba's disappearance. Two heads would have made this burden lighter to bear.

My thoughts led me nowhere. I got out of bed. I took out Wild Animals and began to turn the pages. A lion stared bravely at me. Two elephants were walking away, the tips of their trunks coiled. A gorilla stood up on its legs, looking squat. The gazelle, slender and beautiful, stared at me. The hare was racing across a vast green land.

After going through the book I went to bed, determined to sleep.

The Wind must have brought me here. I look from right to left and turn around. I turn around again. It is not just the vastness of the land, but its lush greenery and smooth terrain that attract me. Where is this? No trees, no hills, no mountains. Nothing to prevent me from looking to the far horizon. Where is the sun? The air is cool, damp. It changes colour from light blue to light green to light brown. I turn instinctively. Behold it comes. A gazelle is racing towards me from the horizon, its legs rhythmically rising above the green undergrowth. I watch keenly, fascinated, entranced. Gazelle! The distance seems great. It comes. It comes. It comes. My fascination suddenly turns into fear. It is coming right towards me, perhaps to attack me.

It stops before me, quite close. I am terrified as our eyes meet. Then laughter fills the air. It's a girl's voice. My terror turns into amazement as I see the gazelle raise its forelegs, standing erect, turning into a human being, with fair skin, young and sturdy bandy legs, smooth thighs, round hips, her crotch slightly darkened by the pubic hair, her torso smooth with a protruding navel and round, pointed breasts. She is charming. Her arms open towards me. I grab her in an embrace. We hold each other tight. She is still laughing, her laughter filling the universe.

'Oh Helen! But why did…'

She interrupts me. 'I miss you.'

'I miss you too. But I saw a…'

'I see you every day, follow you wherever you go.'

Surprised, I ask, 'You see me every day?' I look into her eyes. The eyeballs glow.

'Sure.'

'But didn't I see a…'

'You're always mine. Remember that day?'

'When…'

'We…'

'Cut…'

'Each other's…'

'Palms…'

'And…'

'Sucked the blood?'

She is giggling. I am also giggling, extremely pleased that I have found her at last.

I ask, 'Where is…'

Again, she interrupts me. 'No more talk.' She holds my hand. 'Come.'

Just a few steps away, we find a beautiful raffia mat spread on the floor. She sits on it and gestures me to sit beside her. I find myself stark naked, like her. My erection is sudden, really unwanted. All I want is to be with her, to talk, to admire her body, to listen to her sing, the way we used to do in those days.

'Take the offering.'

Reluctantly, as if mesmerised, I mount her. The sensation is unprecedented. I lose my senses immediately as I slide into her. Then while she is under me, with the sensation rising, I notice something strange happening. Her body, under mine, is shrinking into a hairy skin. Fear grips me. 'Helen! Helen! Helen!' I feel my shout receding into my throat. I want to pull out of her, but I cannot. I'm stuck to a gazelle.

I woke up suddenly and sat up. My penis was erect. My crotch felt wet. I quietly pulled down my shorts and touched the tip of my penis, which was becoming limp now. The wetness felt sticky on my fingers. The room was dark. I felt Yakubu beside me. I heard the heavy breathing of sleepers from the inner room and the chaotic movements of the mice.

Ah Helen! She was full of strange ideas. 'My mama told me that she and my papa sucked each other's blood. They married against their parents' wishes.'

'What do you mean? Does blood make people marry?' I had asked her.

We were seated under a tree, near our primary school, where we usually sneaked when we wanted to be alone. We were both in primary six.

'The blood is the love,' she had said, looking happy that she was telling me what I didn't know.

'But my father and mother married without sucking each other's blood,' I had said.

'I'm talking of love, not marriage.'

'In my case, I want to marry you.'

'You must love me first.'

'Don't I love you?'

'You may love another girl and abandon me. Or your parents may prevent you. If we suck each other's blood, nothing of that nature will happen. '

'How do you know?'

'It worked for my mama.'

Helen had convinced me after a few days. She brought a new razor blade. After school, while everything seemed to stand still in the hot sun, Helen had made an incision at the centre of my palm and sucked the blood. I did the same to her.

Linda stood up from the bench and catwalked towards me

with a charming smile. I stopped walking. My thoughts ceased.

'You don't have to be coming around here to wait for me.'

'I have to, sweetie.'

I felt anger welling up in me. The Hausa traders stared at us. She stretched her hand to give me a wrapped object she was carrying. I refused to take it and began to walk away.

'Why are you rejecting what I've bought for you?'

'I don't need it. Let's go to school.'

We walked side by side, silently. The day was bright and I saw a number of chicks pecking, flapping their wings and jumping happily. I saw a large dog, unusually hairy, walking with a woman, its tail wagging.

Linda cleared her throat. 'Sweetie, I'd like to remind you of the help you've promised to give me in the…'

'I didn't promise you anything!' My voice was loud, tinged with anger.

'You're shouting at me.'

I shouted louder. 'Leave me alone! You're disturbing my life!'

She shouted back at me. 'Why are you being hostile to me?'

I stopped walking and turned to face her. 'Look Linda, I don't want to be hostile to yon. Kindly leave me alone. I can't help you in the exams. Please.'

There was raw hatred in her eyes. 'You're an ingrate! An ingrate!'

I was speechless. I started walking away. She rushed forward and blocked my way. 'I say, you're an ingrate and a shameless wretch, a beggar! Think of how much I've spent on you!'

I glared at her, not knowing what to do. I decided to walk away, but she was still blocking my way. Then I pushed her. She staggered back and then lunged at me, slapping me hard across the face. I stood still, covering my face with my hands. My school bag had fallen to the ground.

'What's the matter, young man?' a man across the road asked.

I raised my head and saw other people watching me. Linda was charging away in front of me. The man asked me again, but I could not answer. Tears kept falling on my shirt. It was not the pain of the slap that made me weep.

25 | *I Rush from the Room*

I rushed out of our room to join those crowding around Baba Peter. An early riser, because of the factory job he had recently secured, Baba Peter had almost reached his workplace when he turned and ran back home. He was panting. 'Haa! My people, dem don begin to kill again o.'

'Wetin happen?' a frightened Baba Eddy cried, his voice filling the whole compound.

'Make una listen, listen first, I say listen!' Baba Peter was desperate as he raised a hand eastward in a dramatic gesture. 'Listen to dat song!'

We all hushed up to hear the distant chants.

'Wetin I see ehn!'

'Be a man and tell us wetin you see,' Baba Fatima said impatiently.

'Dem cut woman head, chuck am for stick and raise am up like dis.' Baba Peter's arms glistened with sweat as he raised them towards the sky.

'Hey Jesus Christ!' Mama Eddy burst into tears.

Omodiale asked, 'What's her offence, Baba Peter?'

'Dem say she tear paper from Koran clean im pikin nyash.'

Omodiale chuckled.

'Why she ma go do dat?!' Baba Tindele yelled.

'Chei! Which kin' wahala be dis?'

'E fit be lie!' Baba Eddy sputtered.

'Which kin' yeye woman go do dis kin' ting?' Baba Fatima asked, deeply sad.

Baba Peter trembled as he said, 'Dey don declare jihad now. Dem wan chase every *kafiri* comot from Kano.'

'Oh our own don finish.'

Baba Tindele went straight to the mosque. I saw Zubairu hurrying into the compound, glancing at us and disappearing into his room. The loud *slap-slap* of his slippers seemed to bear the message of death.

Most people did not wait to hear the end of Baba Peter's story. He shouted at his wife and children to pack their belongings. His wife roared back at him to enter the room and pack himself, else she would smash the same mouth that brought the sad news.

Baba Fatima struck an important pose and began to make a speech. 'My dear brodas and sisters, make you na no run go anywhere. Na Muslim I be. And oder Muslims dey here. We go protect you people wey be Christians. Na one big family we be...'

Omodiale was blunt to him. 'Baba Fatima, you're talking bunkum.'

'Ehm? Wetin be dat?'

'I mean you're talking nonsense! Didn't I tell you of that cemetery?' He pointed in the direction of the cemetery. 'During the previous crisis, many non-Hausa Muslims were buried there. Y'know, don't deceive yourself that you're a...'

Baba Fatima interrupted, trying to control his temper. 'Yes, but na dose people wey no comply.'

'Comply with what? By the way, everybody in Kwanar Jabba knows you Islamised to be among the living in those hours of death. We're in another hour…'

Baba Fatima was enraged now. 'And so what? Abeg comot from here with your big grammar. You get head?'

'They also know you've not been to the mosque after the hours you played the role of a Muslim in order to avoid death.' Omodiale was chuckling.

'God punish you!'

'So allow the people to go wherever they'll find life.' He walked into his room, leaving Baba Fatima fuming.

Apart from the two of them, I was the only one still outside in the compound.

I met Mama in the outer room, very frightened. My siblings were around her, rigid with fear.

'What do we do, Murtala the rational one?' She spoke to me the way she would to Baba.

'We must get to the police station. Everybody in the compound is packing,' I told her.

I asked my siblings to help me pack.

Mama could not move. She was muttering, 'I know the hawks are still hovering on the horizon. That's why I insisted we must go to our village. Didn't I insist?'

We packed those things I knew were important and not too heavy.

When we were ready, I told her. She looked into my eyes in a way she had never done before. 'Murtala the rational one, I prefer to die here. But I'll follow you, because you're my children and I can't let you go alone.'

'Mama, we must leave now. Everybody's gone.'

I did not let Mama carry any load except Oyigwu on her back. Our compound was filled with neighbouring Hausa Muslims who had come to sympathise with us.

'Come into my house; I'll not let them in,' an old woman told us, her voice full of feeling.

'Thank you, but we'll go,' Mama answered.

'Where do you go in this rain? And you are looking sick.'

'Hhm. Thank you.' Mama did not say anything more, though the old woman persisted.

In front of our gate stood many Hausa Muslims, looking at us with sad eyes and promising they would keep our compound safe if the fight finally erupted in Kwanar Jabba.

The sun was trapped behind the clouds.

We took the first turn, the second turn and flowed into a multitude of people on the main road, all carrying heavy luggage, jostling one another. Some children trotted behind their parents. Some parents held their children tightly by the wrist, pulling them, forcing them to keep pace with their long strides. When a girl tripped and fell, her angry mother yanked her up violently. The girl burst into tears. I felt like berating the mother. I was happy when another woman, looking at the angry mother sideways, said, 'How could you be that wicked to your daughter? Isn't it enough that the killers are after her innocent life?' The angry mother did not respond.

The chants were still distant and we could now see curls of thick smoke from afar. I made sure all my siblings were in front of me. Yakubu gallantly carried two bags and tramped ahead like an adult. Now and then Anyaosu and Emayabo disappeared out of sight. I kept calling their names and asking them to keep in front of me. I also kept an eye on Mama who was walking with great effort.

At the police station, we spread our mat and blanket on the very spot we had occupied during the previous crisis. The sun had freed itself from the clouds and risen high, its rays becoming hot. The sky was getting bright.

I searched for food immediately and did not have to go far. A number of food sellers had created a market beside the Hausa man who had a kiosk across the street. I did not ask Mama for money. Instead, I bought food with the money I had found inside my school bag.

Mama did not eat. She had remained mute ever since we arrived. With dismay, I saw that she was giving in to utter despair. Tears would not stop flowing from her swollen eyes.

People tramped to the police station, not with wounds, as it was during the first crisis, but with infinite fears.

I saw Adejo standing near the gate, a bag strapped to his back. He had grown taller and thinner. Not in a mood to chat, I turned my eyes away. We used to visit each other when he was my class monitor in primary school.

I overheard two women talking: 'Na my *oga* make me come back. I for dey for our hometown now. He say him no fit leave his work.'

'Na de same ting my *oga* talk. He get business for Yarkura Market.'

'But dis kin' problem, when e go end sef?'

'Hhm, my sister. Some people na human beings; oder

people na animals. Any day wey human beings like den go begin kill animals.'

'*To*. And God dey dere dey look us.'

There was no wailing. There was no crying for lost fathers or mothers or children. There were no insults hurled at God. But we heard the faraway shooting of guns. The police convinced us that more soldiers had been deployed to the place where the killers were causing havoc. They assured us the killings would not reach us. They advised everybody to not return home, however. Although we felt safe in the barracks, nature was unkind to us in the night. The evening weather had not forewarned us at all. The shout of 'Rain! Rain! Rain!' caused a rumpus at midnight. Those who had fallen asleep woke up abruptly, thinking the killers had descended on us. We scrambled to our feet, shouting. There was total darkness: no electricity. I tried to raise my voice above other voices: 'Oyigwu and Emayabo come to me. Come to me! Mama where are you? Ajara! Anyaosu! Yakubu!'

I stood still, moving my hands around to get hold of them. I almost started crying when I realised I did not have a torch. Through the numerous torchlights shining, I saw Mama on the floor, sitting on the mat, Oyigwu and Emayabo in a tight embrace. Anyaosu and Ajara were standing close to me to my left. 'Yakubu! ' I yelled.

'See me here.'

'Come closer.'

When I felt his hand in mine, I gripped it firmly.

The raindrops came rapidly. People scampered around

helplessly. Lights from several torches dappled the rainy atmosphere.

The inhabitants of the three-block barracks, moved by people's touching cries for help, opened their doors to strangers. All the apartments were soon jam-packed. I held Yakubu's left hand and Anyaosu's right hand, and told Ajara and Anyaosu to hold each other's hands. We moved blindly, stumbling, to the veranda of one of the blocks. 'Sit here. Don't move anywhere, do you hear me? Ajara, hold their hands.'

I returned to find Mama in the very same posture, Oyigwu and Emayabo clinging to her. She held them tight. They were drenched.

'Mama!' I shouted.

She did not reply.

'Mama, you must get out of the rain. The children will catch cold.'

She did not say a word.

'Mama, p-l-e-a-s-e.' I was almost in tears.

I gripped her right arm and pulled. She yielded. I disengaged Oyigwu from her. He whimpered. 'Climb on my back.' I stooped and he mounted my back. Then I disengaged Emayabo from Mama's left arm.

'Mama, don't stand up. Wait for me.' I was afraid she might stray away.

Oyigwu held me tight as I carried Emayabo against my chest. I walked carefully to the veranda where Ajara and the others were. Glad that Ajara, Anyaosu and Yakubu had remained in one place, I gave Emayabo to them.

I returned and found Mama standing on the mat. 'Let me fold the mat,' I said.

As she stepped off, I folded it.

'Let's go.' I led her by the hand and she followed quietly behind me. Then I slipped. She gripped my hand and prevented me from falling.

We huddled into a tiny space on the veranda. The rain intensified. People rushed onto the veranda. We pushed one another, breathing into one another's faces. The space became tighter and tighter and children began to cry. I saw Mama, carrying Oyigwu, struggling to move out of the crowd. She squirmed and pushed her way out into the rain. She stood in the rain, wiping her and Oyigwu's face over and over. The wind blew the rain in gusts our way and soaked our bodies.

It was a sleepless, busy night. After the rain, which lasted more than half an hour, many people unpacked their luggage and emptied it of water. People dried their clothes on the short barbed wire on one side of the barracks.

Next day, the sunrise brought relief.

Mama wrapped Oyigwu in our threadbare family towel. Emayabo was braving it. Ajara shivered visibly, cursing everything that had caused the cold. Anyaosu squatted on the floor and covered herself with her damp wrapper. Yakubu, in a damp jacket, was wandering around.

We heard a loud scream and turned in that direction. It was the voice of a helpless mother. Yakubu rushed to us and reported, 'One baby is dying. He is shaking like this,' and he demonstrated by shaking his body convulsively. I saw Mama's lips move in prayer.

There were many Hausa traders hawking coffee, tea and bread. I called one of them to serve us, to which Ajara protested, 'How can we buy from the same Hausa people causing our suffering? Don't buy from him, Murtala.'

Yet she insisted on having the first cup when it was prepared. Everybody had a cup of tea, a luxury we were not used to. Yakubu finished his in no time, sweating. He was already after Oyigwu's, like a cock after a hen, wheedling his way. 'Let me blow on it to make it cool for you, you hear?'

Oyigwu shook his head, turning his back to Yakubu.

'I'll get you a toy gun if you allow me to take a sip.'

Oyigwu kept shaking his head, growing impatient. Emayabo was taking her time. I brought out one of the plates we had carried from home and, imagining the tea hawker would not have the patience to wait, poured the tea into it.

Oyigwu exploded into tears.

I intervened. 'Yakubu, leave Oyigwu alone.'

Mama did not say anything. She refused to drink the tea.

When I brought out wet money from my pocket to pay the tea hawker, Mama spoke: 'The rational one, how did you get the money?' Her voice was soft, but firm.

'Ola gave it to me,' I lied.

She sighed.

As soon as the hawker left, Mama asked, 'Couldn't you have bought two or three cups and shared them? You could have saved some money. You went for tea when you know that pap is much cheaper.'

Ajara threw a scornful look at her. I did not answer Mama.

At 10 a.m. we were yet undecided about returning home. Other people had begun to leave for their homes, though.

I saw Baba Eddy and drew closer to him. 'Shouldn't we return home now?'

'You no know say when Muslims declare jihad na terrible ting? No mind dose people wey dey go deir house. Na *iyanga* dem dey do. We don see how people wey do *iyanga* for death don die just like dat. No carry your mama and im pikin go anywhere o.'

Baba Eddy continued, telling me that a group of hard-hearted Christians, emboldened by the visit of one great Igbo warrior, had sworn they would confront the jihadists in what threatened to be total war. The group had called on all Christians to form an army. A plane had just arrived in Kano with sophisticated weapons for this army.

'I swear to God I go join de army if dem come.' Baba Eddy touched his tongue with his index finger and shot the finger skyward. His expression was belligerent.

'You'll kill people?' I asked, aghast.

'Wetin you dey talk, Murtala? Anyway, you be small boy. You tink say e no dey pain me as dem dey kill Christians? Wetin we do dem?'

'E better make you keep dat your big mouth shut o!' It was his wife who was breastfeeding her new baby.

'Comot from here! Wetin you know? Dis one na people's army against de devil. I go fight am.' His muscles flexed and his big stomach heaved up and down as he spoke.

To my left, I saw a group of children playing, amongst whom I spotted Peter. He was talking to them, his hand on his waist. Farther away, another group of children was playing soccer.

The sun had risen gloriously. We did not hear the sounds of guns anymore.

My eyes caught a large, dark Mercedes-Benz car coming towards the gate of the barracks. It stopped on the side of the road, near the Hausa man's kiosk. A mobile policeman opened the front passenger door and alighted briskly. He opened the back door and a short, fat, dark man came out.

Baba Eddy, noticing the car, stopped talking in mid-sentence. After a moment he told his wife, 'Dat na Mercedes-Benz V-boot.'

She hissed loudly.

The policeman was on the other side of the car, opening the door. A woman's leg, shod in a beautiful shoe, came out first. The second leg followed. Then the woman emerged from the car, carrying a baby. She stood erect with the baby to one side. I could not believe my eyes.

'Your sister! Na Imatum! Na your sister! Jesus of Nazareth!' Baba Eddy shouted, holding and pulling me in a frenzied excitement.

I stood speechless.

Baba Eddy and his children were creating hoopla.

'Hey Imatum!'

'See how e dey fine!'

'Deni baby big and fine o.'

'She don get money o.'

'Hey Murtala, una wahala don finish! Una don get money!'

I could also see some of our neighbours catching the fever.

'You see how God dey make tings happen?'

To their bewilderment, I remained frozen.

A woman took the child from Imatum and children clustered around her. Imatum was walking gracefully towards me. The fat man walked behind her and the armed policeman behind him. Mama and my younger ones were a few feet behind me. I looked back and saw that my siblings were excited, but did not rush towards Imatum.

Mama was sitting on the mat, stony-faced. When I turned, Imatum was right there, close to me. She looked exceptionally pretty. The fat man was by her side. He had eyes like a frog.

'Good morning, Murtala,' she greeted me.

I merely nodded.

'I hope you're all right, Murtala.' She said it like an adult, graciously asking her younger one.

I essayed a smile.

She walked away from me. The fat man grinned at me and followed her. My siblings were gathered around Imatum now. She was introducing them to the fat man, patting their heads and looking into their eyes. She introduced him as Alhaji Tanko, her husband.

'Ajara, you look emaciated,' Imatum said with concern.

'We don't have food.'

'Baba losh,' Oyigwn blurted out.

'Where is Baba?'

Ajara answered, 'Baba has left us. We don't know his whereabouts.'

Imatum looked at the fat man who expressed surprise by widening his frog-like eyes and canting his head.

'Anyaosu the quiet one, still quiet as ever.'

'Your baby is beautiful.'

'Thank you.'

'I miss you, Emayabo.'

'Mama said we wouldn't see you again,' Emayabo said.

'Now you're seeing me, Emayabo,' Imatum said, her eyes darting to Mama.

Mama remained deadly cool. She narrowed her eyes and stared vacantly, as if nothing was happening. Imatum was taking her time. Her husband was learning to pronounce the names of my younger ones, his thick lips moving slowly.

I moved closer to Mama.

'Na her mama sidon dere,' one of our neighbours was telling another woman, pointing at Mama.

'She no dey happy o.'

'Na so me I see am too.'

Omodiale came around, smiling broadly. 'Y'know, Imatum, you've become a big woman o.'

They exchanged a knowing glance. Imatum rolled her eyes and clucked.

Imatum moved closer to Mama. Loudly she told Ajara, 'Let me greet Mama even if she doesn't welcome me.'

Ajara grabbed Imatum's wrist, preventing her from moving farther. I knew she was saving Imatum from Mama's slap.

Mama rose slowly. 'So you've come to laugh at me,' she began almost inaudibly. 'So you've come to laugh at me.' She coughed and raised her voice. 'So you've come to laugh at me!' She broke into handclaps, giving a short, bitter laugh. 'Imatum the courageous one, you've come to laugh at this wretch of a mother who didn't know the smell of riches like you do, haven't you?'

We all froze.

Though frightened, Imatum still spoke. 'No, Mama. I've come to ask you to come to my house during this unrest.'

'Come to your house! To the house of your Muslim enslaver! Look for other people to kill, not my children and me. Ha! I should come to your house...'

Imatum's husband was visibly embarrassed, nonplussed. Murmuring voices, in favour of Imatum, drowned Mama out. Imatum's husband, perhaps understanding what Mama meant, spoke briefly to his armed police escort who nodded to him, and went back to his car.

'*Chaakokoo!*' Mama let out a loud shout.

Everybody hushed up.

Mama was trembling with anger. Her eyes roamed round the people and her voice was full of spite. She spoke to them in our language. 'Keep yourselves out of this. I say, keep yourselves out of this! And if you really want to be any good to that bastard who calls herself my daughter, advise her to disappear from my presence now. Now!'

'Wetin she dey talk?'

'I know say she no well.'

'She no happy with her pikin at all.'

They looked at Mama with exceeding pity, maybe because she was very frail. It was as though even a mild wind could lift her off the ground.

'And you Imatum,' Mama turned to face her, 'the greed

you've put inside your mouth, you'll continue to chew all your life. It's a stone and you'll chew it forever.' Mama was now hysterical. 'You think you'll finish chewing it? And then drink water to wash it down? No, you'll not. You'll chew it till you die! If you live, if you ever live to see your evening, your daughters will do worse things to you. Since you've chosen to prostitute with a rich man, your prostitution will know no end…'

A crowd had gathered around us. Two policemen and a policewoman came too, glaring at Mama. Mama kept on raving.

One middle-aged woman yelled at Imatum in our language: 'You fool! Do you remain standing while your mother destroys you with curses? Leave here! Save yourself!'

The policewoman drew closer to Mama. Mama ignored her and shouted my name: 'Murtala, the rational one!'

'I'm here, Mama.'

'Where are my children?'

I called out their names. They came towards me reluctantly.

Imatum had turned to go, taking her baby back.

The onlookers, most of them women, regarded Imatum with deep concern. They also looked at Mama with deep sympathy. Their quiet surprised me.

'I'll go with Imatum,' Ajara cried.

'Ha! Ajara the beautiful one, will you walk into fire?' Mama asked.

'I want to go with Imatum.'

Mama lunged at her, giving a hard slap. Ajara was on the ground, rolling, screaming.

A woman shouted at Mama: 'Are you going to kill the good child instead of the bad one? This is nonsense!' Her accent showed she was educated.

'Don't mind her. Wetin dey make am mad sef?' another woman said.

I saw our neighbours go back to their places, disappointed. The policemen and policewoman had left.

Mama returned to the mat and sat down quietly. She did not talk to anyone. She did not even bother that she had created a scene. Her eyes were coldly on us. Her children.

26 | We Wake Up in Ola's House

We woke up two days later in Ola's house. I felt a bit better from the sleep I had managed to have. Mama's eyes were bulbous and red. Ajara was still sulking from the slap Mama had given her. Nobody had apologised to her. Yakubu isolated himself in a world of staring, enchanted by the neatness of the room, the gleaming walls and the designs on the door. Anyaosu and Emayabo whispered to each other about the beauty of the house. Oyigwu lay on the rug, hungry and frail.

I looked outside through the window. The day was bright. No clouds in the sky. My gaze settled on a number of fat fowls with neat legs and feathers, pecking at some grains. The younger fowls were flapping around happily. Farther away from them were some small birds, also pecking.

Anyaosu and Emayabo, after I encouraged them, were able to sit on the water closet in the toilet of the room we occupied.

'It's weird to have a shitting place inside a sleeping room,' Anyaosu said.

'That's how rich people's houses are,' I told her.

'I don't like it.'

'What if my shit smells too much?' Yakubu chipped in.

I did not answer him. Anyaosu and Emayabo giggled.

Oyigwu urinated inside the bathtub. I wondered where I would take him after breakfast, when he would certainly need to shit. Yakubu closed the door and only came out when I bawled at him. He was grinning as he emerged from the toilet.

We did not have morning devotion and that was unusual. Since Baba had disappeared, we had consoled ourselves every morning by talking to God about Baba's fate. Mama insisted that each of us pray. 'Your father doesn't know how to call on God; you must not be like him,' she said, her expression stern.

I argued. 'But if God were interested in helping Baba, must Baba first call on him? Didn't he create Baba?'

'Jehovah Almighty doesn't do things like that. You must follow his way.'

'I understand you, Mama. But God should have listened to you. You've been praying on behalf of Baba.'

Mama's sad gaze fell on me. She picked her words slowly. 'Since you started going to that college, you've developed a tendency to blaspheme. Be careful the way you talk about God.'

I listened to her wordlessly as she continued to criticise Baba's unchristian attitude. Though I did not agree with all she said, I did not want to hurt her by arguing. I was convinced that she was already hurt by the beliefs she clung to.

Emayabo said, 'Mama, we've not prayed today.'

Mama sighed instead of answering.

'Every day, prayer. We should rest today. We should allow God rest too,' said Yakubu.

Mama sighed again.

Ajara eyed Mama contemptuously.

We heard knocking on the door and Ola opened it. He was too shy to enter the room. My siblings stared at him with admiration.

The day before, when Ola had come with his father and their driver to the police station to ask us to come to their house, my siblings were charmed by his appearance. Discernible in their eyes was the wish that Ola were their brother. They had all held their breath, eagerly expecting Mama's consent, when I had spent more than ten minutes convincing Mama to go to Ola's house. I told her Ola's house was the safest because it was in a rich people's area and the crisis, no matter its intensity, would not reach there. She agreed with me that rich Muslims and Christians would never kill one another, but her logic differed from mine: the rich should enjoy their riches and the poor wallow in their poverty. She had taught us a proverb to instruct us never to covet what the rich had: the sweetness of food ended just in the throat; once it entered the belly it became faeces and rich people's faeces were not sweeter than poor people's faeces.

Mama did not want to move. I told her that we were wasting Ola's father's time. She replied that she had not invited him and if I had schemed his coming, I should jump into his car and leave her and her children alone.

Ola was chatting with my younger ones.

Some of our neighbours were happy for us that we knew rich people who could help us. When Imatum and her husband had left the day before, Baba Eddy had said, 'Una get person wey go help you but your mama dey do *iyanga*. If my pikin do *ashawo* reach rich man place, no be blessing be dat?'

'Is it a blessing that she had VVF?'

'But I hear say de man carry am go hospital for London and dey don treat the VVF na. No be so?'

'Yes.'

'If na poor man make am get VVF, she for don die by now. You see wetin I mean?'

I told him I supported my mother and he thought I was stupid.

Seeing Ola's father's Mercedes-Benz, our neighbours watched to see how Mama would react to the gentleman who had come to help us.

Disregarding Mama, I took a decision. I told her, 'I'll carry my siblings to Ola's house. If you like, come with us. If you don't, stay here.'

She sighed heavily and said, 'Wherever you go, I'll go.'

Ola's father's patience, as I spoke to Mama, amazed me. He sat in his car and read his newspapers. Earlier on he had walked over to meet us and sympathise.

'Sorry, Madam. Take heart,' Ola's father said, his eyes going round us.

'Tank you, Sah,' Mama said, bobbing a curtsy.

'Come to my house with the children. You'll be safe.' His gaze was still on us.

'I hear you, Sah.'

Ola's father asked to know the names of my siblings and I told him. He shook hands with them one by one. Then he returned to the car to wait for us. My eyes followed him as he walked away. He walked with style, like Omodiale.

With Mama's consent, I called Ola and told him. He was relieved, having sensed that there was a problem. Pushing our luggage into the boot of the car, we all climbed into the back seats. Mama carried Oyigwu on her lap and I carried Emayabo on mine. Ajara carried Anyaosu on hers. Yakubu carried no one and posed like a son of a rich man. Ola sat in the front passenger seat with his father.

'Breakfast is ready. Would you prefer to eat here or in the dining room?' Ola asked, after we had exchanged greetings.

'We'd prefer to eat here.'

'Okay.' He left.

'Murtala, the rational one.'

I answered her. Apart from attending to Oyigwu's nagging, this was the first time she had spoken.

'We'll all go to the village tomorrow.'

Something leaped in my mind. 'You promised I would write my exams.'

'Our lives are more important than your exams.' Mama's expression was stern.

'Mama, we can stay here while Murtala writes his exams.' It was Yakubu. He stood by the wall, away from Mama.

She threw a cold look at him.

'Why are we even in a hurry to go to the village?' Ajara asked with pursed lips.

We heard knocking again. The door opened. Aunt Becky, her charming eyes as bright as sunlight, entered with a covered dish, a water flask and a huge loaf of bread inside a bag. Ola followed her, carrying a tray of teacups and cutlery, milk and sugar. They placed everything on the floor by the large bed and greeted Mama and my siblings. Aunt Becky asked for everybody's name except Mama's. She tried pronouncing *Anyaosu, Oyigwu* and *Emayabo*, amusing us.

The food flask contained omelettes. My younger ones brought their eager noses to smell it. I could not remember when last we had eaten eggs in our house. Oyigwu's hand, which had almost touched the omelettes, recoiled when I shouted at him. Startled, he burst into tears and went to Mama.

'Get away from me, greedy boy!' Mama shouted at him.

He cried louder and returned to me.

I took my time to share the omelettes equally. I also shared the sliced bread equally, even though I knew Oyigwu and Emayabo might not be able to finish theirs.

'This cup is too small,' Yakubu complained. 'Even Oyigwu can drink up two of it.'

'Why don't you go bring your big plastic cup?' Anyaosu taunted him.

'I wasn't talking to you.'

'Eat in silence,' I told them. 'Mama is watching.'

We ate in silence except for the loud slurps.

Listless, Mama ate little.

Yakubu ate up his in no time. Then he shifted towards Mama, his eyes on her teacup. She barked at him. 'Get out of my sight. The fool who will die for food!'

He moved to a wall and sank into a bad mood.

My mind was not on the food I ate, but on Mama's decision that we would leave for the village. I had been working hard, preparing for the JSSCE. Would Mama not let me take the exams? I would beg her.

'I can't watch my children eating rich people's food,' Mama thought aloud.

I responded, 'Mama, why do you say such a thing?'

'Why did you,' she said without looking at me, 'bring us into this strange life? Don't you see you're eating strange food? This food will turn my children into thieves. We must leave here.'

I became weak and let out a heavy sigh. The slice of bread I was eating fell from my hand. I could not even swallow the piece I was chewing. I knew at once that we would not stay longer than a day here. Maybe we would even have to go immediately. Why had I brought them here? I wondered if I too had changed. Was I taking undue advantage of my friend's riches? Was I escaping from my poverty? But how could I have turned down Ola's offer? Recently, I had been declining when he offered to buy me food, pens, books and other things. But how could I have turned down this offer?

'I was so worried that I persuaded Dad to release the car for me to come and see how you were doing in your place, Murtala. Dad decided to come with me. When we reached your house, they said you were at the police barracks. This place is not safe; let's go to my place.' How could I have refused such kindness?

I wanted us to be away from the violence. I was sure that we could be adequately sheltered at Ola's house. That we could hide our poor selves here until we were sure that Baba Eddy's information about the impending war between Christians and Muslims was either false or true. I wanted us to live as much as Mama did.

I had noticed that she looked at Ola's parents suspiciously. Not a single thing did she admire in the house. Her only remark about the huge, beautiful house was: 'This house is too quiet, as if nobody lives in it. So they live upstairs and only the cook lives downstairs?'

I told her that Aunt Becky, the cleaner and the laundry man lived in a place called the boys' quarters.

The large visitor's room we occupied was downstairs.

After the breakfast the whole family, except Ola, came to greet us. The twins wore jeans and T-shirts. Each girl's hair was neatly combed backward, held in place with a ribbon. When we had arrived the day before, the twins had looked at my siblings strangely and had not shown their usual liveliness. It was as though aliens had invaded their house. I felt both uneasy and sorry for them. Ola's younger brother also wore a pair of jeans and a T-shirt.

'Madam, how are you today?' Ola's father asked.

'I dey fine, Sah.'

Ola's mother added, 'Madam, are you sure you're fine? You look sad.'

Mama's answer was a loud sigh.

'Mariam, she can't be happy after what's happened to her,' Ola's father told his wife quietly.

'Madam, you need rest,' Ola's mother said sympathetically.

'Tank you, Ma,' Mama answered.

Ola's father turned to me. 'Any news about your father yet?'

'No, Sir.'

'Mariam, can't you see we're in a terrible world? Only God knows what has happened to the poor man.'

The twins were looking up at their father, puzzled.

'It's serious, Sam.'

They left the room without saying much.

'Mama, do you know that Ola's father is a Christian and his mother a Muslim?'

Mama sat up and leant her back on a wall. 'The husband Christian and the wife Muslim?'

'Yes.'

'No religion for the family then. What's your friend's religion?'

'He goes to church with his father.'

'I see.'

'The other children are Muslims.'

'And there is peace in the family?'

'Didn't you see them?'

'You don't know things by merely seeing, Murtala.'

Thirty minutes later, I went out to look for Ola. I would not climb up to his room. Instead, I went to Aunt Becky.

'Ha! Mu-ri-ta-la,' she sang my name jovially. 'I hope you're all right.'

'Yes Ma, thank you.' I wondered how she could be so cheerful all the time.

'Don't yesma me, boy. You know my name, don't you? By the way, you've got a beautiful mother there. I can see why you're a fine boy.'

'Thank you, Aunt Becky.'

'And what's this thing I hear about your dad?'

'We can't find him.'

'*La ila ha ilalahu Muhammadu rasullilah!*' she exclaimed.

'I want to see Ola.'

She was not happy that I had changed the topic. In her eyes was the desire to know more about my father. She stared at me pitifully for a moment before she stud, 'You know his room, don't you?'

I only stared at her.

'Don't want to go up?'

I nodded.

'Shy boy. I see that the whole of your family are shy. Don't you want to feel at home?'

Despite her garrulity, she dialled the phone on the kitchen table. 'Murtala is here. Wants to see you, but won't come up.'

In a short while, Ola joined me in the kitchen.

'What's it, Murtala?' He had read my eyes. This aspect of him made him unbearably intrusive.

I told him we should go out under the tree. He followed me with ease even as his curiosity mounted. I leant against the tree. 'My mother insists we return to our house now.'

He was shocked. 'Is anything wrong? Has anybody hurt her?'

'Certainly not. It's the trauma of my father's disappearance. I reckon that the way she's going, if she's not given what she wants, she might do something harmful to herself. My father's disappearance began with such a depression.'

I said all this because I did not want Ola to argue widi me. Indeed, it had dawned on me that I could not afford to take chances with Mama's depression. If she had attended to Baba's distressed mood, he probably would not have vanished. At the moment, Mama was growing alarmingly distraught and I had to do what was practical.

Ola sighed painfully.

'What exactly does your mother want, Murtala?'

I opened up entirely: 'She wants us to return to our homeland.' I sighed.

'But you have exams.'

'To her, that's beside the point,' I said, bowing my head sadly.

After a moment of silence, Ola said, 'Okay, I'll go tell my father now. You wait for me in the sitting room.'

We went back into the big duplex. My heart was heavy. I would miss my exams after all, despite my intense preparations. I had braved the emotional chaos in my family, vowing that I would do all I could to achieve the best results. I had forced myself to study while listening to Mama's nightly wailings. I had forced myself to read while thinking of what Imatum had become. The thought of her dying of childbirth complications had haunted me. I had forced myself to study, my mind seized by the bizarreness of a lost father.

Ola and his parents came down the staircase.

Tension was building up in me. I would summon up the courage to tell them the truth. I knew they would not be happy, having their offerings of genuine kindness rejected so soon. In spite of our poverty.

'Murtala,' Ola's father called.

'Sir.'

'Call your mother, let's talk.'

As I stood up slowly, I knew the matter would be complicated. Mama was in a calamitous condition. Would she be able to express herself coherently? Would Ola's parents pressure her into agreeing with them? Would their attempts to persuade her provoke outrage? Mama was, to me, a gathering fury, fragile, likely to explode any moment, not minding where she was, whom she faced. I felt too inadequate to tell Ola's father that the best thing was for him to agree to our decision.

Mama was a heap of lean flesh on the rug. She lay on her side, her knees packed up, her head between her arms, her fingers locked behind her head. My siblings, even the adventurous Yakubu, had assumed different positions, napping.

When I called Mama softly, she raised her head, sat up and looked at me, red-eyed. Would Mama ever stop weeping? It was amazing the store of tears she had.

Mama hesitated at first, but followed me.

We sat on a lavishly cushioned settee on the right side of Ola's father who sat with his wife on two adjacent chairs.

'Madam, your son told us you want to leave our house. Have we done you any wrong?'

Mama raised her head, looked at Ola's father and shook her head slowly.

'Can't you stay until the crisis is over?'

She shook her head again.

'Do you want to take your children to Kwanar Jabba where they're killing people?'

Mama shook her head a third time.

I grew afraid. Could Mama not talk?

'Where do you want to take them?'

'We dey go our village,' Mama said, raising her head.

I sighed.

'Listen to me, Madam.' Ola's father cleared his throat importantly. 'This family has a good plan for you. It's our wish that you stay here for the moment, until the crisis is over. If you don't want to stay inside here, we'll ask one of the boys to vacate a room in the BQ for you. When it's safe to return to your house, we'll take you home. Thereafter we'll assist you with money to return to your business. What do you think about this plan?'

Mama answered, 'Tank you Sah, but I dey go to my village with my children.'

Ola's mother spoke. 'Why would you carry your children to the village? In the city here they'll attend good schools. Your son, Murtala, is brilliant and I suppose the others are also good. Remain here and train your children in a modern way.'

Mama replied, 'Tank you, Ma. De city no good for us.'

'Oh my God!' Ola's mother exclaimed. She looked at her husband who did not show any surprise.

Ola's father said, 'I can see your mind is made up, Madam. I'll advise that you leave Murtala here in our house and we'll educate him. He's a brilliant boy and the village will do him no good.'

Mama shook her head elaborately.

'But if he is educated he will grow up to help you and the children,' Ola's father pressed.

'I no fit leaf Murtala for Kano. Dem go kill am.'

I wanted to shout at Mama to be quiet. To shout that I would remain and go to school. That I would not die in the city. That she was denying me the future I had been dreaming of. How could Mama be so unkind to me?!

Ola's father said, 'Nothing would happen to him if he stayed with us. Once they take their JSSCE, I'll change their school so that they don't go all the way to Sabon Gari. And after their secondary education, I'll send them abroad for further studies.'

'I dey go home with Murtala,' Mama said simply.

Ola's father let out a heavy sigh, relaxed his back against the chair and looked sideways thoughtfully. Frustration was written on his face. His wife stared at him. Ola sat almost frozen on a chair opposite Mama and me. I held my head in my hands and wept in my mind.

Ola's father spoke again. 'Madam, if you leave here now for Kwanar Jabba, I don't know what'll happen to you and your children. In order not to run into any trouble, I'll suggest you sleep here today while I get a lorry that'll pack your belongings from Kwanar Jabba tomorrow. I'll arrange for the lorry to convey you to your village.'

After a moment of thought Mama agreed. 'Tank you Sah, Almighty God go bless you for your good mind.'

Later at night, Ola and I were in his room. I was so sad

that I could not eat and Ola felt helpless about the whole situation. He told me, 'I'm sure you found an envelope in your school bag.'

'Yes.'

'I put it inside.'

'Thanks, Ola,' I said, ashamed.

'Please, don't reject anything from us. We've more than enough for ourselves. I wish your mother had accepted my father's offer.'

But why is my family only created to accept charity?

My lips trembling, I told Ola, 'Please tell your dad I'll escape to Kano to continue my schooling. I will return.'

'I had it in mind to suggest that to you, but I didn't want to offend you. We'll arrange that.'

I felt a heavy burden lift.

27 | *A Whirlwind Descends*

A whirlwind descends from the clouds. It circles me, at first violently and then gently. It is a sunless day at the cemetery near our house. I am standing, stripped of clothes except for my underpants. I am panting like someone who has been running for a long time. But I cannot remember anything pursuing me. I stare, conscious that I am alone, as the whirlwind settles and finally becomes Ukpo. Ukpo! He wears a tattered shirt over khaki shorts. His body is all dusty. He looks sad and angry and does not welcome my broad smile. 'Where have you been, Ukpo?'

'Two brothers were foraging and a violent death snatched one.'

'You've eluded me. For…'

'Even here, we're not happy.'

'Our father is lost and…'

'Come with me.'

In a split second, I am suspended in the air behind Ukpo, the wind bearing us gently as we move along Airport Road towards the town. It is a long straight road with several roundabouts. We emerge on Murtala Muhammad Way and make a detour to reach the main road that leads to Unguwa Uku. I recognise the road that leads to Hotoro, to the government house, to Ola's house. We pass the Bank of the North, the tallest building I have ever seen. We fly past Zoo Road and Unguwa Uku to Naibawa. It is here our legs touch the ground. We are on the outskirts of the city where there are only a few houses. We turn to the right, into a sandy road, and walk ahead. Ukpo's strides are so unnaturally long that I must trot to keep up. Then we reach a huge storey building under construction. It has no fence. He stands away from the entrance.

'Look into the entrance of this house.'

I move to the entrance and look into the house. At first I do not see anybody, only planks and mason's equipment in the large room. Then I look round and see a human figure, silhouetted, sitting in the doorway of one of the rooms opening onto the large room. Its back is to me. I want to approach the figure, but hesitate. I decide to talk to Ukpo first. When I turn round to see Ukpo, however, he has vanished. Astounded, I look round. The clouds begin to murmur, thickening, darkening. I run round the house, searching for him. Frustrated and angry, I scream his name.

I started awake.

'The nightmare, at last! Why Ukpo?'

I did not answer Mama. I screwed up my eyes at the electric lamp. She was standing over me. I sat up abruptly and held my head in my hands.

'Tell me, the rational one. Is your father no more? I knew you'd see it.' Mama's voice was shaky.

'Ukpo has shown me where Baba is. I'll go get him.' I stood up quickly.

Mama grabbed my arm and pulled me down. 'Even

dreamers have their limits. Where are you going at this time of the night?'

I looked at the wall clock. It was 2.40 a.m. I calmed down. Mama sat beside me, curious and sad. My siblings slept heavily.

'Mama, I know where Baba is.'

'Don't talk out of sense, because of a nightmare.'

'I'm sure, Mama.'

'You can't be sure of a dream in this perilous time.'

'I'll go there when it's daylight. I'll try to locate the place I saw in my dream. We'll come here together if I see him.'

'Where did you see in your dream?'

'Naibawa.'

'On the way out of Kano?'

'Yes.'

'And Ukpo showed it to you?'

'Yes.'

Mama fell silent. I heard whistles from afar and distant footfalls.

'You won't go anywhere. They're killing people all over.'

'I'll go, Mama.'

'Have you been there before?'

'Yes, Mama.'

'You really want to go?'

'Yes, Mama.'

'No, you won't. We can't take such a dangerous step.'

'Joseph dreamt,' I said, surprised at my own utterance.

Mama stared at me. 'Yes, he dreamt in Egypt.'

'I've also dreamt. Just give me a chance, Mama.'

Mama was silent for a while, thinking. 'You'll not go. I can't let you out of my sight. If your father is alive, he can find his way to the village.'

I awaited the coming of dawn with anxiety. Numerous thoughts flitted through my mind. My attention occasionally focused on Mama's moving lips. Would she ever tire of reminding God of her travails?

Mama fell asleep at 5.30 a.m.

I opened the door gently and sneaked out of the room. The parlour was colder than the room we slept in. I opened the kitchen door and surprisingly found Aunt Becky. She started as the door creaked open.

'Are you a ghost, Murtala?'

'Good morning, Aunt Becky.'

'Morning. Why out so early? Need something?'

'I didn't know I would find you here,' I said, dodging her questions.

'Oh you should know, Murtala. I have to be up on time to prepare food.'

I moved towards the door. 'I'm going out to get something for my mother.'

'But you don't know this area, do you?'

'I know where I'm going.'

'What are you going to buy, Murtala?'

'Just let me go and…'

She opened the door for me to go.

The watchman posed no difficulty. I trekked some distance to the main road before taking a bus. Inside the bus, I tried to recall my dream vividly. The direction. I succeeded in trapping some images: the tall building, the Unguwa

Uku main park, the baobab tree, the turn to the right, and the green undergrowth.

I alighted where I thought was the right place, at Naibawa. There I saw Adejo walking towards me. Adejo! What could he be doing here, so early in the morning? I could not dodge, because he had already seen me.

'Hey Murtala, nice to see you again.' He beamed, stretching his hand out to shake mine.

'Nice to see you, too. What're you doing here?'

He looked haggard. He was carrying a loaf of bread inside a polythene bag.

'Moved in to stay with my uncle. Where is your house? I saw someone like your dad yesterday.'

I was wide-eyed, drawing closer to him. 'My dad?'

'Oh yes. Around there.' He pointed at a *suya* spot. 'The man I saw was bearded and wore a jacket. In fact, I wanted to greet him and ask about you, but changed my mind because I wasn't sure if it was him.'

'I'm sure you saw him. I hope you didn't lose anyone in the crisis.'

'We can't find my mother.' His voice was weak.

'Oh my God! You mean…'

'She never returned from work.'

'Ukpo died.'

'That strong brother of yours? Accept my condolences.'

'My condolences, too.'

The mood was getting heavy.

'Show me your house, Adejo. I'll come see you later.'

He pointed at a house. After telling me to take care, he turned and walked gawkily away.

My dream would come true after all. If I looked for Baba and did not find him, I would return to Adejo, tell him more and ask him to help me.

I walked some way before I saw the turn to the right. A huge baobab tree stood by the roadside, immediately beyond the intersection. I tried to focus on the images of the green grass, the farm and the uncompleted storey building. I tried to keep in mind the shape of the building. The upper part was larger than the lower part. There were pillars outside. There were doubledoor shops at the front of the house. The house was not plastered and a heap of sand stood in front of it.

As I walked down the lonely lane I saw a farm of young com stalks on the right, handsome and dewy. I stood for a moment to admire them. I trod gently past the farm. Then, raising my head, I saw a lone storey building under construction a little distance away, surrounded by small clumps of reeds.

I looked at the sky. It was bright. Far in the sky two birds, close to each other, flew towards the east. On both sides of the road were ferns, shrubs and young trees, green and full of life. Happy small birds, in their morning splendour, were flying from one tree to another.

A Hausa man, tall, dark and clad in *riga*, came out of the frameless door. I walked towards him, speaking in Hausa. 'Good morning, *mallam*.'

'What're you doing here?!'

There was suspicion in his eyes. I drew closer to him. His lips were thin and dark. He stood, nervous, visibly embarrassed that I had drawn so close to him. I noticed a fat spliff in his right palm, which he was trying to hide. His anxiety was putting him on the defensive. His eyes were restless. I said loudly, 'I'm looking for my father, please.'

'Your father?' The scowl on his face changed to a squint.

'Yes.'

'Your father?' he asked again.

I nodded.

He canted his head to the left. He drew closer to me. 'I can see you resemble that ex-policeman.' He pointed towards the entrance of the building.

'I'm his son!' I almost jumped up with happiness.

He looked me up and down, the suspicion not totally gone from his eyes. He drew on his marijuana, then gestured towards the entrance.

I saw the figure straight ahead of me. He was sitting in the doorway to one of the rooms, his back to me. I could see that his arms were folded over his chest. He faced an influx of light from the large window of the room. I heard news being broadcast on the radio. I stepped into the house and took two quiet steps towards him. At the sound of his voice, I froze.

'And the children shall seek their father.' He did not turn.

'Baba! Baba! Baba! Why have you…'

He interrupted me, standing up. 'Murtala, I'll prefer us to avoid the whys in this matter.' He turned to me. 'Consider my leaving home an act of freedom. The cage has burst open for all of us.'

The influx of light presented him to me in utter clarity. Baba's face had grown very hairy. He obviously had not shaved since leaving home. He walked to me and gestured that we should go out of the building. He led the way, his small radio, now turned off, dangling from his left hand. Outside the building, I studied his features. His face had become thinner, more wrinkled and dissipated, with his beard threatening to swallow his lips. His lips had turned quite dark and assumed the perpetual shape of a chuckle. His eyeballs were bloodshot, but sharp. His neck had grown leaner, veined. He wore a tattered, long-sleeved shirt torn at the elbows and a pair of faded jeans. His body stank of marijuana.

'Are your younger ones as healthy as you?'

'Yes, none of us is ill, except Mama. Because of your absence.'

Baba smiled. 'Not because of my absence, but because she's in a prison called the city. Take her to the village and her health will return. She was quite robust in the village, before I married her.'

'We're planning to go to the village. She's waiting for you and me. We're in my friend's house, because of the riot.'

'Oh! The religious killers. Avoid them as much as you can. Most people in our country are enslaved to Islam and Christianity, two foreign religions tied together by violence.'

'I hear you, Baba.'

We stood outside the house, looking at the sun as it rose with alluring rays. I saw two beautiful butterflies flying around.

'Murtala, life turned into an enigma for me; to confront it, I have become an enigma too.'

He walked to the heap of sand and sat on it. I sat beside

him. He raised his head, that chuckle refusing to leave his lips. 'I've become an enigma to confront life.'

'I understand Baba,' I said even though I really did not understand. I wanted him to stop talking so we could leave. I was filled with joy.

'When the cage finally burst and I left home, I walked towards the sunrise. Persistently. I was angry at the sun. Unlike my age-mates in the village, I was born when it was rising. Didn't the sun owe me some explanation for the mess I lived as a life? Don't ask me whether I've found the sun or not, whether I've had the explanation or not. I'm just resting. And learning. I shall rise with the sun again.'

Baba chuckled. He was full of life, happy, happier than I had ever known him to be. He draped an arm over my shoulders and held me like a friend, as he had never done before. My attention was not on what he was saying. I wanted to shout with joy that I had found Baba, that Baba was after all alive, that at last Mama's boiling emotions would calm. I was eager for us to leave here. Why did Baba choose to carry on talking?

'Mama and the younger ones are waiting for us, Baba.' My tone was impatient.

'Don't be in a hurry, Murtala. I hurried and hit the rocks. Now I live my life gently, gently and thoughtfully. I seek knowledge. I seek inner peace and energy.'

'But...'

'Have you heard of Martin Luther King Jr, Malcolm X, Kwame Nkrumah, Marcus Garvey, Frantz Fanon, Patrice Lumumba, Jomo Kenyatta, Julius Nyerere, Nelson

Mandela, Thomas Sankara, Bob Marley and Fela Anikulapo Kuti?'

I stared at Baba, surprised. Was he all right? Why the question? Baba looked at me intently, expecting an answer, that chuckle still playing on his lips.

'I've heard of Mandela and Fela and...'

'Good, Murtala. Tell your mother I've begun a new life. My previous life was one long sleep.'

'I don't understand, Baba. Aren't we going to meet Mama?' I was anxious and angry.

'You will, I won't. I left the village in search of something I haven't found yet. Tell her I'm sorry for having kept her in the city all along.'

I simply stared at Baba, baffled.

'All of you, my children, are free to search for light in your own ways. Do not cast Imatum away. Tell everyone, including my parents, not to blame me. Beware of pointing your tiny finger at someone. Tell them none of them has fought life the way I have.'

Baba stood up from the ground, dusted his trousers and offered me his hand. I took it and averted my eyes. He pulled me up. He was energetic.

'You're weeping. Aha! The world doesn't need weeping but bravery. People have wept, wept and wept, and yet have perished. Have you heard of the slave trade? The centuries of continental weeping. Where has weeping taken Africa? Tell my children that they should be brave and radical in their youth.'

I cleaned the tears from my eyes and followed Baba inside the building. He did not seem to be tired of talking. We entered the room in whose doorway he had been sitting when I found him. A small stool stood on the floor beside the door frame.

'Each morning I sit here,' he pointed at the doorway, 'to embrace the sunrays from that window,' he pointed to the window. 'The sun must give me an explanation, Murtala.'

It was a large room with a plastered floor. A spread mat – with a threadbare blanket, a wrapper and a dirty pillow – lay to the left. At the head of the mat, I saw a pile of books of different sizes. They all looked old and dog-eared. I squatted to touch the books, fascinated, and skimmed the titles, recognising some: *The West and the Rest of Us, The Wretched of the Earth, Petals of Blood, God's Bits of Wood, Violence, The House of Hunger, The Poor Christ of Bomba* and *Two Thousand Seasons*.

'I'll write a note with which you'll convince your mother that you've seen me. And I'll give you some money to give her. I've been working at this building both as a mason and as a watchman. When you leave, I'll vanish from here. So don't even attempt to bring your mother to see me. But if you happen to see what I wrote in one of your new notebooks, read it to her.'

I stared at Baba, flabbergasted. He sat down on the mat, retrieved a sheet of paper and wrote the note. Then he counted some money and handed it to me. He stood up and gestured that we should go out.

We walked out of the building. My heart was heavy. It all seemed to me as though I was watching a bad movie. I still wept, averting my eyes.

He placed his right hand on my shoulder. It felt warm.

'Murtala, your path is that of light. Pursue it with strength and courage.'

We walked on towards the main road. My heart was pounding. I felt like exploding with rage. I felt like kicking Baba. I felt like killing myself.

I saw a number of small birds, flying happily, their wings making *prr-prr* sounds.

Baba stopped walking when we sighted the main road. I wanted to tell him that I would not be able to take the JSSCE with Mama insisting that I follow her home, yet I could not. All I felt like doing was exploding with a cry.

He looked into my teary eyes and grinned, a painful grin. 'Tell everyone that I await the triumph of my soul.'

Acknowledgements

When I attended the nine-month Per Sesh Writing Residency coordinated by the Ghanaian novelist Ayi Kwei Armah, I brought with me an old fiction manuscript which I hoped to rework. However, meeting and working with Mr Armah proved so inspirational that I relinquished the old manuscript and fervently embarked on a new book. *Sterile Sky* was therefore conceived in the seaside village of Popeguine, Senegal, while living with Mr Armah and other residency fellows. I remain grateful to this programme for giving me the very rare opportunity of working under the mentorship of my favourite novelist (which was the very reason I applied for the residency). My thanks go to Mr Armah, an amazing talent and mentor. My profound gratitude to TrustAfrica (Akwasi Aidoo and his vibrant team) who sponsored the residency.

Of all my works – both literary and scholarly – not one has benefitted from friends, colleagues and editors as much as *Sterile Sky*. From conception to writing and production, the novel has had many insightful inputs, including those of my residency fellows, Aisatou Ka, Mildred Barya and Kofi Doudou, who made invaluable comments on my work-in-progress. I am also grateful to Carmen McCaine who carefully read the manuscript and provided some great suggestions. Chinyere Obi Obasi generously organised a daylong editing session with Ahmed Maiwada, Patrick Oguejiorfor, Spencer Okoroafor, Denja Abdullahi and my student Egbunu Dauda Egbunu. Their discussions proved to be very useful and Maiwada's contribution to the manuscript extended beyond the session. I also received some very useful suggestions from Isaac Attah Ogezi, Crispin Oduobok, the Berlin-based scholar Ineke Phaf-Rheinberger, and the foremost Nigerian playwright Femi Osofisan during one of his stays in Berlin, Germany. I thank my teacher Dul Johnson for reading the manuscript at the shortest possible time and for making great suggestions. I must also mention the staff of the Institute of Asian and African Studies, Humboldt University, Berlin, especially Christine Martzke and Lutz Deigner, who gave me the opportunity to read from the manuscript during a conference in Berlin. It was there that a friend of James Currey showed interest in the manuscript, and it was James who brought it to the attention of Pearson.

I would like to thank my editor, Estelle Jobson, for her patience and profound attention to the manuscript. Thanks also to Alexander Moore of Pearson who made excellent suggestions during the editing process, and to Lynette Lisk of Pearson for her prompt attention in the course of preparing the manuscript. There are other names which this limited space does not permit me to mention. I thank you all.

E.E. Sule
Keffi, Nigeria
2012

About the Author

E.E. SULE is a Nigerian novelist, poet, and professor. He received a Masters in Literature at Benue State University and a PhD from the University of Abuja. He has been granted fellowships from the Alexander von Humboldt Foundation and the African Humanities Program.

His poetry volume *What the Sea Told Me* won the 2009 ANA/NDDC Gabriel Okara Poetry Prize and the AWF/Anthony Agbo Prize for Poetry. His novel *Sterile Sky* was long-listed for the NLNG Prize for Nigerian Literature in 2012 and won the 2013 Commonwealth Prize, Africa Region.

Sule currently works as a professor of African literature and cultural studies at Ibrahim Badamasi Babangida University in Lapai, Nigeria.